GRAY HAIR

KAREN BOOTH

GRAY HAIR DON'T CARE

For anyone who decided to own their gray.
Especially Ashley.

AUTHOR'S NOTE

Donovan, the hero in this story, ignores (more than once) pain in his chest and shoulder. If you experience symptoms like Donovan, don't be like him—please see a physician. These symptoms could be signs of a serious underlying condition.

CHAPTER ONE

Three years ago

DESPITE HER 0-1 record with marriage, Lela Bennett was kind of a sucker for a wedding. There was something so recklessly optimistic about it—two people lashing themselves to each other, hoping it would last for eternity.

Lela's love affair with nuptials was born at the age of eleven, when she watched two epic weddings on TV. In July of 1981, Lady Diana Spencer and Prince Charles of Wales were wed in London. Back home in Wisconsin, Lela watched every minute of it with her mom, perched on the edge of their brown pleather sectional. Then, in November, fictional couple Luke and Laura tied the knot on every teenage girl's favorite soap opera, *General Hospital*. Actress Genie Francis wore a bizarre head-hugging veil and a dress that looked like a marshmallow. Her groom, Anthony Geary, rocked his deceptively fluffy '80s hair. Lela couldn't help but be transfixed. It all felt larger than life. And her little eleven year-old heart gave into it lock, stock and barrel.

Even now, more than thirty years later, Lela's reaction would have surprised exactly no one when she stepped out of the Japanese stationery store near New York's Bryant Park. Minding her own business on a Friday afternoon, she spotted a bride and flower girl standing in the cathedral of trees across the street. Like a well-tested reflex, she instantly knew she had to go. Even though she wasn't a guest. Even when she was newly divorced and likely to ugly-cry if she subjected herself to vows, the exchanging of rings, and 'I do'. Still, a wedding was a wedding, and at forty-seven years old, Lela didn't get invited to many.

There was no time to waste. Not only did she have no idea when the ceremony would start, the Belgian waffle stand on the corner of the park had no line, and that almost never happened. She had extensive experience attending weddings to which she had not been invited. This was a spectator sport. She needed snacks.

Fast-walking her way along the bustling city sidewalk, she managed to hit the signal with a few seconds to spare, and her feet flew through the crosswalk and up to the order window. "One, please." Lela handed over her credit card and peeked around the tiny outbuilding to make sure she wasn't missing anything. It looked as though this was going to be a quickie ceremony. Most likely the couple hadn't taken the time to get a permit from the powers-that-be. She liked the idea of getting married like a rebel. Now that she was free of her husband and staring down a wide-open future, coloring outside the lines held a certain appeal.

Hot and tasty treat in hand, she jogged up the stone steps, past the forest green bistro tables teetering on gravel, and ducked under the dappled shade of a looming tree. It was a gorgeous early May day, with New Yorkers starting their weekend early by picnicking and sunning themselves on the impressive expanse of the park's lush green lawn. The couple hastily assembled in front of the woman officiating, who wore a deep purple robe. The bride took the flower girl's hand, then the groom did the same. Lela's heart lurched. A plot twist. *She's their daughter.* Another middle finger to convention. Lela was all-in for that.

She took an eager bite of her waffle, crispy on the outside, yeasty and chewy on the inside with sweet bursts of pearl sugar lacing the batter. She couldn't hear what was happening with the ceremony, but she simply liked watching the bride and groom and imagining their story. Maybe they met at work. Or at school. Or perhaps they'd literally run into each other on the subway, knocking foreheads, just like in a movie. Lela dismissed the idea that they might have used a dating app to connect. Lela had tried them for one week—last week, to be exact—but couldn't hack it. Too many fifty-something men looking for twenty-something hook-ups. *Such utter bullshit.* The whole thing made her feel old and she was *not* old. On the inside, she felt almost exactly like she had when she was in her twenties.

Other people were taking notice of the proceeding, looking up from their conversation or their coffee—or, unbelievably, their phones. Love was at center stage. It was worth rubbernecking. A few more onlookers gathered, including a tall man, who had stepped into Lela's peripheral vision. He had a spectacular head of thick and shaggy brown hair and was wearing dark jeans and a black blazer, but his back was to her and she couldn't see his face. From behind, he looked exactly like someone she'd once cared about a lot. It was a distracting thought, so much so that it was hard to focus on the reason she'd stopped in the park in the first place. "Damn, that looks like Donovan," she muttered to herself, taking another bite of waffle.

He turned to the side and she immediately knew it *was* him. *Holy crap.* She hadn't seen him since the end of her junior year of college. He hadn't been sporting the beard back then, but everything else was the same. The posture, with his hands jammed into his pockets. The propensity for wearing black. The aura of a person who wasn't like everyone else.

In fact, it had been twenty-six years since she'd last seen Donovan. They met when she was a freshman and he a sophomore, both at NYU. They became instant friends, primarily bonding over music, particularly anything of a 1980s vintage. They gloated about liking The Pixies before anyone knew who they were, spent entirely too many hours dissecting the lyrical poetry of The Smiths, and decided there was no way Prince wasn't from another planet or at least another time—he was too singular an artist. They gobbled up The Beastie Boys and U2. Public Enemy and The Clash. The Cure and INXS. Their scope was broad, and they listened to very few things ironically. Everything was fair game.

For three blissful but super confusing years, he was her best friend. Then they crossed that invisible line one night, the one that always seems to be there when men and women manage to forge a friendship. Donovan freaked out, Lela wanted to shrink into nothing, and the next thing she knew, he was graduating and getting married to someone he'd dated off and on—Genevieve, easily the most beautiful woman Lela had ever seen.

That had been an all too common refrain in Lela's life—being set aside in favor of something or someone more sparkly. Not that she had *zero* appeal. By this point in her life, she was confident she was smart, talented, and decent looking. She just wasn't sure she was smart, talented, or decent looking *enough*. Divorce did that. It rattled your foundation.

Donovan turned to the side again, but this time, he actually looked at her. As his gaze met hers, his face lit up with recognition. She didn't want to overstate the importance of the moment, but the clouds over Bryant Park *did* part. Hell, he had biblical sunbeams shining down on him. He adopted his predictable and potent self-satisfied smirk, the one that was certainly on his face the moment he left the womb. If she ever met his mom, she would have to ask.

"Lela?" he mouthed as he marched in her direction, answering his own question with forward momentum. He knew it was her. Earwormy strains of *You Make My Dreams Come True* popped into her consciousness. Not Hall & Oates's deepest song, but a true hallmark of pop music. It worked. And it was making one million memories rush back.

Lela realized she had the remnants of her waffle in her hand and something told her she had to get rid of it. There was no trash can in sight, and she didn't want to put it in her purse. Only old ladies put half-eaten bread products in their bag. So, she shoved it into her mouth.

She instantly regretted the decision. She felt like a hamster. *Chew faster.* She wanted to avert her eyes, but she couldn't stop looking at him. All while her mouth was working *hard* on that waffle. This was such a perfect illustration of their entire friendship—Donovan floating through life like Mr. Perfect while Lela was knee-deep in some half-baked plan she hadn't taken the time to think out.

Luckily, she choked it down just as he arrived with open arms.

"Lela," he said. "I cannot believe it's you."

She went in for what she thought would be a quick hug, but he wasn't about to let her off the hook so easily, holding her tight. Part of her wanted to push away. All these years later and she already felt herself falling under his spell. Still, she soaked up his embrace, the side of her head against his solid chest. Funny how so much early-twenties longing still resided in her body. Donovan was stirring it up like a wizard over a cauldron. "Donovan. Wow."

"Let me guess." He released his rein, but his gaze locked in on her. "Spotted the wedding and had to stop?"

"Old habits die hard." It was almost annoying how well he knew her. "What's your excuse?"

"I enjoy being reminded of my personal shortcomings."

Oh, right. His marriage to Genevieve hadn't lasted. Nor had his second. Or third. At least according to Facebook. "A divorce isn't necessarily a failure. Lots of people get divorced." Lela struggled to get the word out. Her split was a recent thing. As in two months. The only person she ever talked to about it was her best friend, Tammera. "Like me."

Donovan's eyes went wide with shock. "No. You're one of the most loyal people I've ever met."

"To a fault. I didn't have the guts to walk away even when I knew neither of us were happy."

"Hey. It takes two to tango. He could've walked away, too."

"Oh, he did." She spotted the pity on Donovan's face. If

anything killed a conversation, it was a discussion of the many ways love could die. She was desperate to change the subject. "You're still in San Francisco, right? What are you doing in town?"

"I'm seeing my daughter, Echo." Lela had forgotten Donovan and Genevieve had named their daughter after his favorite band at the time—Echo and the Bunnymen. "She went back to school and is about to get her master's. She wants to start a business and was hoping for my insight." Donovan was a marketing genius. Companies all over the world hired him to reposition or rebrand all sorts of ventures.

"She was going to F.I.T. the last time I saw you post about her. Did she stay in fashion?"

"She did. Now she's hoping to build her own little empire." His eyes found hers again. The whole world seemed to stop turning. "Care to talk about it over dinner?" He shifted his glance to the rumpled napkin in her hand. "Tell me that wasn't your dinner."

A blustery breath left her lips. "Pfft. No. Just a wedding snack."

"Come on. I'll take you for a real meal. So we can catch up." He reached for her hand, but took only the very tips of her fingers. Yet another perfect example of their dynamic— he'd give Lela just enough to leave her hungry for more. "Unless you have somewhere else you need to be."

Lela wanted to hate the excitement bubbling up inside her, but it was nice to have the attention, especially from Donovan. Especially out of the blue like this. They'd been so close at one time. She'd never thought she'd see him again, let alone share a meal. "I have no plans. I'd love to go."

The crowd in the park began to clap. Donovan and Lela

turned and joined in as the bride and groom kissed, then scooped up the little girl into their arms.

"I don't believe in happy endings, but that looks like a pretty happy beginning." Donovan's comment came as no surprise. He'd taken his dismissiveness of love to near-academic levels when they were in college. Apparently some things never changed.

"I see you haven't lost your sunny disposition."

"Never." He delivered one of his penetrating glances. "You, Lela, seem exactly the same."

She choked back a sigh. Was she supposed to be radically different? Was she supposed to have let life, love, and divorce change her? Maybe. Probably. "Thanks. I guess."

"I mean, way less eyeliner. Obviously."

"What can I say? My eyelids were getting droopy." Lela laughed. He wasn't wrong about that. "Where should we eat? You're the visitor. I get to eat in the city all the time."

"John's?"

Lela and Donovan had frequented the Bleecker Street location of John's Pizza countless times when they were in college. Even though they didn't sell slices, it was the best pie in the city and not far from campus. But now there was another, closer option in midtown and Lela wanted to keep herself wedged in the here-and-now. "We can walk to the Times Square location."

"Not quite the original, but I'm game if the pizza is just as good."

"It is. The bonus is there's usually less of a line."

He bounced his expressive eyebrows. "I've always liked the way you think."

Lela's traitorous cheeks flamed, but it was nice to feel alive. She'd been mostly numb for the last two months.

They walked down the promenade on the north side of the park and if Lela hadn't been wearing a dress and a pair of shoes that cost several hundred dollars, she would've sworn they were back in college. There was something so familiar about strolling along with him again, striking out on an adventure. Of course, Donovan was dressed quite differently now, too. Gone were his ripped jeans, dingy white Converse high tops, and distinctly untidy hair. He also hadn't come to scoop her up on his mint green Vespa, the sort of scooter that begs to be stolen in NYC, although Donovan managed to zip around the city for years with nary a problem. No, today he was wearing a jacket that cost more than her mortgage, his hair was nearly respectable, and this little jaunt was on foot.

But he was still just as mesmerizing, more than twenty years later.

CHAPTER TWO

I'LL BE DAMNED. Lela still wandered into Donovan's thoughts every now and then, but today, she'd wandered into his life. In a city filled with millions of people, they ran into each other at Bryant Park during the wedding of strangers? How did that even happen?

John's pizza hummed around them, a cacophony of chatter in the echo-prone restaurant, which had once been a church. A heartbeat away from the chaos of Times Square and surrounded by off-Broadway theaters, it was an eclectic space, with a fresco ceiling and brick pizza ovens crammed into the corners. "So. The wedding today," Donovan said. "Is this still a normal thing for you? Because it seems a little weird given recent events in your life."

Lela wiped her mouth with a napkin. Even in the room's dim lighting, her deep blue eyes were as bright as ever. He had a lifetime of memories of looking into them, late at night when they were in her dorm or his apartment. He and Lela used to sit up for hours listening to music and talking about everything. She'd always been so earnest, and her eyes had always reflected it. "Not really. I sort of OD'd on it for a while there. I started my career in makeup with bridal work. It *is* possible to get sick of weddings."

Lela had been an art history major when he first met her, but after he graduated, she dropped out of NYU and went to beauty school in the Bronx. In the days before the Internet, he'd had to hear about it through friends. He hadn't entirely understood the shift at the time, and a huge part of him had wanted to call her and ask what the hell she was doing, but it clearly worked out for her, so it was best that he'd kept his mouth shut.

Plus, he'd also had his own stuff going on. He was married to Genevieve just one month after commencement, then their daughter arrived six months later. He was trying to start his consulting business. Life was crazy, and not always in a good way. "Now you're doing more high fashion work, right?"

She smiled sweetly and he instantly knew he was out of the loop. The question was how far. "I did. For a while. But doing runway and magazine shoots can be brutal. It's not always the healthiest environment. I mostly have individual clients now. Celebrity chefs. Actors. A few pop stars. Internet influencers. Stuff like that."

"Anyone I know?" He took a swig of his beer and grabbed another slice of pizza.

"My best client is Tammera Beyer. She's on the Cook It! channel. She was my hair stylist for a long time while she was trying to break into TV. She's even better with food than she is with hair, and she was great at that."

"I've heard of her. Haven't seen her show, though."

Lela grinned warmly. "She's always trying to get me to do

crazy stuff. Right now, she's trying to convince me to start my own line of cosmetics."

He swallowed down another drink of beer and plopped the bottle on the table. "Yes. You should totally do that. I could help if you want. I'm good with start-ups."

"Maybe. One day. I'm not there yet." Lela shrugged it off. "Anyway, Tammera's my best friend."

"That used to be my job."

"A million years ago, maybe."

"Maybe? What are you talking about with maybe? We were definitely best friends." Just thinking about it, Donovan couldn't help but long for the simplicity of the relationship he'd had with Lela in college. It had always been so easy to be with her. She never expected anything from him. Everyone else—his mom, his brother, girlfriends—all loved to build him up just to tear him down. He didn't want to be on a pedestal, or as he liked to think of it, a hook.

"Hey. You're the one who went and got married," Lela said. "We couldn't stay best friends after that."

That was indeed true. Genevieve had demanded he cut all ties with Lela after they got engaged. All these years later, he hated hearing the hurt in Lela's voice. Had she been holding onto it this whole time? Or was it cropping up because they were seeing each other again? "You're right. I'm sorry." He had the distinct impression he'd let down his best friend twenty-some years ago. Like most days, he was filing away a mental note to do better next time. "I still hate that things changed."

"The earth spins. Life goes on. Yada yada yada."

"I know. It sucks."

"Look at it this way. Genevieve barely tolerated us as

friends when you guys were dating, then not dating, then dating again." Lela bounced her head from side to side, her sandy brown hair flopping along with it.

"You're right, but you must've had a guy who didn't like it either." Although, come to think of it, Donovan didn't remember Lela having many guys around at that time. He'd probably blocked it out.

"There was no guy."

"Sure there was. What about that guy who wore all the flannel shirts? With the glasses?"

Lela narrowed her sights on him, making him wonder if he was nuts. "Are you talking about Max? He was in one of my study groups. He had a very serious girlfriend."

"Oh. I guess I didn't realize that." She was such a spectacular human. There was no way he was the only guy who ever saw it. "Well, you got married, didn't you? So there was eventually a guy."

Lela bunched up her lips then finished off her beer. "Eventually. Yes."

He sat back in his chair and rested his hands on his belly. The pizza was mostly gone. So was the beer. But he wasn't ready for his night with Lela to end. "What now? The night is young."

"What'd you have in mind?"

"Grab a beer from a bodega and walk around the city? It's too nice out to stay inside."

She shook her head. "People don't really do that anymore. The cops actually enforce open container laws now. Plus, I have to go feed my cat. He's probably used his claws to carve a murderous manifesto into the hardwood floors."

"Can I come with you?"

"You want to meet my cat?"

"Of course. I have a million questions to ask him."

An effortless smile crossed her face and Donovan had to catch himself. There'd always been a glimmer of attraction between them, circling overhead. One time, it swooped down and flew right into their faces. He'd devoted a lot of energy to ignoring it. She was the first real friend he'd ever had. No one had come close to eclipsing her in that regard. "Yeah. Of course."

After he paid the bill, they walked outside. The sights, sounds, and smells of the city were coursing through his body like he'd just plugged into a limitless power source. It was invigorating. "Why don't I come back to New York more often?"

Lela took several steps down the sidewalk, then turned to him, walking backwards. "Maybe because I'm here?"

He hustled to catch up. "That was never the reason."

She arched her eyebrows and lifted her chin. It was her way of calling him out. "Or is it just because you can't stay in one place?"

He did move around a lot. He'd lived all over the world since college—Chicago, Miami, Dallas, a short stint in Albuquerque he'd rather forget, Tokyo, Madrid, and London. "Probably. You're the steady, dependable one."

"You make me sound like a washing machine."

"I mean it in a good way."

"Right."

"Seriously. The best possible way." He slung his arm around her shoulder and squeezed her closer. There was a part of him that knew he shouldn't do it. Every other time in his life he'd pulled a woman in, it ended in a fight, a relationship, or sex. He absolutely did not want the first two. The third could be amazing, but he didn't want to repeat old mistakes. He hadn't dealt with it very well the one time he and Lela had wound up in bed. Although, hopefully, he wasn't that same guy anymore.

CHAPTER THREE

DONOVAN AND LELA walked over to 7th Avenue to catch a cab down to her apartment. They rode through the night, the taxi popping over bumps in the road as the driver sped up to red lights and lead-footed it away from the green. This was not how they'd traveled together when they were in school. Back then, they explored on foot, took the subway, or when his Vespa was working, he'd take her on that. He had so many incredible memories of running around the city with Lela that it would be difficult to pick a favorite one. Hell, it would be hard to untangle them. There were the nights they went to see bands at CBGB or The Pyramid, crushed up front against the stage and ferrying beers to each other. Or rainy afternoons spent hanging out in his apartment, studying or reading, always talking. And of course, there been the Saturdays sneaking into churches.

Lela admitted early in their friendship that she had a thing for weddings. They made her happy, and as her best friend, he'd felt obligated to enable her somewhat odd hobby. So, they would dress up—Donovan in a laughable wide-lapeled tux he found in a secondhand store, and Lela in a lavender dress she'd Frankensteined together by cutting up a few thrift store finds. He'd called it the *Pretty in Pink* dress, just like the one Molly Ringwald's character put together for prom. He attached no romantic feelings to the vision of them dressed like that—it was more astonishment that no one had ever kicked them out of a church sanctuary.

"You realize, Lela, tomorrow is Saturday." The cab slowed down and turned onto West 21st Street. "We could go to a wedding. Sneak in and sit in the last pew. People-watch."

"Maybe. I'm still not on super steady ground after my divorce. Today was more of an impulse."

"Well, I'm glad you took a chance. Otherwise, we would've been half a block apart and still not seen each other." That was a truly depressing thought. He hated the idea of missed opportunities. The cruel twist of fate.

She smiled at him warmly and placed her hand on his thigh. She likely meant nothing by it, but his crotch did not get the memo. Everything in the vicinity of his hips went tight. "I'm glad we both decided to do it, too." Lela scooted forward on the backseat to better talk to the driver as they crossed 8th Avenue. "It's up here on the right. Middle of the block. You can pull over anywhere."

Donovan fished his wallet out of his pocket to pay, leaving a fat tip, then slid across the seat to climb out. Lela was already halfway up a flight of stairs leading to a picture-perfect brownstone. "You've really moved up in the world."

"I should hope so. I might not be rich, but I do make decent money."

That was a bit of a shot at Donovan, who came from considerable wealth on his mom's side. He didn't like to dwell on it or even talk about it. In fact, Lela was one of the only people who knew, although she'd never experienced in person what it was like to be fully immersed in the James's world of money, guilt, and questionable intentions. "I wasn't trying to say that you didn't."

"It's okay. I know that."

She keyed her way inside and Donovan followed, stepping into a beautiful foyer, with a black-and-white checkerboard landing and a vintage chandelier overhead. Ahead was a long stretch of what looked to be original hardwood floors, leading all the way to the back of the house. Down the stairs came a fluffy orange cat, meowing with every other step. Lela crouched down to rub his head. "Donovan, meet Rio."

"Duran Duran?"

"Of course."

"You could've gone for a less obvious song."

She swatted his arm. "Don't be a snob. That's one of my favorites. Plus, what was I going to do? Name him The Chauffeur?" She cocked her head to one side and adorably stuck out her lower lip. "Actually, that would've been pretty cool."

"Maybe you can get Rio a friend."

"I don't need more responsibility in my life." Lela kicked off her heels. "Do you mind taking off your shoes?"

"Oh, yeah. Of course." He untied his Tom Ford oxfords and set them to the side.

Lela strode down the long central hall, flipping on lights as she went. He hustled up, wanting to take in everything, but quickly realizing that however this place was decorated, it was not Lela's style. As he stole a glance of the large living room running along one side of the house, the furnishings were not only spare, they were super modern black leather, when he'd always known her to be far more colorful, never so bleak, and definitely much more cluttered.

"Is this where you lived with your ex?"

She grabbed a bag of cat food and filled Rio's dish. "Yes. It's a work in progress right now. I need to make a bunch of changes. He refused to take the furniture, which is really stupid since he picked it out."

Donovan leaned against the kitchen island and sighed. He'd done that routine more times than he cared to remember, separating himself from the material goods acquired during a relationship. "What was he like? Your ex."

"That topic requires a drink." Lela headed to the far end of the kitchen and opened the upper cabinet. "I have tequila, vodka, and gin. For mixers, I have tonic and soda. Otherwise, red wine."

"Gin and tonic?"

"Sounds like a plan."

Donovan didn't want her to have to play bartender. "You sit. I'll make the drinks."

"I'll help. You don't know where everything is."

Donovan pulled out the gin bottle as Lela grabbed two pint glasses from a cabinet.

"I see we're going for the supersize." He gestured with a nod to the glasses.

"This is not a super fun conversation."

"Got it. Fill those to the top with ice. Then we need tonic and lime."

"Refrigerator."

Donovan went hunting, finding the fruit in the crisper

drawer and the half-size tonic cans at the back. "I see you still have a thing for pickles."

"Hey. Did you agree to this just so you could snoop?"

He turned back and smiled at her. "Maybe." He free-poured the gin, then the tonic.

Lela cut slices of lime and squeezed them into the drinks, then stirred them with a butterknife. She raised her glass. "To friends."

"Yes. To friends." He sipped his drink, the bubbles and citrus tickling his nose. Their gazes connected, and even though he got a little zing of electricity, it felt like the most natural thing in the world. Two people picking up exactly where they'd left off. "So. Your ex?"

She took his hand, her fingers warm and perfectly coiled around his. "Come on. Let's get comfortable."

He trailed behind her, his body buzzing from the effects of the drink and of Lela. He had to make a conscious effort not to run off to the circus with his thoughts. Because here in this moment, all he could think about were decisions and mistakes and the course of his life. Should he have been less committed to keeping Lela in the friend zone when they were in college? Was she what had been missing from his life?

They sat on one of the black leather couches, which looked truly out of place among the original elements of the home, like the white carved stone fireplace surround or the old cast iron insert. "If your ex picked out this furniture, I already know why it didn't work. It's cold and totally lacks character."

Lela pulled her leg up on to the sofa and faced Donovan. "Mark was a good guy. But, honestly, I think I talked myself into the idea of loving him. All of my friends were married and having kids and I felt like life was passing me by. So he came along and swept me off my feet, and I went along with it." She took a long sip of her drink then cradled the glass in both hands. "I know that sounds terrible."

"We're wired to do crazy things for love and sex." Much of Donovan's life could be summed up by that statement, although he would vote to substitute stupid for crazy. "So no kids then?"

She shook her head. "That's one of the worst parts. I really wanted them, but he was dead-set against it. Of course, I knew this when I married him, so I have zero business being upset about it."

"You can't change your feelings."

"That's very insightful."

"I went to therapy for a while, but that's the only part I really remember."

"I guess you're right." She lazily rubbed the glass with her index finger. "Tell me about the wives after Genevieve."

Donovan hated that it was wives, plural. He felt like a cliché. To cope, he gulped down a good third of his drink. "There was Tess, the dermatologist. That lasted two years. Then Nadia, the yoga instructor. That lasted eight months, I'm afraid to say."

Lela shook her head then raised that same finger she'd been massaging the glass with. "Let me guess. Tess was younger than Genevieve, and Nadia was younger than Tess."

Donovan swallowed hard. "Why does it sound so horrible when you say it?"

"Because men are painfully predictable?"

"Please don't lump me in with the other dudes of the world."

"I'm merely pointing out a pattern. You happen to fill it."

"I like older women, too, Lela."

She arched both eyebrows at him then took another long sip of her drink. "Don't tell me. Women your own age?" Her eyes went wide as saucers in feigned astonishment.

He laughed and smacked her leg with the back of his hand. "Yes, women my own age. I like you."

Their gazes connected again, completing a circuit. "I like you, too."

His breath became heavy, so much so that it felt like it had to be heaved out of him. He found himself leaning closer to Lela, drawn to her in the inevitable way metal couldn't stay away from a magnet. "I hate that our friendship ended. I know it was my fault and I'm sorry."

"I'm sure I share just as much of the blame."

"No. What you said at John's was dead-on. Getting back together with Genevieve ended everything. I should have said something. Just so you wouldn't have to wonder what I was thinking."

"We weren't a couple. We were friends. I don't think you owed me that explanation."

Donovan felt the need to bring up one of many elephants currently occupying the room. "But we slept together. So we weren't strictly friends."

"That was a one-time thing. You get a free pass on that."

"I don't want a free pass. I know I messed up by leaving the next morning."

Lela shot him a quizzical look. "Um. If I were you, I'd take the free pass."

"Why?"

"Let's just say it wasn't the absolute best."

"What? It was amazing, wasn't it?"

"Mostly? I was just left a bit..." She was clearly searching for words. "Unsatisfied."

That word. It was a dagger to his heart and his ego. "Hold on a minute. The one time we had sex you didn't have an orgasm?"

She shook her head, looking sheepish. "Nope."

"Did you fake it?"

"No. You just didn't happen to notice."

He slumped back on the couch, feeling more than a bit defeated. His entire memory of that night was now cast in a far less flattering light. "Wow. I'm so sorry."

"It's not a big deal. Plenty of guys in college didn't really know what they were doing."

"Uh, I definitely knew what I was doing."

She unleashed a patronizing smile. "You don't need to get defensive."

"I'm serious."

"Okay."

"No. I'm absolutely dead serious. More serious than I've ever been in my entire life." He put his glass down on the coffee table, feeling like if he could only right one wrong in the world, this was it. "Let me prove it to you."

"This isn't darts. Don't treat me like I'm the elusive bullseye."

"I'm not. That's because the bullseye, for me, is not elusive. It's not only attainable, it's an imperative. Your bullseye, of course. Not mine."

"You're drunk."

"A tiny bit tipsy. That's it." He cleared his throat, if only to let some noise fill the silence between them. "Of course, if you don't want to have sex with me, I understand."

Lela traced the top of her glass with her finger, not taking her eyes off him. "Okay. But I get to be in charge."

Donovan could hardly believe what she was saying. And he had no earthly idea what it would mean for her to be in charge. But he answered the only way he knew how. "Perfect."

CHAPTER FOUR

LELA'S HEART was about to pop out of her chest and run laps around the living room. What had she just agreed to? Only the thing that she'd wanted the entire time she and Donovan had been close, the thing that she'd only had a taste of, once. Today couldn't get any more surreal. Or amazing. And even though Donovan was going to return to San Francisco in a few days and he'd be out of Lela's life just as quickly as he'd managed to walk back into it, she was still on board. She couldn't deny that she longed for another chance at the guy she'd always wanted.

She was, however, questioning the idea of taking charge. Allowing those words to pass her lips had been a misstep. Or... perhaps this was the universe telling her it was time to try new things. As she mulled it over, poor Donovan was sitting on the other end of the couch, looking like he was truly at a loss. This came as some amusement. After all, he was the man who seemed to breeze through life with everything and everyone at his whim.

Lela got up and took the two steps it required to be standing next to his legs. She peered down at him as he looked up. Everything about him was raw and breathtaking—the untamed hair, the unruly facial scruff, the way his eyes shifted darker like sex was the only thing worth thinking about right now.

"Are we doing this?" His voice hitched adorably at the end of his question. He was at least a little bit vulnerable. Just like her.

"We are." She planted one hand on the back of the couch near his head, then a knee to the cushion next to his thigh. The next thing she knew she was straddling his lap and wondering how she'd so quickly shoved aside her more docile ways.

She settled her weight on his legs, closed her eyes and took what she wanted—a kiss. She felt her insides soften at that first touch. His mouth was warm and soft like she'd remembered, this time flavored with gin. But there was an urgency that hadn't been there before. It felt like he truly wanted her. Was that convenient thinking? She didn't want to believe it, and if this was a one-time thing, she had to make the memories she wanted, which meant telling herself that yes, he did want her. It felt especially true when he flattened one hand against the center of her back and pulled her closer while his other hand slipped under her dress, palming the bare skin of her thigh. She combed her fingers into his generous head of hair, curled the tips into the back of his head, erasing any empty space between them. She breathed in at the same moment that he groaned into her mouth, and that filled her with new confidence. She was invincible. For now.

"Do you want to go upstairs?" she asked. She really didn't want to have sex with Donovan on the stupid couch her ex-husband had picked out. Yes, she'd slept with him in her bed, but at least that had new, post-divorce bedding.

Donovan kissed her cheek, dragged his lips along the line of her jaw, then skimmed the sensitive skin of her neck, especially the spot right below her ear. "I do."

Lela felt dizzy, but wasn't about to let her unsteadiness keep things from moving forward. She scrambled off his lap, grabbed his hand and made for the stairs up to the second floor. All the while, her needy body was screaming at her to go faster so she could tear off his clothes, while the out-of-practice seductress in her brain wanted to go for the slow burn. She settled on a medium simmer, making quick work of the trip to her bedroom.

As soon as they were inside, clothes started to go. His jacket. His shirt with what seemed like the most ridiculous amount of buttons she'd ever encountered. And the cuffs she hadn't thought to undo first. He turned her around and unzipped her dress, pressing kisses along the channel of her spine and sending tingles over her entire body. If this little prelude was any indication, Donovan had definitely expanded his skillset. Of course, she'd been wearing jeans and a sweatshirt the first time they'd done this.

As she stood before him, she was glad for a few things— she'd worn exceptionally nice underwear, it *matched*, and she'd shaved her legs a few days ago. Still, she felt truly on display, and every little worry a woman has about her body, especially after forty, tried to creep into her thoughts. She fought them back, shutting out doubts about the perkiness of her breasts or how her ass simply wasn't in the same zip code it had resided in when they were in college. Donovan didn't seem to care as he unhooked her bra and slipped her panties past her hips. He didn't care at all when she unzipped his jeans, took off his boxer briefs, and finally got a chance to wrap her fingers around him. His body wasn't disappointing either of them. Of course, she wasn't the only one who'd picked up a few tips and tricks along the way. Donovan seemed to appreciate every pass she took with her hand, especially as he kissed her hard and cupped her breasts with both hands.

Lela felt her body temperature spiking, or maybe that was just what Donovan was doing to her, but it wasn't worth debating for too long because the reality was that the urgency between her legs was immense. This was impatience like she'd never experienced. She needed him to touch her there, set her on fire, and leave her in a breathless heap. Or however close he could get to that. No matter what she'd said downstairs, if sex was darts, she wanted the damn bullseye.

She walked backwards to the bed, learning how easily you could get a man to follow you if you had his dick in your hand. When her legs met the mattress, she sat, then released her hold on him and scooted back to the center of the bed, conjuring every seductive scene she'd ever seen in a movie, where a woman takes control.

Donovan seemed to take her lead, admiring her as he stood over her like a monument to sexiness and the maintenance of core muscles. "How did you get to be even more beautiful, Lela?" he asked.

The old Lela would've blurted something about how she was only better looking now because it had been her mid-twenties before she lost her baby face. But the Lela of tonight, the one who was seducing her college crush? She had a way better answer. "I take excellent care of my skin."

He smiled and stretched out next to her, smoothing his hand over her bare belly. His skin against hers brought her back to life in a way that shocked her. She hadn't thought of herself as asleep, mostly because everything had hurt so damn bad over the last few months. But apparently she'd at least been dozing, because right now, with Donovan, she felt wide awake. "What do you want, Lela?" he huffed the question into her ear with hot breath.

She took his hand and placed it between her legs. "This. I want this."

Donovan knew exactly what to do, quickly finding the spot that made her suck in a sharp breath. He rotated his fingers in languid circles, and Lela closed her eyes and arched into him, kissing him softly while she gave in to every heavenly thing he did. She let her brain go, every negative thought, and simply focused on the sensation. The warmth pulsing through her body, the tension coiling in her belly, the need quickly doubling inside her. As good as his hand felt, it wasn't enough. She wanted all of him, everything she'd wanted more than twenty years ago.

She gently broke their kiss. "Let me get a condom." She didn't wait for an answer, rolling to her bedside table and pulling one from the box. She didn't think about the reason they'd been there in the first place. She was tired of the bad parts of her past. She wanted to gravitate only toward the good, and Donovan was one of the best things that had happened to her in a very long time. She didn't want to wait any more, so she tore open the packet and rolled on the condom.

Donovan pushed Lela's hair from her face as she settled in on her back and he loomed over her. There was a moment or two where all Lela could hear was the sound of her own heartbeat pounding in her ears. It was like he was marking the moment with a pause for dramatic effect, but then he thrust inside and it was yet one more thing about that day that made her think... *wow*. He was somehow different and familiar. She felt satisfied, yet still wanted more—which would always be her biggest takeaway with Donovan. As they found a rhythm, Lela focused on the present. The feel of his muscular ass beneath her calves. His soft, but white-hot, wet and craven kisses. The realization that she was free to do this now. As much as she wanted.

The pressure began to mount faster, and Donovan became more earnest with his charge. He was trying. Hard. She almost felt bad for admitting that he hadn't given her an orgasm the first time... then again, men needed to know these things. They needed to understand that as much as they loved their penis, it was not magical. One had to exert some effort and pay attention. As if he'd heard the random string of things running through her head, Donovan adjusted the angle of his approach, leaving more of his bodyweight to ride over the exact perfect spot. Lela's mind went blank, then black. And then white. And then pink, which seemed totally random. Just like that, the peak knocked her over like a steam-roller. Her body froze, she threw back her head, and that was when she heard and felt Donovan, groaning his approval as his hips slammed against her one last time.

He collapsed on top of her for a moment, kissing her

neck, then shifted on to the bed, letting his arm hit the mattress when he rolled to his back. Lela's eyes opened and closed, over and over, as she had nothing to look at but the ceiling and she struggled to catch her breath. As the waves subsided, she was overcome with the warmest, most wonderful feeling. It was like a big fat piece of chocolate cake on an epic hair day in early spring, when the air is breezy and everything is blissful. Donovan was in her bed. They had a whole weekend ahead of them. Maybe they *would* sneak into a wedding as he'd suggested earlier, or maybe they would just stay naked for two days. If he could make her feel even half of what she felt right now, she'd be stupidly happy.

"Please tell me that was real." He rolled back to his side and kissed her shoulder.

She snuggled closer to him, inhaling his scent, feeling drunk on the beauty that was Donovan. "I solemnly swear that was mind-blowing."

"I'm so relieved."

Lela's brain was delightfully frothy, like a root beer float. Her thoughts were lighter than air, like brightly colored helium balloons floating off into space. "It's not just about an orgasm, you know."

"Sex?"

"Sex with you. I think I was so disappointed the first time because it felt like it meant so much. It was my only chance to get you to see me as something other than just your friend Lela."

"Don't say 'your friend Lela' like that doesn't mean anything. You were always important to me."

"Not as important as you were to me." The words were flowing from her mouth now. She couldn't stop them.

"I don't know about that."

"But you were my everything." Lela closed her eyes, breathing in the heady aroma of Donovan and sex, as sleep was about to pull her into a deep slumber. "I loved you. So. Much."

CHAPTER FIVE

EVEN THOUGH IT was keeping him awake, Donovan was oddly thankful for the near-chainsaw level of Lela's snoring. The buzz helped to drown out the sound of his own hyper-ventilating. His chest was tight. He was sweating. He felt like he might get sick. Lela had unburdened herself from a secret that might have changed the entire course of his life. She was in love with him? Why in the hell hadn't she said something? Why had she chosen to keep that to herself?

He couldn't get comfortable in her bed. The sheets were almost too soft, the mattress too perfectly supportive. The tingling sensation in his shoulders was compounding his rest-lessness. Meanwhile, he couldn't stop thinking about how his life would've turned out differently if he'd had that bit of information at the time. Would he have still married Genevieve? That would've broken Lela's heart. *Oh, wait—it probably did break her heart, dumbass.* Just because he hadn't known about the way she felt, didn't mean her feelings hadn't been there.

That made his stomach churn, because he knew deep down that the minute Genevieve called him and told him about the positive pregnancy test, it was game-over for Donovan. He'd had no choice but to marry her. There was no way he would've shirked the responsibility of a child. He was *not* his dad. Or at least he'd been sure at the time that he wasn't. Then he'd gone and repeated his mistakes just a few years later. So maybe he was at least a little bit his dad. At forty-eight years old, he doubted he could shake it now.

Panic coursed through him. He felt like he was caged in his own body, a prisoner of his thoughts. *Go. Go. Get some fresh air. Get back your freedom.* That seemed like the logical next step, but he'd taken off the only other time he and Lela had slept together. He had to stop repeating the mistakes of the past.

Lela snuggled closer to him and Donovan was truly torn. Last night was supposed to be pure fun, but Lela's words had changed everything. If only he hadn't been such a macho dickhead, wrapped up in the fact that the first time he and Lela had slept together, he'd failed to accomplish his mission. *The* mission. He wanted so badly to be someone different right now—the guy who wouldn't think twice about pulling her closer, who'd have no problem drifting off to sleep, and spending a weekend with her. But would it ever be that simple? For him? The answer was no. It was never, ever that easy. The minute you introduced the idea of becoming entangled, the expectations kicked in, and Donovan always failed. Case in point, the way he was feeling right now, in Lela's bed.

The faintest strains of moonlight filtered through the shades of her bedroom window, lighting up her face. Even though they'd spent so many years apart and not communicating, her friendship still meant so much. She deserved better than this. She deserved better than him. Donovan would bring nothing but misery and bullshit to her life and Lela was the last person he wished that on. As if his body wanted to push him closer to a decision, he felt a zap from his chest to his shoulder. *Am I having a heart attack? WTF? I run like three miles a day. Although, I also eat too much cheese.* He decided that this wasn't physical. This was all in his head. And the sooner he pried himself from this situation, the sooner he and Lela could both return to their lives.

Silently, he peeled back the sheet and slipped off the mattress, doing his best to not disturb Lela. Unfortunately, he couldn't turn on the light to find his clothes, so he was left shuffling around the floor, searching with his feet, then picking up the found clothing and determining whether said garment belonged to him or Lela. He located his boxers. Then his jeans. He was stepping into the former when behind him, the door to Lela's room creaked.

A howl of a meow broke the silence. *Ma-rowwwr.*

"Shhh. Shhh. Shhh," Donovan whispered at Rio.

The cat scampered through the dark and head butted Donovan's leg just as he was balancing on one foot to put on his pants. He stumbled across the floor, his footfalls like boulders tumbling out of the back of a truck. He caught himself on a chair. Rio meowed again. Donovan froze at the earsplitting silence that followed, waiting for several heartbeats, which came lightning fast as he worried Lela was awake.

Snoooooooort. Shhhhhhh. She went back to snoring.

He finally felt like he could exhale. *Shit.*

His escape plan was not going well. He decided he should finish getting dressed downstairs, so he hunted down his shirt and jacket and tiptoed out of the room. With every step down the stairs, guilt hit him a little harder. All he could imagine was Lela's face in the morning and how grossly disappointed she was going to be with him. He would prove himself to be exactly what she'd most likely been thinking all these years—a total loser. It wouldn't be pretty, but it was for the best. Lela had her entire life ahead of her now that she was free of her husband. Donovan was only going to hold her back.

He quickly finished dressing in the kitchen, then looked everywhere for something on which to write a note. He wound up in the living room, where a small desk was tucked into one corner. But when he reached it, there was no paper to be found, and he didn't want to dig through the drawers. He then spotted the printer. *Paper.* The instant he slid it open, it started beeping like a garbage truck backing up. He grabbed a piece and slammed it shut, his heart thundering yet again. He plucked a pen from the coffee mug, but as soon as he clicked it, he was stuck with a new realization—he had no clue what to say. No excuse was going to make him sound like less of an asshole. And he didn't want to lie. Not to Lela.

So he decided that he wouldn't say *why* he was leaving, only that he was.

Dear Lela,

Thank you for an amazing night. It was so good to reconnect. Hopefully I'll see you before another twenty-five years go by.

Love,

Donovan

He sighed, knowing exactly how piss-poor this letter was. It was like a knife in the center of his chest to leave. But he didn't see that he had another choice.

So he left the note on her desk, unlatched the deadbolt, and slipped out through Lela's front door.

CHAPTER SIX

THE MINUTE LELA WOKE UP, she was overcome with another stupidly happy wave of bliss. Her night with Donovan had been wonderful. And there was more ahead. But then she cracked open one eye, saw that he wasn't in her bed, and she immediately knew what had happened. *Fuckity fuck fuck.*

"Donovan?" she called. There was no answer.

He'd taken off. Again.

She rolled to her stomach, face-down in the pillow, wondering if it was possible to smother oneself. It wouldn't be the worst way to go. Simple. Elegant. No blood. Although whenever the paramedics arrived, they would see her butt first and that simply wasn't a fate she was willing to accept. How would they describe her in their report? Old divorced woman found dead face-down and naked on her bed, with cat lovingly curled up at her side.

Nope. Donovan might have done exactly what she'd feared, but she wasn't going to let it defeat her. And least not right away. Lela forced herself to roll out of bed, then grabbed her robe. Not wanting to be the most hopelessly pessimistic person in the world, she tried his name one more time in the hallway. "Donovan?" She didn't wait long for an answer. She was optimistic; not stupid. She started off for the kitchen, Rio threatening to trip her by snaking between her ankles, meowing his little furry head off.

Sure enough, the kitchen was empty. "Donovan, you are such an asshole," she said out loud, if only for her own satisfaction.

Rio, having zero regard for Lela's personal problems, nudged his food bowl with his nose then voiced another plaintive meow. Lela put coffee on, then poured a scoop of kibble. She watched him eat, realizing what an enviably simple life he had. Seriously. The biggest stressor of his existence was the fact that he relied on a human to feed him. Otherwise, he napped in sunbeams, rolled around on the carpet with toys, crouched around corners and attacked unwitting victims who ultimately showered him with affection.

Coffee ready, Lela poured herself a mug. What would this scene have been like if Donovan had actually stuck around? Probably awkward as hell. She knew what he was like, only really willing to dig in when things were fun. He didn't handle serious very well, and what had seemed so carefree at midnight was definitely going to be far less so in the light of day. What in the world had she been thinking? It was too easy to get caught up in the whirlwind of Donovan, enticed by his charm and good looks, by his brains and the easy way they fell in together. Stupid. The whole thing had been incredibly stupid.

Lela wandered into the living room and spotted the note.

She ran her fingers over the scrawl of ink, wondering what had been going through his head when he'd written it. She wished she understood his unwillingness to stick around for her. There had to be something more to it than the simplest conclusion—that something about her drove him away. Maybe it was the same thing Mark hadn't liked about her. Or, perhaps some men were fickle creatures who deserved to fuck off. She remained undecided.

She took her coffee cup to the kitchen sink then went back upstairs to shower in her bathroom. Her phone rang with a video call from Tammera. Lela laughed quietly before accepting the call. Tams had a sixth sense about Lela's life crises. She'd literally called Lela to check in with her less than five minutes after Mark asked for a divorce.

"Hey, Tams." Lela nestled the phone in the old-school toothbrush holder hanging on the wall next to the equally antiquated medicine chest, with the mirror's silver peeling at the corners.

"Something is wrong. I just know it." Tammera was sitting on her couch, her dark natural curls gathered on top of her head. She had the most enviable complexion—a warm brown, glowing and made for television.

"How do you know these things?" Lela scrutinized her face in the mirror. She'd earned every line, especially that crease between her eyes, but they didn't feel like a badge of honor today. The same for every gray hair—had they been multiplying while she slept? There were twice as many as yesterday. It felt too much like the fickle finger of fate reminding her that she didn't have her whole life ahead of her. She had half. Probably less.

"Well, let's see. You didn't return my phone call

yesterday and now you're in your bathroom staring at your wrinkles. It's pretty obvious to me that things aren't all right in your world."

Lela blew out a breath picked up her phone and sat down on the closed toilet lid, resting an elbow on the vanity. "I slept with my college crush last night and he left before I woke up."

Tammera wasn't fazed by much, but this prompted a hand clamped over her mouth. "No fucking way."

"Yep fucking yep."

"Is this what happens when you get divorced? You make poor decisions about sex?"

Lela shrugged. "Maybe? Probably? I don't know, Tams. This is my first time at this rodeo."

"Was it good?"

Lela couldn't contain the traitorous smile that cropped up on her face. Her cheeks flushed with a mix of embarrassment and pride. Last night had been fantastic. So, no, it wasn't a total loss, even if her ego was dinged. "Way better than the other time we slept together. Twenty-five years did wonders for his skills."

"Then why did he take off? Did something happen?"

Lela was about to answer that everything went great, but as the details rifled through her mind in fast fashion, something popped into her memory. It was like a brand new pimple dead center on your forehead when you were about to walk out the door for a date. "Oh, shit."

"What?"

Lela squinted, wincing at her own stupidity. "I told him that I was in love with him in college."

"Why did you do that?"

"I don't know. I was delirious from the most epic orgasm of my life?"

Tammera shook her head like a damn metronome, then took a patient sip of her coffee. The whole sequence was silent, but felt super judgmental. "Oh, that's bad."

"You're my best friend. You're supposed to say something supportive."

"Like what? That he probably didn't hear what you said? He snuck out in the middle of the night. It's pretty clear you freaked him out."

Lela was so pissed at herself she could hardly stand it. Here she'd been thinking this was all on Donovan, when the reality was she'd contributed to this nightmarish outcome. Why had she felt the need to make such a confession? That was the past. Ancient history. Not worth repeating. "Ugh. You're right. You're so right."

"Think of it this way. It's probably better that he left. The belated I love you doesn't make great breakfast conversation."

"No. It doesn't." Lela sighed. "I need to get my act together."

Tammera waved it off and sat back on her couch. "Cut yourself some slack right now. Acting erratically isn't a personal shortcoming. Anyone would in your situation."

Lela stood and looked at herself in the mirror again, returning her phone to its previous perch. She threaded a finger through her hair, flipping strands back and forth. The gray had gotten crazy. Like out of control. "What if I dye my hair purple? Or red? Or something totally out there and dramatic?"

"You could do that, but I'll tell you what I used to tell my clients who wanted bangs after a big breakup. Wait a few days. Let the sting of this incident fade a little bit." Tammera was tapping the expertise she'd gained during her previous career as a hair stylist. "Or maybe don't color it at all. I like gray. A lot."

"Maybe..." Lela couldn't help it. Something deep inside her was yearning for change. She'd been feeling that way since the divorce. So why was she looking to her past? Going to weddings and sleeping with Donovan? Those weren't steps forward, they were stumbles back. "I just need something new and exciting in my life. Something to look forward to. Something that helps me get my mind off the fact that I'm forty-seven and divorced in New York and that I might as well be dead as far as most men are concerned."

"I know honey. I'm sorry you're feeling this way."

Lela shook her head. "But you don't know. You're in a relationship. You're in love." Lela willingly admitted to her envy of Tammera's life—stability, a killer job, and love. What more could anyone want? "How is Delia, anyway?"

"Good. Her lease is ending in two months, so we're thinking about moving in together."

Lela felt as though her heart might swell to twice its normal size. At least her best friend was happy. "That's so wonderful. Are you excited?"

"I love her, so I'm excited about seeing her everyday, but I'm also worried I might be too set in my ways. I've been living by myself forever." She shrugged. "We'll see."

"It's still nice."

"Yes, it is. But stop trying to change the topic. You're in crisis, Lela. You're not being yourself."

There was the pity people had slathered on her the moment she split from Mark. It made her cringe. Maybe because she simply had never wanted to be in a situation requiring sympathy. "It is what it is."

Tammera unleashed a distinct frown. "Don't resort to corporate clichés. You deserve better than that."

"I don't know what I deserve at this point. All I know is that I'm tired of letting men have so much influence on my happiness. First Mark, now Donovan." Maybe it was time to worry about the one person men always worried about first— themselves. "I need to focus on me. Get my act together."

"Maybe you should think about what that actually looks like." Tammera leaned forward, peering right into her phone. She had an uncanny ability to buzz the lens, as they liked to say in film and television—connect with people, even via a camera. It was undoubtedly part of what launched Tammera's career as a celebrity chef. "Look. You are an amazing, beautiful, brilliant and vibrant woman who happened to marry a bowl of mayonnaise."

Lela snickered. Mark *was* pasty. "And your point is?"

"That is your old life. Think about what you want your *new* life to look like. I mean really think about it."

"Okay. I will."

"No. I mean right now. Close your eyes and try to envision what you want."

"While we're on video chat?"

"Yes. The sooner you do this, the sooner you and I can go back to talking about *The Great British Baking Show* and why Paul Hollywood is the only man who has ever done it for me."

"He does it for everyone who appreciates good bread and steely blue eyes."

"Shush, Lela. Close your eyes. Do it. Now."

This seemed like a peculiar exercise, but Lela put a lot of trust in her best friend, so she did as Tammera asked, dropping into near darkness when her eyes fluttered shut.

"Now relax," Tammera said in a voice similar to the ones used in guided meditation recordings. "I want you to see yourself. A year from now. Two years from now."

"Okay..."

"What do you look like? What are you doing that makes you happy? Don't think about relationships or love. For once in your life, just think about you. Nobody else."

"Okay..."

"What do you see?"

Lela felt a bit like she was groping for nothing in the dark, but she pushed herself to concentrate. *What do I want? What do I need?* "I'm happy. I'm smiling." Lela felt a tug in the center of her chest, like an invisible force was pulling her in a new direction. She let it take her, just to see where she was going.

"Excellent. What does your life look like?"

"I got new furniture for my apartment. I finally got rid of Mark's ugly-ass stuff."

"Praise the lord."

"And I'm wearing much girlier clothes, all the time. Everything Mark thought was ridiculous."

"I love it. And what about your career?"

This was a big one, the step she'd been too scared to take. "I've started Lela B. And it's going well. People like it."

"Yes!" Tammera clapped so loudly it sounded like a crack of thunder.

Lela jumped. Her eyes popped open. Before her, in the mirror, was only her reflection. Every wrinkle and acne scar that had been there before. But there was fresh color in her cheeks. A bright pink. Her eyes were clear. She turned to the side and the sun caught a few silver strands of hair. They glinted in the morning light. They practically sparkled. Why was she hiding her sparkle? Why was she waiting for any of these things she wanted? She was done delaying her dreams, and she was over trying to make anyone else happy. "And I think I'm going to try going gray."

"Wait. Really?"

"I think it's pretty, but the hair dye aisle at the grocery store says I'm supposed to cover it up. Why does gray have to be bad?"

"It doesn't. At all."

"Exactly. Going gray is normal. And like every other bull-shit standard of beauty, society wants me to hide my age. I'm tired of hiding."

"It could end up being super cute. If nothing else, I bet you end up with one of those wickedly cool streaks."

"Yes. Like Stacy on *What Not to Wear*." Lela was convinced. This meant something. Silver could mark her future. And while she was at it, she might as well start transforming her career. "Also, I'm dropping my makeup clients."

That got Tammera's attention. "No. You cannot do this to me. You make me look amazing on camera."

Lela picked up her phone and looked her best friend in the eye. "Do you really think I would do that to you?"

"Maybe? I don't know. You just got ghosted after a one-night stand with a guy you haven't seen in twenty years. Anything is possible."

"I'm not letting you down. I will do your makeup for as

long as you want me to. Until I'm so crippled with arthritis that my hands are like claws and I can hardly stand up."

"I doubt my show will be on the air for that long, but thanks." Tammera cocked her head ever-so-slightly. "Does this mean what I think it means?"

Lela nodded eagerly. "Yep. I'm going full throttle on my skincare and cosmetics line. Lela B is officially a go."

CHAPTER SEVEN

Three years later

LELA HAD KEPT HER PROMISE. She had not dropped Tammera as a makeup client, even when squeezing her in became a bigger and bigger challenge as Lela B slowly took off. Some days, Lela's little company took a baby step—a new retailer, some praise from a beauty influencer, or a new product that had gone over well with customers. But she'd had her share of setbacks, too—failed formulations, colors that flopped, and stores where Lela B simply never got any traction.

But two years in, a tiny miracle happened. JTI, a consortium of fashion and beauty brands, made an offer to bring Lela B into their corporate family. It meant that Lela could finally move her office out of her house, pay herself more money, and streamline production. It also meant a vast array of opportunities—connections, partnerships, and relationships that would've taken Lela years to establish. But all that good fortune also translated to a lot of irons in the fire, making it even more difficult to find time for Tammera.

"Thank you for coming today, love. I know work is crazy right now." Tammera turned her head back and forth, admiring herself in the mirror of her dressing room at the Cook It! studios. "Looks amazing. As always."

Lela grinned. "Eighty percent of that is you. I can't take much credit. Now look up." She swiped a second coat of thick black mascara onto Tammera's lashes.

Tammera blinked at herself in the mirror. "Ooh. My lashes are so thick and lush. Is this a new product?"

"It is. I'd love to hear what you think. I feel confident in it, but I figure that if it holds up to you standing over a steaming pot of whatever goodness you're cooking while under studio lights, it's definitely good to go." Lela applied a final coat of powder, then removed the tissues protecting Tammera's clothes. "You're all set."

Tammera got up from the chair and gathered her things—a bottle of water and a notebook that never left her side. She often said that recipe inspiration could come at any time. "What do you have going for the rest of the day?"

Lela consulted the time on her phone. "I have to run home and change for a meeting at JTI. They're shifting Lela B to another division."

"They're moving you again? Do you think that's a bad thing?"

"I don't. I talked to my dad about it. He said it's just part of what corporations do."

"Your dad's a retired chemistry teacher. What does he know about it?"

"Actually, he worked for a big company before he transitioned into teaching. He developed patents on all kinds of household products in the seventies."

Tammera nodded. "Huh. And now he's helping you with makeup. Talented guy."

"He just consults now. The scientists in the JTI labs do the heavy lifting." Lela's dad, Ben, and her mom, Deb, were incredibly supportive, but they'd also become far more present in her life since the divorce. They were visiting New York three or four times a year now, just so they could make sure she was "okay". It was incredibly sweet and adorable, but Lela couldn't ignore the central conclusion her parents had made—even though the divorce had happened three years ago, Lela was still in a vulnerable space. She didn't feel that way, but she wasn't about to tell her parents not to come.

"Are you worried about this shift?" Tammera made air quotes for added effect.

"It sounds scarier than it is, which is sort of funny, because I think they call it a shift to make it sound less frightening." Lela started packing up her rolling makeup case. "But no, I'm not worried. I mean, we're doing well, but we're still small potatoes. I don't have that much say in it."

"It's probably all numbers to them."

"Exactly."

Tammera raised her hand to her lips to blow a kiss and say goodbye. "I should get into the studio. I'd hug you, but it'll mess up your hard work."

"I appreciate that."

"Good luck today, honey. I believe in you." Tammera underscored her good wishes with a wink. "Oh, and by the way, you're looking fabulous today. Especially the hair." With that, she disappeared down the hall.

Lela hustled to pack up the last of her things, then ran downstairs, and hailed a cab to her apartment. It took about twenty minutes to get changed, fix her makeup and hop into a different taxi to hightail it to the JTI offices in the garment district, which wasn't far but she was on a tight schedule. As they whizzed through the city, Lela couldn't help but feel like today was going to be a big day. A good day. There was a flutter of excitement in her chest. JTI had every reason to put Lela B in the best possible situation. If nothing else, at least they were paying attention.

When Lela stepped out of the cab, it was the first time she'd picked up on what a truly beautiful day it was—warm and sunny, like a reminder from Mother Nature that summer would arrive any minute now, even though it was still May. As she strode down the sidewalk, she felt eyes on her. This was a recent phenomenon in her life, happening more and more often in the last year. Before this, if people were staring, she either had toilet paper on her shoe or food on her face.

Now that her gray had fully grown out, people took notice. A lot of people. Lela had never, *ever* been "that girl", the one who turned heads. She'd been to a million parties in her life and had virtually no one take a second look. Things were a little different now. She might have devoted her career to making other women beautiful, but for the first time in her life, she felt that way about herself, and a big part of that was her glorious silver hair. She wasn't about to let it go to her head, but she was glad that going gray had a silver lining.

Inside the building, she swiped her ID across the security turnstile scanner, then made her way to the elevators. A super handsome, younger man stood next to her, and flashed her a flirtatious smile. "Which floor?" he asked when they stepped on board.

"Twenty-two."

He pushed the button for her floor, then another for sixteen. They rode together in silence, but there was an undercurrent of sexual tension ping-ponging off the walls. It was awkward as hell. So much so, that she was thankful when the elevator dinged. She had work to do, not sex to think about.

The man stepped out, then looked back at her. "Love the hair, by the way."

"Thank you." Lela felt her face flush with heat. She might be done jumping through hoops for men, but she still appreciated tastefully delivered attention.

Up on her floor, Lela's office was tucked into a corner with a smallish window that mostly had a view of the ugly 70s architecture of the building across the street. She had no staff, just an admin she shared with another of the small JTI brands, and she got marketing and advertising support from various teams within JTI. She benefited from the muscle of a large multinational corporation, but she also felt like a tiny cog in the machine.

She dropped off her things, then headed up two more floors to one of the more modest conference rooms. She lost some of her earlier confidence when she stepped inside and saw the panel of four JTI staffers she'd never met before. Across from them was a lone chair, apparently destined for her.

"Good afternoon, Ms. Bennett," one woman said as she flipped through a binder. "Please. Take a seat."

Lela did as she was asked. "Good afternoon, everyone."

"This will be quick. We just want to get you up to speed on some reorganization we're doing. We're hoping we can help your company..." The woman consulted the paperwork before her, drawing her finger down the page. "Lela B, step onto a larger stage."

Okay, so they didn't know the name of Lela's baby. At least they were talking about better prospects. "Yes."

"One of our subsidiaries, Echo Echo, is interested in working with you, and we think the move makes a lot of sense. They're primarily a collection of niche fashion brands, but they're doing a deeper dive on beauty. Apparently, they heard about Lela B and thought it could be a good fit."

Lela's heart swelled with pride. She'd heard about Echo Echo. It was a big deal. Unfortunately, she knew almost no details, but this seemed promising. "Can you tell me more? How things will change for me?"

"Well, I believe they want you to move your offices up where they are. They have three floors upstairs. Thirty-nine and up from there. They have their own marketing and advertising departments, so that will be a change for you as well."

The idea of working with a dedicated team held great appeal. Lela often felt like she was just an item on a to-do list, rather than a real priority. "Great. When does all of this happen?"

"It'll be effective immediately. We went ahead and took the liberty of setting up a meeting for you and the Echo Echo founder today at two o'clock. Does that work for your schedule?"

Like Lela wasn't going to rearrange everything to get this

ball rolling. Of course she was. "Absolutely. Who's the founder?"

The woman looked at her like she was nuts. "Echo James. That's how the company got its name."

Echo James. Echo James. *Holy crap.* Lela felt like a complete idiot. And also like the universe might be punking her. Echo James was Donovan's daughter. Echo Echo must have been the company he'd been helping her with when he'd been in the city three years ago.

Luckily, Lela was certain that Donovan was out of the picture. As far as she knew, he was still living in San Francisco. Plus, she wasn't worried about any potential run-ins with him. It might sting a little, but he had just as much to be embarrassed about as she did. Maybe more. It was all water under the bridge as far as she was concerned. Old news, and Lela spent zero time worried about the past. There was too much to look forward to.

"Just tell me where I need to go."

CHAPTER EIGHT

FOR DONOVAN, the best part of being back in New York full-time was working with his daughter, Echo. It had only been a few weeks of consulting for her fast-growing lifestyle company, Echo Echo, but he already felt like this had been the right move.

This was a big step forward in their father-daughter relationship. When he'd first tried to help her three years ago, things hadn't gone so great. Echo had been leery of his advice. She was fresh out of grad school, eager to make a name for herself, and determined to do everything on her own. That left Donovan out in the cold, which was probably what he deserved anyway. He hadn't been there much for Echo when she was growing up. And that was a problem born of unmet expectations and broken promises. It couldn't get fixed overnight.

Three years had made a world of difference for Echo's business. It had taken two for her to get her company off the ground, and since then, it was as if the accelerator had dropped out from under her foot. She was acquired by JTI, given three floors of a beautiful building in the garment district, and granted a substantial influx of funding to bring more brands on board. More important than any of that, she had carte blanche to do whatever the hell she wanted. From Donovan's extensive experience helping entrepreneurs navigate the never-ending maze of corporate structures, he knew very well that his daughter had a rare opportunity.

"Dad. Are things always going to feel this crazy? Like my whole life is going completely off the rails?" Echo stabbed at her salad. This was their now-weekly lunch date, eating takeout and sitting on the couch in Echo's office.

"Probably. At least a little bit." Donovan took a bite of his sandwich—low sodium turkey on whole grain bread. He did his best to eat well, since the occasional tightness in his chest still didn't have a medical explanation. The one time he'd been to a doctor, the EKG and every other test came back normal.

"Thanks. That's exactly what I did *not* want to hear."

"Honey, look. This is what happens when you have a hot commodity. It was only a matter of time before the powers-that-be decided to put significant resources into what you're doing. And with more money, comes more responsibility."

"There are so many moving parts."

"That's why I'm here. To help you through all of it."

"And I'm glad you were willing to move all the way across the country to do it." She smiled warmly at him, her big brown eyes flashing so much genuine affection it made his heart hurt. Donovan knew life was giving him a second chance with his daughter, and he was not going to blow it.

"I will do anything for you. I hope you know that."

"I do. And I appreciate it."

"Let's take a break from work. How are things going with wedding planning?"

Echo closed her eyes, sucked a slow deep breath in her through her nose and forcefully blew it out. She was all about relaxation techniques and being mindful, and this was one of her most tried-and-true methods. After three cycles of in-and-out, her eyes popped open and she looked right at him. "Fine. Everything is fine."

Donovan sat back and crossed his legs, ready to do a whole lot of listening. "Clearly, it's not."

"I'm trying to manifest a state of fine, okay? I keep telling myself that if I say it's all going well, it will actually go well."

"Is there anything I can do?"

"Not unless you want to call Mom and tell her to back off."

Donovan cleared his throat. On a very long list of things he did not relish, at the top was getting into anything with his ex-wife, Genevieve. She had a lethal way of shutting down anyone else's thoughts, opinions or ideas. It was part of what led to their divorce. Genevieve had gotten tired of him. Or his apparent stupidity. "I think we both know she's not going to listen to me."

"True." A grumble left Echo's throat. It was the same noise she used to make when she was a little girl and had reached peak frustration.

"The only approach with your mother is a direct one. Tell her that she's stressing you out."

"She wants to be involved. I can't cut her out of the planning."

"I'm not saying that. I'm merely suggesting you try to get

her to ease up. She'll listen to you, honey. You're probably the one person she'll actually listen to."

"I hate that I have to say anything at all. I'm a grown-ass woman. I should be allowed to organize my own wedding." She kneaded her forehead for a moment then took another of her cleansing breaths and grabbed her phone from the coffee table. "Oh, shoot. I have fifteen minutes until my meeting with the founder of the cosmetics line JTI is moving over to us. Do you want to sit in?"

"Sure. I don't know a thing about makeup, but if you want me there, I'm happy to do it."

"Let me show you the website." Echo got up and grabbed her laptop from her desk, then returned to the couch and plopped down next to Donovan. "Depending on how the meeting goes, I'm thinking about asking her to help me oversee the beauty division. She's been a professional makeup artist for over twenty years and really knows her stuff."

"What's the company called?"

"Here it is." Echo pulled up the website. "It's called Lela B."

Donovan nearly choked on his sandwich. "Wait. What did you say?"

"Lela B. They specialize in products formulated for women over forty. I'm sure you saw in the JTI market research that we're reaching a much broader age demographic than we first thought. Plus, these are customers with a lot more disposable income."

Echo began scrolling through the website. Meanwhile, Donovan was starting to experience that tightening in his chest again. "Is there an About page?"

Echo scanned the screen. "Yep. Hold on."

The page loaded and Donovan did a double take. Because there was Lela, looking completely different. "Holy crap." The words spouted from his mouth like water from a faucet.

"What?" Echo reared back her head.

"She's completely gray."

"Dad. What the hell? She's gorgeous. Who cares if she has gray hair?"

Donovan rattled his head back and forth, if only to shake himself into the present. "No. That's not what I mean." Although Donovan could admit to himself that it was unusual to see a gray-haired woman at the helm of a beauty company. "I know her."

"Who? Her?" Echo pointed to the photo of Lela.

"Yes. Lela Bennett. We went to college together. We were good friends. The last time I saw her was three years ago. When I came to New York when you were finishing grad school." A sharp pain sizzled in his stomach. He winced at the discomfort.

"Dad. Are you okay?" Echo gently placed her hand on his shoulder, her face painted with concern.

He nodded, willing it all to go away. "I'm fine. Probably just my lunch disagreeing with me."

"Are you sure? I feel like you tell me that and you aren't actually okay."

"So says the woman who's trying to will herself into a state of fine with her wedding. I'm good. Don't worry about me."

Echo narrowed her stare on him, seeming unconvinced. She returned her sights to the computer, then back again to him. "Is this going to be a problem? Is there something I need to know about Lela Bennett? Because you're acting super weird."

He cleared his throat. He would not lie to his daughter, but he also wanted to reassure her. "This is not a problem. If you want to work with Lela, I think it's a fantastic idea. I can assure you that she's wonderful."

"Were you two an item at some point?"

"Not exactly."

"Boyfriend-girlfriend?"

"Never that serious."

"Friends with benefits? Fuck buddies?"

"Echo. Seriously? You use that terminology with your father?"

"Just be straight with me, Dad. Because I know you, and when you and women are involved, it never ends well. Ever."

He sucked in what felt like his forty-seventh cleansing breath. "Lela and I were best friends in college, okay? Very close. We grew apart when I married your mom. We ran into each other three years ago and that was the last time I saw her."

"And? Is there more?"

It wasn't easy for a dad to divulge his bad behavior to his daughter, especially since he'd actually managed to make amends with Echo. But he was going to have to own up to this. Echo would see through his facade the instant he and Lela were in the same room. "We slept together. Twice. But it was nothing. There was no romance. It won't interfere with any working relationship we might have."

"Okay. Well, that's fine, but I need you to promise me that there will be zero funny business."

"Don't worry. Zero funny business."

"I'm serious."

"I've told you a hundred times. Dating and all of that isn't for me anymore. I'm done."

"I'm not entirely sure I believe you, but I'm going to hold you to your word." She got up and offered her hand. "Come on. Let's get to reception and grab her for this meeting."

As they walked down the hall, Donovan sensed he was about to meet a very uncertain future. It was confirmed when they rounded the corner into the reception area, and he saw Lela. Her hair was the most striking difference—it fell in luminescent ribbons around her face, lighting up the features he'd always found so attractive—her big blue eyes and slightly off-kilter smile, framed by what he could admit were very kissable lips. As she stood and their gazes connected, it brought back that moment in Bryant Park three years ago, when they'd both been watching a stranger's wedding. That had been such a fun day. An amazing day. But like so many things in his life, what had started out great had not ended that way.

"You must be Lela," Echo said, eagerly shaking her hand.

"Hello." Lela's face absolutely lit up. "You must be Echo."

Donovan hoped to discern Lela's attitude toward him from the tone in her voice, but unfortunately, a handful of syllables were not going to be enough. "Lela. How funny is this?" He reached for her elbow and went to kiss her cheek but before he got anywhere close to accomplishing either, Lela stuck out her hand, effectively distancing herself from him.

"It's so funny, isn't it?" She gave him just enough of a

death stare to illustrate that she did not find this situation humorous. Not at all.

"I cannot believe you know my dad," Echo said. "It's fate."

"Something like that," he mumbled, not acknowledged by either member of his audience.

"Let's sit down in my office and have a chat about our partnership," Echo said. "I'm really looking forward to this."

"Me, too." Lela glanced at Donovan, then promptly disregarded him, focusing on Echo. The two women quickly became a flurry of conversation.

Suddenly, his golden opportunity to earn a real relationship with his daughter was not so shiny. His past mistakes were catching up with him. Again.

CHAPTER NINE

FREAKING DONOVAN. Back in Lela's life. Except this time, it wasn't going to be for a few hours or a night. He was working for Echo, and for all intents and purposes, so was Lela. Which meant, by some bizarre alignment of the stars, she and Donovan were now co-workers. Life had officially jumped the shark.

Lela settled in at a round glossy white table for four in Echo's office, while Echo took a call and Donovan was somewhere off in the hall. She stole a chance to admire Echo's workspace with a mix of black, white, pale pink, and matte gold accents. It was so much more chic than Lela's office. She'd have to do something about that when she made her move.

Of course, furnishings were simply a distraction. The real task at hand, balancing her distrust of Donovan with her need for the Echo Echo arrangement to succeed, would be a monumental task. Sitting alone and feeling more anxious by the moment was not putting her in a great headspace to accomplish either of those things, so she made a mental list of dos and don'ts to keep herself on track.

Do remain unflappable, professional, and above it all.

Do appreciate that this is ultimately the opportunity of a lifetime.

Do find a way to establish ground rules with Donovan.

Don't think about kissing Donovan.

Don't look at his ass in those jeans.

Don't forget that Donovan broke your heart. Twice.

As if he'd heard the thoughts in her head, Donovan strolled into Echo's office. He hesitated for a moment, eyeing his daughter, who was standing near the tall window, still talking on the phone. His sights fell on Lela at the table, and she could see the moment when he resigned himself to his fate. There was no obvious choice for him in this situation other than to sit down with her. So he did. Right next to her.

"I need you to not mess this up for me, okay?" Lela asked out of the side of her mouth, smiling like an idiot so Echo would be none the wiser.

"I need you to not mess this up for *me*. So we're even."

Why in the hell was he being so bristly with her? "Nice of you to let me know you were back in New York."

He cleared his throat, a habit that she'd once found sort of charming, but now grated on her nerves. "It's only been a few weeks. I've been busy. I would've gotten around to it."

Likely story.

Echo got off her call. "Sorry about that. Should we go ahead and get started?" Echo scooped up a notebook from her desk and took a seat at the table next to Lela. "I just want to have a conversation about our next steps."

Lela snapped to attention, opening her planner to a blank sheet in the back. "Yes. I'd love to hear more about that."

Donovan cleared his throat again and leaned his elbow on the table, a bit too close for Lela's taste, but she decided that she might as well start practicing the art of not falling under Donovan's spell.

"Me too," Donovan said. "Since this is my first time sitting in on one of these meetings."

Echo sat a little straighter. She was a stunning and dynamic young woman. That was no surprise—she was the product of an excellent gene pool. Her wavy brown hair, flawless olive complexion, and big brown eyes, coupled with her warm and generous personality, made it impossible to look away. "So, Lela, my whole philosophy behind Echo Echo is the marriage of story, creator, and approachability. I want our products to tell a story. I believe that our creators are an essential part of that story, since they are the origin of everything we sell. And I want everything we offer, whether it's a beautiful dress or a casual pair of shoes or a pair of earrings—or now, an amazing mascara—to be accessible to everyone."

Lela furiously scribbled down her notes, duly impressed that Echo had a mission that went beyond merely hawking products. When she'd first met Echo in the lobby, Lela had seen the effortless radiance of her mom, Genevieve. But now, Lela saw Donovan. He'd always had a knack for picking things apart and examining them, trying to make them better or more than they were. This ability was surely part of what had made him so successful. Now Lela was seeing the same in his daughter, and it quite frankly, made her adore Echo. Lela was falling. Head over heels.

"This all sounds amazing," Lela started. "I feel so privileged that you see Lela B being part of what you do. I also appreciate that you've put so much time and thought into the vision of your company. I love being a part of JTI, but this makes me feel like there will be more purpose behind what I'm doing, which is great. I'd like to do more than simply sell makeup." Lela hoped she wasn't laying it on too thick, but her words were sincere.

"Fantastic. I think our first step is a whole new media campaign. Electronic billboards, web advertising, bus wraps. The whole nine yards. We need to position you, and put the Lela B name out there." Echo knocked her head to one side and pointed her pen at Lela. "Which means we need to get *you* out there."

"You mean the products?" Lela asked.

"No. I mean *you*. You are the face of the company. You're the expert and the one with the passion. You are the campaign."

Donovan had been remarkably still, but he was now squirming in his seat. Lela could relate. This wasn't going down easy for her, either. She liked being in the background. She wasn't used to center stage.

"We'll do a photo shoot. Dad has an amazing photographer friend who I think could be perfect for this." Echo turned to Donovan. "Do you think Nico would be open to photographing Lela? He's got that raw Annie Leibowitz vibe that I just love."

"Are you serious?" Donovan and Lela asked the question in unison. Lela felt she was entitled to her surprise. It was insulting coming from him.

Echo reared back her head. "Whoa, you two. That was freaky."

"Was it?" Donovan tapped a pen on the legal pad he had taken exactly zero notes on.

"Yes. The timing. The same words."

Donovan shrugged. "It's a logical question. You're trying to sell beauty products." For a moment, stone cold silence fell over the room as they all seemed to pick up the thread Donovan was about to pull on. It went something like this—selling beauty products required beautiful people, and that was not Lela. "I mean, Lela is an attractive woman, but I'm not sure she sends the right message."

Lela planted an elbow on the table, propped her head on her hand, turned to face Donovan while wishing she could shoot laser beams out of her eyes. "And what message is that, exactly?"

She relished his initial look of uncertainty, but then she witnessed the moment when something else clicked in for him, and he regained his natural arrogance. "Look, Lela, I say this for your benefit as well as Echo's. I know you want Lela B to do well and be successful. And I know that Echo wouldn't bring you on board if she wasn't confident in the line's ability to do exactly that. But I sincerely have to wonder if a campaign with a gray-haired woman is going to help us achieve those goals."

"Dad. I can't believe you said that," Echo said.

Lela slowly shook her head, not taking her eyes off Donovan while addressing Echo. "It's okay. I understand what he's saying." It took an iron will to remain composed. Hearing that from the man she'd once cared about so much was a punch to the gut. And there were so many damn layers to what he'd said, it felt impossible to pick it all apart. She wasn't about to launch into the personal, so she focused on the larger issue. She and Tammera talked about this often, and it was a topic that burned hot inside of Lela—her belief that no woman should be pushed aside because of the way she chose to present herself to the world.

"So you agree?" Donovan asked.

Good God, she wanted to slap him. Right across his handsome face. Really hard, creating a noise so loud that it could be heard out in the hall. Or maybe in outer space.

Obviously she wasn't going to resort to violence. Donovan was an ass, but she knew what she was dealing with. And she wasn't about to take a flamethrower to her new partnership with Echo Echo. "I don't agree, but I'm biased. I made the choice to let my hair go gray. I made the choice to stop trying to hold on to my youth. It takes entirely too much energy. I'd rather focus on the here-and-now, which is me, exactly the way you see me. So, I'd like to hear what Echo thinks. It's her company, after all." Lela eased back in her chair, feeling satisfied that she'd said exactly what she needed to say. Even so, her heart was pounding fiercely.

"Dad, I've made a point of challenging all sorts of standards of beauty. They're so ridiculously narrow. Size, color, shape. The list goes on and on. Why not tackle age? I think the time could be right."

"I don't make the rules," Donovan said. "I think it's great that you want to change the narrative, but some standards will be harder to do away with than others. Age is a tough nut to crack. It's so entrenched. And you're trying to do this with a brand that hasn't fully established itself in the marketplace."

"But everyone gets older. Doesn't it make sense that we would celebrate that rather than devoting so much energy to hiding it?" Echo countered.

He doodled a few circles on the corner of the paper before him. "Maybe. Or maybe we let someone else blaze that trail with a more well-known commodity. Some of the bigger brands are in a much better position to do it."

Echo blew out a frustrated sigh. "I feel really strongly about this. Lela is gorgeous, her hair is rad, and I love Lela B. So, we're doing this. If it fails, we pivot. But I don't think it will."

Donovan smiled, but Lela knew for a fact that it was forced. "Okay, then. You're the boss."

"Great. We'll get the production team on it. First step is to get the photographer booked and we'll go from there."

Lela could hardly believe she'd made an argument for doing the thing she didn't want to do—the photo shoot. But she had to stick up for herself. And Echo's idea, for that matter.

"I'll call him right after this meeting," Donovan said.

Echo smiled and reached over to touch Lela's shoulder. "The only other thing we need to go over is moving your office. That'll happen later today, if that's okay with you. Our office manager will pull it all together. Then you can be up and running tomorrow morning."

"Where are you putting her?" Donovan asked.

"In that empty office right next to you."

Fantastic. Just what I don't need. "Great."

CHAPTER TEN

DONOVAN FELT a little beat down after his meeting with Lela and Echo, but what could he do? He was committed to forging a stronger bond with his daughter, and also determined to help her reach a greater level of success. The comment about Lela's gray hair was completely valid as far as he was concerned. He knew his stuff. Gray meant old, and old was not a beauty ideal anyone was willing to put down cold hard cash to achieve. It wasn't his fault. He did not make the rules.

Even so, he felt a twinge of guilt over Lela being on the receiving end of his comments. It wasn't about her. It was all about the bottom line.

When their meeting broke up, Echo hopped on a call, which left Lela and Donovan walking out into the hall together. Lela immediately beelined her way toward reception, but Donovan felt like they had to clear the air. "Lela, wait."

She came to a halt, but didn't turn around. "What?"

He took several strides to catch up with her. "We should talk. In private."

"I don't want this to be weird, Donovan. You do your job, I'll do mine, and we can simply try to stay out of each other's way."

That was a valid approach. It still didn't sit well with him. "Five minutes. I'll show you where your new office is going to be."

She managed an exasperated smile. "Okay. Fine."

"Come on. We're going this way." Donovan led them in the opposite direction down the hall, pointing out the various offices occupied by Echo Echo staff. When he was close to the end, he walked into what was about to become Lela's new work abode. "Here you go."

She froze in the doorway. "Is this a joke?"

"No. Is something wrong? Not nice enough?"

Lela proceeded in slow motion, like she didn't trust what he was saying. "Do you have any idea what my current JTI office looks like?" She peered out through one of the towering windows, which had the same halfway decent view Donovan's office did. The JTI building was one of the tallest in this part of town, so you could see a few stretches of the city.

"No clue."

"I'm down on twenty-two, in what is essentially a janitor's closet with a window. I have a lovely view of the building across the street. In the afternoon, I can watch a man take off his socks and rub his bare feet on his desk."

Donovan winced. "Sounds gross."

"It's disgusting."

"Well, I'm glad this is a step up for you." He stuffed his hands into his pockets and leaned against the wall near the window. "I'm sorry about what I said in there. I have to protect Echo and her interests."

"I get it. I still think you're a jerk, but I get it."

"I am a jerk. We've established that."

"You made it that way. I'm just stating the obvious."

That was fair, but Donovan still felt a need to explain himself. "I think we should talk about the elephant in the room."

"Any more elephants and one of us is going to need a degree in zoology."

Donovan snorted.

"I don't know that we need to talk about it," she continued. "Just let it go."

"I feel bad about what happened."

"And I'm supposed to relive it so you can unburden yourself?"

"Hey. You're the one who unburdened herself by saying that you used to be in love with me." In fact, three years later, Donovan still wasn't over the realization. He kept mulling over his past, wondering how things would've been different. Would he have been happy? Would he have ended up with Lela? Or would that relationship have ended the same way his marriages had? He knew none of the answers to these questions, which really bothered him. Why did his own life have to be such a mystery? "Why did you do that? You seriously messed with my head."

"I barely remember it, Donovan. I was half asleep and delirious."

He had to fight the smile that wanted to cross his lips. Despite the way things had ended, their interlude in her bed had been pretty spectacular. "It was still hard to hear."

"Look, we wouldn't be having this conversation at all if we hadn't had this little instance of happenstance." She circled her hand in the air above her head. "Talking about any of this doesn't change what happened. You still would've left in the middle of the night, and I would be walking through life, tired of feeling like I was never good enough for you."

For a moment, Donovan was stuck. Stuck between his two pasts with Lela—the recent and the more distant. "Is that really what you think?"

She looked truly startled, in a way that could only suggest that Donovan was the biggest moron to ever walk the earth. Frankly, he didn't disagree. "I did at one point. The first time. Don't worry, the second time cured me of it. I'm over it."

What she really meant was that she was over *him*. "So that's it, then?"

"Yep."

Okay. Apparently the case of Lela and love was an open and shut case. The past was the past, and it was time to move forward. "Okay, well, I'm still sorry I left. But clearly, it was for the best. For both of us."

Lela turned away from the window and walked to the center of the room, still admiring her new office. "Are we going to be able to work together? Because I really need this to pan out. At this point in my life, I can't help but think that I have a limited number of chances at success. If you're going to stand in my way, I need to know now."

He wasn't going to hold her back. Hell, he didn't see how he could stop bold, silver-haired Lela from doing anything. "We both have a vested interest in Echo Echo. That's a good thing. I think we keep things professional and cordial, remember we're on the same team, and try to forget anything that happened before today."

"Fine. Good."

"Okay."

"Just no more cracks about my hair, okay? I love it, and I'm proud of it."

"It's gorgeous." He tamped down his urge to tell her that *she* was gorgeous. It would only make their working relationship more difficult. But he not only felt that way, he felt it in a way he hadn't before. This new version of Lela, with her own brand of confidence and a distinct air of not giving a fuck, was extremely appealing. Too bad he was done with women. Too bad he was done with love. Too bad he'd promised Echo that he wouldn't go there.

"Thanks." An off-kilter grin bloomed on her face. "In an odd way, I have you to thank. I decided to start Lela B and go gray the morning after you left three years ago."

"Really? The morning after?"

She nodded eagerly. "Yep. I knew that between my divorce and what happened with you, I was just spinning my wheels. I knew then that I simply needed to move on."

CHAPTER ELEVEN

TWO WEEKS IN, being under the Echo Echo umbrella had proven to be a whirlwind inside a tornado brought on shore by a hurricane with a bonus tsunami. Also, an earthquake. The pace was unrelenting. Lela worked twelve-hour days, dragged her ass home at night, lucky if she had the energy to feed Rio before she collapsed on her couch. Going upstairs to her bedroom was too exhausting a proposition.

Donovan, for his part, was giving Lela space, which she appreciated. Of course, there were the moments, mostly late in the day when Lela was tired and prone to weak thoughts, when he'd walk past her office not noticing her and she would wish that things were different. But there was no longer room in her life for regret, or pining for someone who didn't want her.

So Lela kept her eyes on the prize. She conferred with graphic designers on the rework of packaging. She had meetings with the ad team about campaigns, and strategy sessions with the sales department. At every step of the way, Echo was remarkably hands-on. Honestly, Lela couldn't figure out how she did what she did. She was involved with everything, never seemed to miss a beat, was always cheery yet stone-cold sober about business decisions, and a dream to collaborate with. She brought zero ego to her role, even though she had every reason in the world to be as much of an asshole as she wanted. In short, Lela was in awe of her unflappable brilliance.

Case in point, Echo's latest brainchild. It was completely counterintuitive—when the ad campaign featuring Lela was launched, they were going to mark every product in the Lela B online store as "Sold Out". Echo's thinking was that web sales were for later. They wanted to build buzz, and the only way to do that was to drive people into brick-and-mortar stores, clamoring for something they believed to be scarce. As Echo said, nobody wanted to be left out on something super cool. It was a brilliant plan.

Unfortunately, said plan put a whole new level of pressure on Lela now that the thing she'd been dreading—the day of the photoshoot—had arrived. Echo had asked Lela to do her own makeup, insisting it would lend authenticity to the story behind the campaign, as the PR department planned to have Echo and Lela do lots of interviews once the much anticipated buzz had been achieved. Lela's previous experience with "much anticipated buzz" was limited to tequila shooters after Tammera landed the pilot for her cooking show, and that time Lela went to Vegas and slurped a syrupy vodka slushie through a three foot-long straw. She still couldn't imagine this actually working.

The photographer's studio was only a few blocks north and one avenue west from her apartment, so Lela walked over with her rolling makeup kit in tow. She embarked with confidence, head held high, which was mostly the product of too much coffee. The weather, however, had other plans. Even though it was only the beginning of June and not quite nine in the morning, the day was already sweltering. By the time she reached the studio, she was sure she looked like the Little Mermaid after a bender—dripping wet and disheveled.

To make matters worse, she was prone to hot flashes if she'd had too much caffeine. Or when she was already overheated. And also when she was nervous. One step into the studio and it started. This was a familiar cast of characters before her—the wardrobe person, the hairstylist, the lighting guy and a handful of photographer's assistants milling about. The difference was that they were all there because of *her*. She didn't get to hide today. She had to step onto the stage.

The oven-hot heat crawled up her back, rolling over her shoulders, and flooding her face and neck. Sweat ran across her scalp and down her upper lip. This was going to ruin everything. No makeup, however good it was, would stay put if her face was like Lake Erie. No amount of Aqua-Net was going to hold her soggy hair.

"Find a fan," Tammera suggested when Lela called her in a panic. "Every photographer has one."

"Good idea." Lela frantically scanned the studio. "The only one I see is huge. Like wind tunnel huge."

"Any port in a storm."

Lela glanced at the time on her phone. Echo was going to arrive at any minute and Lela did not want to look like a complete disaster. She already felt like one. "Okay. I'm going for it." She casually sauntered across the room, holding her sweaty head high and smiling at anyone who made eye contact, until she reached the opposite corner where the fan sat.

"So is you-know-who coming to this thing?"

"Donovan? I don't know, but I hope not. He'll just make me more nervous."

"Interesting."

"What? Why is that interesting?"

"I've just never seen you nervous. So I'm wondering what sort of influence this mystery man has over you."

"He's not a mystery. It's a pretty open-and-shut case." *I liked him. He didn't like me back. Mystery solved.*

"Maybe if I met him, I wouldn't feel this way anymore."

"Maybe. Some day." Tammera had been angling for this ever since Lela had told her the whole crazy story about how she ended up at Echo Echo, working with her former-college-crush-two-time-one-night-stand. "In the meantime, thank you for listening to my neurotic ramblings."

"It's not like you don't listen to mine." Tammera had a lot going on in her career right now, too—a publishing deal for a cookbook and a licensing deal for a line of kitchen gadgets. They hardly saw each other. In fact, Tammera had to use the network's makeup artists last week because their schedules were so incompatible. Lela felt incredibly guilty.

"Dinner soon?" Lela asked.

"Yes. Delia and I really want to see you." There was an edge to her voice that made Lela thing something might be up, but she didn't have time to dig for more info.

"Want to come over to my place?" Lela found the switch for the fan.

"Can we do takeout? I never get to order in. Delia always wants me to cook."

"Sure."

"Maybe you can invite Donovan."

Lela grumbled. "I'll think about it. I should go. I need to lower my body temperature by ten degrees."

"Good luck, darling. You're going to be awesome today."

"Thank you. Love you." Lela ended the call and tucked the phone into the pocket of her jeans. She flipped the switch. With an enormous whoosh, it was like a jet taking off. Everyone in the room stopped what they were doing and turned their head. Meanwhile, Lela's tresses blew back like streamers on a kid's handlebars. The blast of air plastered her clothes to her sweaty body. "Fuck it," she mumbled to herself, gathering her hair, raising both arms, and resting her hands on top of her head. She closed her eyes and let out a sigh of relief. The air was cool. The sweat was drying. If everyone wanted to watch her be a weirdo, let them.

"Hey there, rock star," Echo called.

Lela jumped, dropped her hair, and turned around. Echo was strolling toward her, and although her words had made her seem like her normal, chipper self, her face told another story. "Hey." Lela flipped off the fan.

"Just cooling down?" Echo asked.

"Hot flash. You'll learn all about it in twenty years."

"Ah." Echo nodded. "Are you ready to do this?"

Lela smiled like she was self-assured and at ease, even though she felt like nothing of the sort. "Of course." She wasn't sure if she should bring up the subject, but something told her she had to. "Is everything okay?"

"Do I look that bad?"

"No. You look amazing. I'm just sensing that something is wrong."

Echo folded her arms across her chest. "You know I'm getting married in two weeks, right?"

"Yeah. Of course. I've heard both you and your dad talk about it."

"Well, I got into a huge fight with my mom last night. She's been so overbearing about the planning, and Dad told me that I should just tell her to back off, so I did, and it blew up in my face. She totally flew off the handle, calling me ungrateful, saying I was being a brat." Echo's face seemed to fall a little more with every word. Lela felt so bad for her. When Lela had planned her wedding to Mark, her mother had been nothing less than a godsend. She never complained. Never made a fuss. Never even expressed her opinion. "So there's that, plus, the woman who was supposed to do my hair and makeup had an accident at freaking Cross Fit and broke both of her arms."

"Yikes." Lela wanted nothing more than to help. "I'm not a total whiz with hair, but I'm not bad, and I will gladly do your makeup. I can drive up that morning and get you all taken care of."

"You'd do that for me?"

"Of course I would." Lela reached for Echo's arm. She'd never felt maternal about anyone in her whole life, but she was starting to wonder if this was what it felt like to be a mom. The thought of Echo unhappy was almost too much to bear. "Anything you need."

"I don't want to make you drive all the way up to Connecticut for that. My grandmother lives in the middle of nowhere."

"Well, now I have to go. I've heard stories about the James family estate, but your dad never invited me." Echo's grandmother was the heiress to a silver fortune and had raised Donovan and his brother in what was reportedly a completely over-the-top mansion. Donovan had once said that when he was a kid, he'd figured out that he could hide from his mother for days in the house if he wanted to. And apparently, he often did. "I'm dying to see it. And get a chance to meet your grandmother, too."

Echo rolled her eyes. "She's a trip."

"So I've heard."

"This would be such a godsend. Thank you." Echo's eyes brightened, even as she slanted her head to one side and a curious look crossed her face. "But hold on. This is stupid. You should just come to the wedding. Dad will be there and you know my mom, so you'll have people to hang out with."

Lela was about to have another hot flash. "You don't need to do that. I'll be fine. And I'm sure it's impossible to book a hotel this close to the date anyway."

"Oh, no. There's plenty of room at the house. We kept the invite list small. All of the guests are staying on the grounds."

"Oh."

"And you can ride up with Dad."

"Well..."

"Lucius and I are going up with him, too. Seriously. Lela. I won't take no for an answer."

That was all she had to hear. She wasn't about to state any more objections, no matter how much she was incredibly unsure about how this would go. "It sounds lovely. I sincerely appreciate the invitation. Thank you."

Echo clapped her hands in gleeful fashion. "Awesome.

Now let me show you the dress I think would be perfect for the shoot."

The pair walked over to the clothing rack in the opposite corner of the studio. Echo pulled a garment from the middle —bright pink with tiny black polkadots, a fluttery hem, and a plunging neckline. It was exactly the sort of thing Mark would've criticized, telling her it was ridiculous or that she was dressing too young for her age.

"Do you think it'll look good on me?"

"Are you kidding? It's going to look freaking amazing. Go ahead and put it on."

Lela disappeared behind a gray velvet curtain in a small dressing room and peeled off her clothes. Slipping both sleeves of the dress up over her shoulders, she held the bodice against her body with one arm, turning in the mirror. The horrors of the hot flash and subsequent sweat-fest faded. She not only loved the way she looked in the dress, she loved the way she *felt* in it, like a glamorous superhero. She poked her head out of the fitting room and waved Echo over. "Can you help with the zipper?"

Echo stepped inside and cinched Lela into the dress, which fit like a glove. "It's gorgeous. It pushes boundaries, but it also just looks flat-out incredible with your hair. I can't wait to see how it photographs."

Lela looked down at herself, surprised that she now found the prospect of this whole thing somewhat exciting. Why she'd spent any time at all stressing about it was beyond her. "Thank you so much for this. I really appreciate it."

"Thank you for trusting my ideas, especially the ones that my dad thinks are harebrained. It's so great to work with someone who understands what I'm going for."

"I just feel lucky to have the chance to be around you and have any input at all." Lela had to ask one question, if only to figure out precisely what level of nervousness was appropriate. "Speaking of your dad, is he coming today?"

She shook her head. "No. He thought you would do better if he wasn't here. He said he'll meet with us when it's time to choose images."

Lela couldn't figure out exactly why this disappointed her at all. The truth was that Donovan was only going to make this more difficult. But she also looked kick-ass in this dress, and part of her wanted him to see her in it. She wanted to prove him wrong about the idea of her being the face behind the campaign. Hopefully she'd have her chance. "Got it."

Echo's beautiful smile graced her face. "Perfect. Now let's get this show on the road."

Lela quickly got to work on her makeup, Echo standing by for some of the process and asking questions. Once that was done, the hairstylist stepped in. As luck would have it, she liked the way Lela's earlier sweaty episode had added some lift at the roots. All it needed was a curling iron and a metric ton of hairspray. With every step closer to the moment when she'd have to be in front of the camera, Lela was surprised to find her confidence growing. She looked good. Better than good. She looked amazing.

And for once in her life, she was ready to be the center of attention.

CHAPTER TWELVE

IT HAD BEEN two days since Lela's photo shoot, and Donovan was on pins and needles, anxious to see the pictures. Scratch that—he was *dying* to see them. It wasn't helping that Echo and Lela had been talking about the shoot non-stop, Echo insisting that Lela had looked "too hot for words", which only sent his brain on a fool's errand of attempting to answer the impossible: exactly how hot could Lela get?

Even though Donovan had been unconvinced of the wisdom of the campaign, things were moving forward. Ad buys had been placed. Bus wraps had been booked. If Echo disliked the photos or if Lela didn't feel good about the way she looked in them, it would be a fiscal disaster to postpone or cancel anything. He could see a scenario in which he would be partly to blame, either for the fact that the photographer was his friend, or perhaps because he had opted to not be there that day. He'd said it was because he didn't want to make Lela nervous, but the truth was that he was the one on edge.

Echo and Lela planned to meet Donovan in Echo's office so they could look over the photo proofs. But when he showed up, exactly on time, everyone in the room was several steps ahead of him. A handful of people from the marketing team were on hand, staring at the large computer monitor on Echo's desk and spouting "ooh"s and "ahh"s—it was annoying, like listening to someone else describe fireworks. Meanwhile, Echo and Lela were a study in contrasts—the former ebullient, practically floating around the room, while the latter looked like she wanted to crawl under a rock.

"I take it you've already got the proofs?" Donovan asked. He was a little irked that no one had waited for him before they started.

"Dad, they are amazing." Echo turned to the marketing folks. "Guys, can you clear out for a bit so my dad and Lela and I can go over these?"

Several members of the team grumbled, but they willingly departed, leaving him alone with Lela and Echo.

"Well? They're good?" Donovan asked.

"Better than good," Echo spouted, sitting at her desk and looking at the computer. "Come see."

"I'd actually like to hear from the subject of said photographs before I look at them." He directed his gaze to Lela, who was sitting on the couch, legs crossed, arms folded at her waist. "Because you don't look like you feel that great about them."

Lela gnawed on her lower lip, her eyes full of uncertainty. "They're good, I think? I mean, I'm not really capable of being objective in this situation. More than anything, I would say that it's weird to look at dozens and dozens of photos of myself. It's cringeworthy."

It was now clear that Donovan had to decide this for himself. "Okay. Let me see." He plucked his reading glasses from his shirt pocket and dragged one of the chairs from Echo's meeting area around behind her desk.

It only took a glimpse, a nanosecond of a look, before he knew that Echo was right—there were zero words. Lela looked drop-dead gorgeous, like a freaking sex kitten, a goddess, her skin glowing and her hair as lustrous and beautiful as ever. The dress she wore managed to distract him for a heartbeat or two, especially since the neckline plunged toward her belly button, revealing the most inexplicably alluring stretch of cleavage he'd ever seen. Lela was not full-chested, but she was working what she had with aplomb, and that made Donovan's palms get antsy with the memory of what it was like to have her velvety breasts in his hands. The poses were somehow both raw and glamorous at the same time—Lela confronted the camera with her steely blue eyes, or she sat in a chair, toes pointed in like a little kid while the dress was hiked up and showing most of her thighs. One made him lose all train of thought, with Lela laughing, hands on her hips as she tossed her head back and her silvery locks trailed down her back. *Maneater* popped into his head. Not helpful, Hall & Oates.

His entire body started buzzing, but his dick and his brain were humming the loudest, having an extensive back-and-forth about the situation he found himself in. *This could be great for business. You're an idiot for leaving that night. We'll make millions. Maybe you should've been smart enough to support this from the very beginning, asshole. And while you're at it, have you thought about swallowing your pride and asking Lela out again? No? Oh, right, because you're trying to build a real relationship with your daughter. Boo. Hoo.*

He'd seen more than his fair share of photographs of beautiful women. Hell, he'd been married to a model for three years. But this was something entirely different. He saw Lela in these images, the good friend, the woman he'd known since they were in their late teens. And he also saw the woman she had since become. He could even see the woman he'd flirted with and taken to bed, the person whose bare skin he'd caressed and kissed. But beyond all of that was a new person, someone he felt lucky to have met—a supercharged indestructible version of Lela.

"Wow. These really are amazing. I am completely blown away. They totally exceed my expectations."

Lela tutted out of frustration. "You didn't want to do this in the first place, so I'd say your expectations were probably pretty low."

Echo picked up the water glass that sat on her desk. "I'll be right back. Need to get a refill."

Donovan understood why Lela was angry with him, or at the very least, annoyed. Still, he hated it. She should be happy. This was a good day. For all of them. "Lela, are you okay?" he asked once Echo was gone, strolling over and taking a seat next to her on the couch.

She pulled her arms even tighter around her waist. "I'm great. I'm just in a bad mood. Maybe it's hormones or low blood sugar."

"I really don't understand. You look incredible in the photos."

She pointed in the direction of Echo's desk. "This is what getting out of my comfort zone does to me. This feeling that

I'm having right now is the whole reason I dragged my feet on starting Lela B in the first place. I don't like it. I feel so damn anxious. That's my face in those pictures and it's going to be on the side of buses, Donovan. Goddamn *buses*."

Donovan removed his reading glasses, sat forward and rested his elbows on his knees, turning his head so they could have at least a little bit of eye contact. "I get it. I do. You know, I think there's something about getting older that makes it easier to take more chances, but it doesn't always mean you feel comfortable the minute you jump out of the plane."

"Yes. That is totally it." She exhaled loudly through her nose. "I also think there's too much midwestern politeness in me. I grew up thinking that you weren't supposed to put yourself out there. Be quiet, and be a hard worker, and don't make too much trouble. Those photos feel like trouble."

"If it helps at all, I think that trouble is going to make Lela B a massive success." How he wanted to take her hand to comfort her, but he knew it wouldn't play well, especially if Echo were to walk in. He and Lela were colleagues now. That was it. Well, they were friends, too, but that wasn't the central role he played in her life anymore. "Also, I want to apologize. I was wrong. You and Echo were right. This was absolutely the correct call, and I think the campaign is going to be a massive success. That's all because of you."

"You're not helping me feel any less self-conscious, you know." She picked at one of her fingernails, dropping her head so that her hair tumbled perfectly over her shoulder. "But thank you. I do like hearing you say that you were wrong. I like it a lot."

Echo reappeared, waltzing into her office in what was

honestly the best mood Donovan had ever seen her in. "Dad, did Lela tell you that she's doing my makeup for the wedding?"

"Actually, no. I didn't know that." He watched as Lela and Echo exchanged looks of pure affection. He'd seen that they were forging a bond, but it now seemed even stronger. "When did that happen?"

"At the photo shoot. I invited her to the wedding, too."

"Oh, wow. Okay. Great." But was this great? Maybe? Sort of?

"I told her she could ride up with us. If that's okay with you."

"Yeah. Of course." Donovan smiled and nodded like a good dad, realizing that Echo and Lela's now-closer relationship made it that much more definitive—there would be no romance with Lela. Echo didn't want it and neither did Lela. He had to shut the door on that forever.

CHAPTER THIRTEEN

DONOVAN WALKED to and from work every day. The distance between his new apartment in the Murray Hill neighborhood and the JTI building was minimal by New York standards—only a twenty-minute jaunt since he had a pretty long stride. Normally, he used that time to decompress, but now that they were several days into the Lela B ad campaign, Lela was everywhere. In fact, he'd had to change his route completely to avoid certain spots where the sexy images of her in that dress were omnipresent, like along Broadway in the windows of the big cosmetics stores. And Times Square? That was a non-starter, and not just because there were entirely too many tourists for his liking. Lela's face graced one of the electronic billboards, looming over him, reminding him of his shortcomings.

But one thing he hadn't taken into account was the buses.

He was nearly to JTI, about to cross the street, when the light turned red. He and several dozen other people came to a halt, just as a bus pulled up to the curb to let off its passengers. And there was Lela plastered to the side of the metal transport, with her big blue eyes seductively boring into his soul, and her sumptuous hair blown back from her flawless face.

"Ugh. It's that picture again," a twenty-something man in a too-slim suit said.

"Seriously. Enough with the old lady side-boob. It's everywhere," his similarly-dressed companion added.

Donovan had never been the sort of person who got into fist fights, but he was seriously considering starting now. Could he take two guys at once? He might have to try. They were being so rude.

"I don't know shit about makeup but do women really want to see their mom in an ad campaign?" the first man asked.

"Or their grandma," man number two added.

Donovan willed the light to change, but it stubbornly remained optimistic Kelly green in the other direction and angry red in his. Something in him couldn't let this go. He had to say something. "She's not a grandma."

"What did you say?" the first man asked.

"She's not a grandma. The woman on the bus is not a grandma."

"I wasn't talking to you."

He knew he was about to sound exactly like a trifling old man, but he couldn't let this go. "No. Hold on a minute. That woman is a friend of mine, I think she looks amazing, and she's not a grandma. Not that it would matter if she was a grandmother. There's nothing wrong with that. A grandma can still be sexy."

"Whatever, grandpa."

The light changed and the men brushed past him and

started off across the street. The bus was long gone. And Donovan's cheeks were dry and hot with fury. *Punk-ass jerks.* He silently blew out a breath and stormed through the crosswalk to JTI.

Upstairs at Echo Echo, things were always busy, but today there seemed to be a new level of hectic. The phones were ringing like crazy. People were darting down the hall, and in and out of offices. Donovan had no clue what was going on, but something was in the air.

Echo was on the phone when he stopped by her office to check in. As he darkened her doorway, she noticed and waved him in. "Yeah. Yeah. Okay. Just call me back." She hit the screen on her phone and cast the device aside. It landed with a thud on a pile of papers.

"What's going on?" Donovan asked.

"Everything's falling apart."

He stepped inside and closed the door behind him. "Define everything."

"I thought we were off to a great start with the Lela B campaign, but we're suddenly getting complaints. Some of the retailers are saying they don't want the displays up in their stores, and some religious group started picketing a cosmetics store in Dallas. They said the photos are lewd and inappropriate for a woman Lela's age. What is wrong with people? How could anyone get so triggered by a fifty year-old woman?"

Normally, Donovan liked being right. But this was not what he'd wanted to happen. And after encountering those two assholes down on the street, he knew exactly how pigheaded and narrow-minded his original appraisals of the campaign had been. "What do you want to do?"

"I don't know. It's going to kill me to tell Lela. I had to talk her into doing this in the first place. And this isn't like a rejection of her products. People are complaining about *her*. They're criticizing the way she looks. It's awful."

Donovan agreed. It *was* awful. "Have you looked at the sales numbers?"

Echo blinked back at Donovan. "Actually, no. I haven't."

"Let's do that before you make a decision about anything."

"Smart. That's so smart." She turned to her computer and hit a few keys on the keyboard.

Donovan fished his reading glasses out of his laptop bag and rounded behind her desk, planting one hand on the back of her chair so he could look over her shoulder. "Well?"

"It's not a big wave across the board, but there are hot spots."

He moved in closer to see better. "Chicago looks pretty good. So does Seattle."

Echo nodded slowly. "And look at Dallas. Those look solid, and that's where they're picketing."

Donovan removed his glasses and tucked them into the pocket of his suit jacket. "Do you want my opinion?"

She turned in her chair and looked up at him. "I not only want it, I want you to tell me what to do. We leave for the wedding in two days and I literally cannot make one more decision. My brain has no more room for choices."

"Do nothing. Stay the course."

"No tweaks?"

"If anything, I might move into a few more secondary markets. Talk to the sales team and see if they have any ideas."

"You want to double-down?"

"Maybe not double, exactly, but a hell of a lot of resources have already gone into this campaign, and I don't think it's wise to scrap the whole thing and start over. I would wait it out."

Echo kneaded her forehead. "No one has ever protested one of our products before. The whole thing is weird."

"It's impossible to predict how everything will land, honey. This is just part of the game. But I say we wait it out."

She sighed. "Okay. You're right."

"The good news is you're about to get married and go on your honeymoon. If things blow up, it'll be my job to deal with it."

She laughed, her eyes flashing brightly from what seemed to be relief. "True. You can take the heat."

Donovan couldn't contain his smile. It felt good to help her through this, but more than anything, it was one of the rare times he felt as though he could protect her, or at the very least insulate her. After a lifetime of falling short, he was making up for some of it. "Does Lela know?"

Echo shook her head. "I don't think so. She had to take her cat to the vet this morning, so she's coming in at ten."

"Oh, no. Is something wrong with Rio?"

"Is that her cat?"

Donovan realized he'd just tipped his hand. He didn't want to share the specifics of the one time he and Rio had met. "Yeah. She's always talking about him."

"Ah. Gotcha."

"I think we should plan to tell Lela as soon as she gets here. A few steps into reception or down the hall and she's going to know something is up. It's nuts out there."

"I know. And I feel sick about the whole thing. I worry she's going to be crushed."

"Maybe. Maybe not. She's pretty resilient." Donovan shrugged. "Do you want me to talk to her?"

"That doesn't feel fair to you. I'm still the boss. Shouldn't this all fall on me?"

He walked over to grab his bag. "And I can't help but feel that as the guy who stupidly voiced concerns over a woman with gray hair in an ad campaign, that I should be the one to tell her that despite everything, this was the right move."

Echo pointed at him. "That is an excellent point."

"It'll give me a chance to tell her that I was wrong. Again."

"Again?"

Donovan stuffed a hand into his pocket. "Yes. I also told her the day we first saw the proofs. When we saw how gorgeous she looked."

Echo narrowed her sights on him, seeming suspicious, but then her phone rang again. "Sounds good. Catch up later?"

"Yes." Donovan ambled down the hall, got settled in his office, and cleaned out as much of his inbox as he could while keeping an eye on the clock. At five to ten, he wandered to reception and waited for Lela. He didn't want to risk her finding out about recent developments from anyone other than him. He might not be the most diplomatic person in the world, but he did feel as though he knew how best to handle her reaction and potentially soothe her ragged nerves.

Lela stepped off the elevator a few minutes after ten, and Donovan caught himself holding his breath. In figure-hugging jeans with heels and a silky black blouse, she was confident elegance defined. Her hair was up in a high ponytail, and she was wearing swingy silver earrings that showed off the brilliant blue of her eyes.

"How's Rio?" he asked, getting up from the couch.

"Fine. Just a checkup." She narrowed her eyes and scanned the reception area. "Are you waiting for someone?"

"You, actually."

"Let me guess. Is this about the campaign?"

Donovan's eyes darted all over the room. Luckily, no one seemed to hear what she'd said. "You know?"

"Obviously, you do." Her words came out like an accusation, but if the roles had been reversed, he would've been thinking something was up, too. Before today, he'd gone out of his way to give her space at work. Possibly too far out of his way.

"Can we talk about this somewhere with a little more privacy?"

"My office?"

"Sure."

Lela led the way, closing the door behind them once they were inside. She'd done an awesome job with decorating her office. It was fun and bright, with lots of teal, aqua, and brass. "I figured Echo would be the one to tell me about this."

"How did you find out?"

"I saw something on the news about it."

"The news?" He didn't let on that he found this an exciting prospect. If journalists had picked up on the story, that might be a good thing. Any free publicity, good or bad, could be beneficial. "Are you doing okay? Because you seem like you're fine."

She shook her head. "No. Of course not. It's mortifying. I never wanted this kind of attention. Ever." Despite her words, her voice was remarkably steady. "But it also pisses me off. I'm fifty. People are acting like a freaking mummy posed for those pictures. And I'm sorry, but I look pretty damn good."

Donovan loved everything about her reaction to this—the fact that it had lit a fire in her rather than letting it defeat her. "You look better than good. You look amazing." *So amazing that I have to take a different route to work.*

"What is Echo saying about it?"

"We just had a quick meeting, took a look at the sales numbers, which are promising in several markets. I told her that I think it's way too early to back down. If anything, I think we should expand the campaign into a few larger secondary markets. We need to do some analysis, but off the top of my head, I'm thinking Denver, Portland, and St. Louis. Maybe Raleigh-Durham and Baltimore."

Lela nodded slowly, the gears in her head clearly turning. She'd learned quite a lot about the sales and marketing side since coming on board. "Okay. Yeah. If Echo's cool with it, I say we plow full steam ahead."

Donovan was excited by the prospect. He liked the idea of taking on the world with his two favorite women. "Echo will be really happy to hear you feel this way." He glanced at the clock on the wall. "I should go. I have a conference call in a few minutes." He headed for the door.

"Hey, Donovan?"

"Yes?" He turned back, catching her biting down on her lower lip. Dammit, that did something to him.

"Are you free for dinner tonight?"

He was so unsure if he'd heard her correctly that he nearly knocked his head to the side to his rid his ears of what-

ever might be plugging them up. "Are you asking me out?"
Because I wouldn't say no.

"No. I'm not."

"Oh."

"Remember when I told you about my best friend, Tammera?"

It still bothered him that he no longer held that title in her life, which he knew was a stupid reaction, but was true nonetheless. Perhaps it was because Lela had long since moved on and he hadn't come close to finding another human being who could match her. "Yeah. Of course."

"She's coming over with her girlfriend, Delia, tonight. Tammera's mad at me that I haven't introduced you to her."

"Really?"

"Yes. She's tired of hearing about you and not knowing you."

"I see." He stopped short of asking for details like whether or not Tammera knew the bad stuff about him, like his three-year-old panicky exit.

"Also, I think they're going to announce their engagement. Or maybe that they've decided to have a baby. Either would be amazing and awesome, but it would be nice if I didn't have to be the third wheel. You can help me feel a little less pathetic in the life category."

"Because I'm equally pathetic?"

She opened the door to show him the way out. "You said it. Not me."

CHAPTER FOURTEEN

LELA'S original plan to invite Donovan to dinner had been predicated on Tammera's near-constant pestering about wanting to meet him. But there had been more to Lela's decision. She didn't like that they'd been distant at work. It had seemed logical at the beginning, when she was still angry and he was being defensive. But a lot had happened since then, feelings had softened, and she wanted to move forward. That moment when he'd been so kind to her the day they first saw the photo proofs had felt like a step in the right direction, one he'd initiated. He even apologized, which was no small gesture coming from a man who loved to be right. It felt like the rougher edges of their history were finally being filed away. Lela's ultimate hope was that they could fully revive their friendship and work together. Then keep it that way.

The doorbell rang right on the nose at seven. "Oh, look, Delia!" Tammera exclaimed when Lela answered the door. "It's the woman from the buses." Tammera cracked a sly grin and handed over a bottle of wine. She was always dressed impeccably, but there was something about her silk crepe black and white dress that read "special occasion".

"That's me. The bus lady." Lela let out a breathy laugh, even though she did not wish to be identified that way. "Thanks for the wine." She gave Tammera a hug, then Delia.

"I think the photographs are amazing," Delia said as she stepped inside. "Nothing that exciting happens at my job, so I'm officially jealous." The warmth of Delia's smile was echoed in her voice. She was one of those people who radiated calm and ease, which had to be a big asset in her job as pediatrician. Her glossy black hair hung in a perfect shoulder-length bob and she, too, was a little more dressed up than usual, wearing a slim red dress and killer heels.

Lela was glad she'd had the wisdom to also put on something special—a vintage bell-sleeved maxi dress made from a bold magenta and ice blue print. It was a completely impractical item of clothing, which made her love it even more. "It's all the excitement I'll be able to take for awhile." She shut the door behind them.

"So where's the famous Donovan James?" Tammera asked.

Lela was greatly relieved he wasn't there yet. "Famous" might give him the wrong idea about the things she'd said to Tammera. Tams knew that Donovan had once been her ultimate guy, but he wasn't anymore. "He volunteered to pick up dinner. He should be here any minute."

Tammera reached for Delia's hand and they exchanged looks of pure and utter adoration. "Okay, well, I feel like this is probably a better time to deliver our big news. We're getting married."

Funny, but as much as Lela had anticipated this moment,

she hadn't counted on her most immediate and visceral reaction—tears. Buckets of tears. A veritable ocean. "Oh, my God, you two," she squeaked. "Congratulations."

Delia couldn't have been smiling any wider if she'd tried. She planted a soft kiss on Tammera's lips. "We're so happy."

"It's such incredible news." This time, Lela croaked.

Tammera cast Lela a look of surprise. "Are you okay?"

Lela nodded, wiping away the tears. She should probably make a point to drink some water soon, lest she dehydrate. "Come here." The three women got lost in a group hug—two blissfully happy, one a joyful mess.

"Why are you crying? This couldn't have been that much of a surprise. Is this one of those peri-menopausal moments?" Tammera asked.

Lela stepped back and sniffled. "It's been a long time since I've heard any news that was purely good. I feel like everything comes with a 'but' these days."

"You mean like your company's gotten this great opportunity, *but* you have to work with a guy you regret sleeping with?" Tammera asked.

The doorbell rang. Lela held her finger to her lips. "Shush."

"Hold on. What did I miss?" Delia asked.

"I told you in the cab," Tammera answered. "Donovan's the guy Lela crushed on in college. They had sex three years ago and he took off in the middle of the night."

Delia nodded like this was the most sensible explanation ever. "Oh, right."

Lela was standing with her hand on the doorknob, but she wasn't about to turn it yet. "Are you done? Can I answer the door?"

"Yes. Sorry," Tammera answered sheepishly.

Lela opened the door for Donovan, who was completely loaded down with takeout. "Cute" had never been a word she would have attributed to him—it was too gross an understatement. But something about him standing there, smiling and peeking over the top of an armful of brown paper bags, made it pop into her mind. A warm breeze picked up his hair and blew it sideways across his face. He artfully jerked his head to flip it back into place.

"Hey," he said in a voice that Lela would only admit to herself still did something to her.

"Hey. Can I help?"

"This is a very carefully constructed mountain of Indian food. If we move one thing, it could all come tumbling down." He stepped into the foyer.

"Donovan, this is Tammera and Delia."

Tammera was in hyper-drive, sizing him up and shooting Lela inquisitive glances. "Hi, Donovan," she said with a very leading tone.

"Nice to meet you," Delia said.

"Likewise," Donovan replied. "I should probably set these down somewhere."

"Come on. The kitchen. Tams and Delia, do you want to open the bottle of wine? There are glasses under the bar in the living room."

"We're on it," Tammera said.

Lela led Donovan down the long hall. He carefully set the bags on the island, unwrapping his arms from the bundle. And that was when Lela saw it. "Donovan. Your shirt."

He looked down at himself—square in the middle of his

crisp white shirt was a round bright golden stain the size of a dinner plate. "Oh, shit. One of the bags leaked."

"We need to get you out of that. Your shirt's going to be ruined if we don't get it into the wash."

"What am I going to wear?"

Lela snickered. "I have no idea, but I'm sure I can find something."

"Why is this funny? This isn't funny. I just met your friends and now I have to wear your clothes all night?"

"It's a tiny bit funny. Come on." Lela ducked into the living room to tell Delia and Tammera to go ahead and start with dinner if they wanted to, then she and Donovan went upstairs to her room. She got straight to it, sifting through her closet. "I got rid of anything Mark left behind, so that's out."

"I don't think I want to wear your ex-husband's clothes, anyway."

"He had terrible taste, so good call on your part."

"Speaking of which, I noticed you got some new furniture. I liked what I saw."

Indeed, on the one year anniversary of the divorce, she'd had all of Mark's crap hauled away and then had been gradually replacing everything. Her most recent purchase was a sublime peacock blue velvet sofa. "It's a work in progress, but it's getting there."

"I'm glad to hear you continue to move on."

Lela was happy about it, too, although moments like this made her feel a bit like she was once against stuck between the past and the present. "Oh, wait. I have a T-shirt that I think will fit you." In the corner of the closet, she had a set of wire mesh sliding bins crammed with clothes she rarely wore. She had a very hard time throwing anything away. At the bottom of the last bin was an old R.E.M. T-shirt, faded raspberry pink with yellow printing of the band's name and a simple line drawing of a bicycle. It was an XL, and had always been huge on her, so it would definitely be big enough. "Found it." She stepped out of the closet and was quickly confronted with an image she should have prepared herself for—Donovan's enticing bare chest and abs. "Oh. You, uh, took your shirt off."

"Well, yeah. It has a giant yellow stain on the front of it." A smug grin crossed his face as his arms casually hung at his sides. He was so at ease with himself, it always made her a little jealous. "It's okay to look, Lela. You've seen me without my shirt tons of times."

"Of course. Whatever." She averted her eyes, knowing exactly how unable she was to brush this aside with a single dismissive word. Here they were, in the same room where he'd given her the orgasm that made her spill the beans. And his bare chest was calling to her. If things were different, and they definitely weren't, it would've been two seconds before she was spreading her hands over his pecs and asking him if he was cool with dinner getting cold.

"Plus, I see your side-boob every time a bus goes by, so we're even."

Sights squarely focused on a lamp she didn't care about, she thrust the T-shirt in his direction. "Here. This should fit. I'll throw your shirt in the wash."

"Hold on a second... I've been looking for this. For like over two decades." Arms straight, he held the shirt out in front of him. "You had it all this time?"

"Had what? That is *my* T-shirt. I specifically remember

wearing it when we went to see R.E.M. at Madison Square Garden."

"No way. I wore it that night. Not you. You wore a dress. Some green vintage thing with black tights and Doc Martens." Donovan threaded his arms into the sleeves, tugging it over his head. "Look at this thing. This is my shirt. There's no way you bought one this big."

Lela gnawed on her thumbnail, her eyes raking over his too-appealing form. The T-shirt was old and wrinkled, but it fit him perfectly. "Huh."

"Yeah, huh."

"I guess it *is* yours. I wonder how I got it."

He shrugged. "Maybe I loaned it to you one of the times you crashed on the couch at my apartment?"

Lela was transported back in time to the many, many nights she slept over. He'd be in his bed, she in the living room, wondering why he didn't like her more. "How do you remember what I wore to a concert thirty years ago?"

"It's not hard to guess. That was your uniform at the time."

That seemed like a convenient answer. He'd been specific about the color of her dress. What guy remembered that? "I guess."

"That and lots of eyeliner." He clamped his hand on her shoulder and she peered up into his face, wishing things had turned out differently between them, but maybe this was the way it was always meant to be—just friends, a bit of verbal sparring, nothing more. Still, *Out of Touch* insisted on worming its way into her head, a song about longing, love, and contradiction. Hall & Oates were once again way too closely aligned with her psyche.

A loud meow came from Lela's doorway. Rio happily padded his way into the room, straight up to Donovan.

"Oh, look. It's Simon LeBon." Donovan scooped up the cat and gave him a head scratch.

"His name is Rio and you know it."

"I will never forget you gave him the lamest possible Duran Duran name."

"Shut up, or I won't wash your shirt."

"Fine." He smiled wide, then gently placed Rio back on the floor. "I would like to salvage it if I can."

"I'll do my best."

Lela and Donovan returned downstairs, with Donovan going to the living room in search of wine and Lela heading to the laundry area off the kitchen. A thorough spray of stain remover and she tossed it into the wash, then joined her guests. In her de facto dining area, which was really just one end of the living room, Donovan, Delia, and Tammera were already seated, laughing and drinking wine. Placemats and plates were out, a candle was lit, and the vast array of takeout containers snaked across the center of the table.

"Who did all of this?" Lela asked, taking a seat next to Donovan.

"Tammera," he answered.

"The candle was Donovan's idea," Tammera added. "I think we should eat. This food is getting colder by the minute."

They passed the cartons and filled their plates, with everything from saag paneer to chicken tikka masala, plus more garlic naan and pakora than Lela had ever seen in her life. The food was amazing, as was the conversation, especially once they moved on to a second bottle of wine, the plates got cleared, and then they pulled the cork on a third.

"Wait a second. Hold on." Tammera reached across the table and tapped the back of Donovan's hand. "You have to tell me what Lela was like when you met her. In college."

Donovan turned to her before he spoke, his eyes full of amusement and intoxication. Feeling a bit tipsy herself, Lela swallowed a sigh as she scanned his handsome features—the scruffy beard, the lips she wouldn't mind kissing, and his adorable forehead wrinkles. Why did he have to be so nice to look at?

He turned back to Tammera and Delia. "Lela was the most amazing person I had ever met. Smart and funny and incredibly generous of spirit. So pretty, a little weird because she liked to sneak into weddings, and of course, she had the second best taste in music. I, of course, have the best."

Lela smacked his arm with the back of her hand, but realizing how odd it felt to hear him rattle off a list of her good qualities, without explaining the mystery of why exactly they could never be more than friends. "Donovan got that flipped around. He likes REO Speedwagon, so he will always have the second best taste."

Tammera knocked back the rest of her glass of wine. "I'm with Donovan. I love them."

"I'm Team Lela," Delia said. "No Speedwagon for me, thank you very much." Her head dropped forward and she jerked it back, more than a little drunk.

Tammera slung her arm around Delia's shoulder and kissed her cheek. "I think I need to get somebody home and into bed."

Delia squinted as she raised her hand and pinched her

thumb and forefinger together. "I might have had a teeny tiny bit too much wine."

The four of them gathered at the front door for their goodbyes. It was the first time Lela had really noticed what a funny quartet they were—three impeccably dressed women and one bearded dude in a T-shirt that itself could be considered middle aged. "Thanks for coming," she said to Tammera and Delia, giving them both a big hug. "I'm so excited for you both. Congratulations."

"Yes. Congratulations," Donovan said, having been filled in on the happy news during dinner.

Tammera pointed at him. "You, sir, are officially invited to our wedding. Date to be determined, but we're thinking July."

"July? That's in a few weeks," Lela said. "Also a horrible time in New York."

"Thanks for the vote of confidence," Tammera quipped. "We not only have to work around the production schedule for my show, one of the partners in Delia's practice is retiring. It's really the only time we can squeeze it in if we want to actually go on a honeymoon. It'll be something small and quick. No drama. Then we'll have a huge party later." She turned to Donovan. "So look for an invite. I'll get your info from Lela."

He smiled from ear to ear. "I look forward to it."

Donovan and Lela stood in her doorway as Tammera helped Delia down the stairs, taking things very slowly. Luckily, a cab drove by and Tams was able to hail it in time. Lela closed the door when they were safely on their way. "Oh, shit. I forgot about your shirt. Let me go check on it."

Donovan stopped her with his hand on her forearm.

"Don't worry about it. You can bring it to the office. Or toss it if it's ruined. It's not the end of the world."

"I'm sorry. I'll buy you a new shirt. I feel responsible. It's all because you volunteered to pick up the take-out."

He still hadn't let go of her arm, and now the heat from his hand had permeated the thin fabric of her dress. Tingles rippled along her spine.

"You don't need to apologize. I had the best night," he said.

"I'm happy to hear you say that. I think Tammera and Delia had fun, too."

"I don't know how anyone couldn't. Amazing conversation, we laughed our asses off, incredible wine, and good food. That's the perfect combo in my book."

"It really was nice, wasn't it?" she asked, doing her best to not sound so damn wistful.

"It was. Thanks for inviting me. Thank you for letting me be a part of your life."

A soft smile crossed his kissable lips and Lela fought her tendencies to get swept up in the moment. Her heart was pounding fiercely and with great determination. The air in the house seemed to stand still. She felt strong and weak at the same time. The longing for him had never left her body, it had simply gone to sleep, and he was slowly nudging it awake. But she had to be smarter than desire. She and Donovan had finally returned to a good place. It was a bad idea to mess with that. Friendship was too precious. Yes, she wanted him, but what they had right now was enough.

She popped up on to her tiptoes and kissed him on the cheek. "Thank you for letting me be a part of yours." She reached for the doorknob, but she did it slowly, just to give him a chance to stop her. He didn't. "Probably time for us both to hit the hay."

"Yep." He leaned down and kissed her on top of her head. "I guess the next big thing to look forward to is Echo's wedding."

"Only a few days away."

"We can talk about departure times at work."

And there it was—the new normal. "Sounds like a plan."

Donovan jogged down the steps, but he stopped and turned at the bottom one. "Thanks for giving me back my T-shirt."

"Thanks for letting me borrow it for thirty years."

CHAPTER FIFTEEN

LELA HAD HEARD tales of the James family estate in New Canaan, Connecticut. By all accounts, it was pretty dang swanky—a fifteen-bedroom, twenty-bathroom mansion on more than fifty acres, with a pond, a pool, horse stables, and tennis courts. When Donovan had first told Lela about it back in college, it almost sounded like a confession, as if he wanted her to know where he'd come from, but only so he could illustrate that so much privilege had come at a cost. Before that, he'd never come across like a guy from a wealthy background, and it wasn't because Lela had been tricked by the ratty jeans and dingy high-tops. He lived in an absurd apartment for an undergrad—Lela knew something was up. But the fact that he naturally drew attention, but never wanted any part of it, gave her pause. It seemed like such a humble instinct. When Lela later heard the story about how his dad took off when he was a baby, Lela's view of him began to shift again. She'd started to wonder if his disconnect from the big fancy house he grew up in was more of a survival instinct.

Today, she would have her chance to gather information for herself. Donovan drove Lela, Echo, and Echo's fiancé Lucius up to the estate on the Friday morning of the wedding weekend. Lela had asked why they weren't going earlier, since most weddings demanded a lot of family time and preparation. Echo flatly admitted that there was only so much of her mother and grandmother she could take. Plus, work was crazy, as they all were well aware, and Donovan's mom had a bizarro rule when family gathered—no phones, Internet, or TV. He said that it had always been like that, and the more plugged-in the world had become, the more his mother insisted that everyone not participate.

"Here's your warning, Echo. Ten minutes and there will be no more email." Donovan peered into the rear view mirror to look at his daughter, who was sitting in the backseat. She'd asked for a heads-up while she stole a few final minutes on her phone.

"Can you slow down a bit?" she asked.

"Only a little. Your grandmother is expecting us and she won't want us to be late." Donovan's voice had an unsteady edge that was rarely there.

"Maybe it's time to focus on what we're about to do," Lucius said sweetly. Born in Ireland, he'd moved to the states several years ago, but his brogue was still strong. He was tall and a bit skinny, with thick, nearly-black curly hair. A writer, his personality was far quieter than Echo's, but the two made an incredible and beautiful pair.

Lela glanced in the backseat to see Lucius take Echo's hand. Young love was such a sweet thing. Lela not only hoped it would last, she needed to believe it would.

"You're so right," Echo said in response, leaning in to kiss Lucius. "I'm powering down my phone right now."

A few minutes later, Donovan turned in to a tree-lined driveway flanked by large stacked-stone columns. "We have reached the point of no return. Dun, dun, dun..." He sang, his voice gruff and deep.

"Dad..." Echo responded.

Lela peered out the passenger window as they inched along. All around was nothing but endless stretches of grass and landscaping. When they crested a hill, the house revealed itself ahead, cradled in a valley of rolling country-side and centuries-old oaks. As they closed in, the home seemed to go on forever, a three-level battleship of chalky white brick, dotted with dozens and dozens of lead-paned windows and topped with a swooping charcoal slate roof. The foundation was skirted by a riot of rose bushes in full bloom, and the corners armored with ivy-covered trellises.

And of course, there were the turrets. The house had freaking turrets.

"Wow," Lela said, knocking her head against the passenger-side window.

"Don't say wow," Donovan said.

"It's stunning. Am I not allowed to admire it?"

"Dad's sensitive about how over-the-top it is," Echo said from the backseat.

"It's ridiculous and wasteful. Especially since she and her boyfriend of the moment are the only occupants. What's his name again? Stuart?"

"Yes. Stuart. But don't forget the dogs. And the cats. And the rabbits. And the emu," Echo quipped.

Donovan blew out a breath through his nose, shaking his head. "How could I forget the emu? The thing pecked me on the forehead the last time we were here. I had a bruise for a week."

"Things are never dull at Gram's," Echo said.

"Well, I think it's a beautiful spot for a wedding." Lela was determined to not let Donovan's view of his family color her opinion. She'd decide for herself whether his mother truly was "detached from reality". And whether his half-brother Austin was actually "a fun-loving narcissist".

Donovan pulled off to the side and put the car in Park. Mere moments later, as they were climbing out, a pack of dogs escaped from the front door and scrambled out onto the lawn. "Oh, great."

Trailing behind them was a woman Lela could only assume was Eileen, Donovan's mother. Like Lela, she had long gray hair, although Eileen's was more white than silver. It was piled on top of her head, held in place by black enamel chopsticks. She wore a shapeless linen dress in a color that could only be described as periwinkle. But that wasn't what Lela was focused on right now. It was the dogs surrounding them and barking their heads off.

Eileen came to a halt, stuck her thumb and middle finger in her mouth, and unleashed an earsplitting whistle. The dogs scampered off and were at her heel in a flash, except for a Pomeranian that decided to pee on a rose bush instead.

Lela, Donovan, and Echo started up the walk with their suitcases while Lucius veered off, trying to coax the one stray dog to join the group. Eileen greeted Echo first, taking both of her granddaughter's hands and peering up into her eyes. "I'm excited for you to marry Lucius, darling. He's so handsome," she muttered under her breath. "That's important. If you ever want to kill him, it'll make you think twice."

"Grams..." Echo leaned down to hug her grandmother.

Donovan snorted, which caught his mother's attention.

"My handsome son," she embraced him warmly, making Lela doubt at least some of what he'd said about his mom.

"Hi, Mom. How are you?" The tone of his voice was quiet and resigned, but there was a glimmer of affection.

"I'm happy as a clam. I have my two boys here and my granddaughter is getting married. I can't think of a single thing I might want. Except perhaps a gin and tonic." She glanced over at Lela. "You must be Echo's new business partner. And the makeup artist."

Lela tamped down any disappointment she might have had at the fact that however Donovan had briefed his mother, he had not mentioned that he and Lela had been friends in college. "Hello, Mrs. James. It's very nice to meet you."

She waved it off. "Please. Call me Eileen. Life is too short for formalities."

Out through the door came a bald, muscle-bound man. He was wearing khakis and a button-down shirt, which first read "banker", but he was also barefoot and wearing chunky diamond stud earrings, so Lela was unable to draw any conclusions at all about what he might do. He was holding a sizable carved wood box with a brass lock on the front. "I'm here for everyone's phones."

Eileen smiled wide. "Stuart, this is everyone. Everyone, this is Stuart."

He kissed Eileen on the cheek, then presented the box to Donovan. "You must be the oldest son."

"You must be the new boyfriend."

"Donovan. Manners," Eileen said.

"Mom. I'm fifty-one. Plus, isn't he *actually* your new boyfriend?" Donovan dropped his phone into the box.

"I don't mind. It doesn't bother me at all." Stuart moved on to Echo and Lucius, then made his way over to Lela.

In many ways, she was happy to be rid of her cell for a few days. Work had been so non-stop, that the idea of forced unplugging for a weekend was like to a trip to a spa. "Thank you."

"Wonderful," Eileen said. "Let's go inside and get you all settled. We'll meet for cocktails at five, and dinner will be at six. For now, I need a nap."

"Where's Austin?" Donovan asked her.

"He got here a half hour ago. He's upstairs unpacking. Genevieve's flight was delayed, by the way, so she won't be here until later."

As they all filed inside, Lela overheard Eileen. "Lucius, do you know the origin of 'happy as a clam'?"

"I don't," Lucius said.

"It refers to a clam at high tide. They're happy because they have a short reprieve from death," Eileen said.

"Oh," Lucius replied.

Lela felt as though she was getting her first glimpse of what might be off with Donovan's mom.

As they walked into the yawning yet cluttered foyer, it took a moment for Lela to take it all in. Kitschy 1950s-era floral wallpaper in aqua and cream blanketed the walls, while a Louis XIV settee upholstered in what was surely historically inaccurate lime green velvet sat waiting for a visitor to rest their tired feet. There was a carved marble bust of a man topped with an actual fedora, and a vast collection of nudes—

sketches, oil paintings, and watercolors, in mismatched candy-colored frames. Ahead was a grand flourish of a staircase with a delicate wrought-iron handrail ascending to the right, then looping back around to a landing on the other end. Anyone who went upstairs had no choice but to go out of their way.

Suitcases in tow, Lela and Donovan started up the hardwood steps, which were covered in an ornate eggplant carpet runner. "Did it look like this when you were growing up?" she asked.

"Sort of. She's constantly at rich people's estate sales, so she's added quite a bit since I was a kid."

She followed him down one of several halls. "But isn't she a rich person herself?"

"Yes, but she'll never come close to spending it. She's cheap as hell."

"Did she grow up poor?"

"No. I think she enjoys squeezing the life out of things."

Lela couldn't ignore the possible double meaning in this answer. "And she grew up in this house, too?"

"Virtually all by herself, other than a caretaker, gardener, and a nanny. She was an only child and my grandparents traveled extensively." Donovan stopped in front of a door and opened it. "Mom said she wanted you in here. We call this the pink bird room."

"Like flamingos?"

"No. Pink. And birds."

Lela stepped inside and immediately caught Donovan's drift. She really loved pink, but this was a whole new level of rosy adoration. Everything, from the bed to a mountain of throw pillows, from the heavy Dupioni silk drapes to a pair of chairs near the window, and even a faux-fur ottoman were decorated in shades from soft and pale to vibrant and electric. Littered about the room were dozens of antique bird cages, painted in a non-pink array of colors. They hung in clusters from the ceiling and two had been turned into lamps on the bedside tables. They were perched on shelves, and a few had been left on the floor in the corner. "Got it. Pink. And birds."

"Except no actual birds. Just their little jail cells."

"That's a lovely thought."

He laughed quietly. "I'm sure you know by now to ignore me."

She sat on the edge of the bed and bounced up and down to check the firmness. She patted the spot next to her. "Come here. Sit."

Donovan artfully arched both eyebrows. "I thought we decided we were done with that."

"We did. This is just you and me, talking as friends."

He did as she asked, sitting next to her. "I like the idea of that. As long as this isn't a lecture."

"Maybe a little one."

"Can't wait."

"I want to make sure you're going to take the time to enjoy this weekend. I understand things with your mother are complicated, but your daughter is getting married. It's a big deal. It would be a shame if you didn't have at least a little fun."

He cleared his throat and leaned back, propping himself up with one arm. "I'll try. I feel like I have one foot in the grave. How do I have a daughter that's old enough to get married?"

Indeed, as slowly as time moved when you were young, it

moved equally fast when you got older. "Don't think about that part. Just try to enjoy it."

He looked over at her and allowed himself a smile. "I'm glad you're here."

"I am, too."

"I hope you still feel that way after spending time with my mother."

"She's fine, Donovan. Really. She's quirky, but who doesn't love that? My mom is perfectly predictable."

"Your mom is awesome."

"There you are." A good looking man who resembled Donovan ever-so-slightly appeared in the doorway. Lela could only assume it was his half-brother Austin. He was nearly the same height, similar thick brown hair, although Austin's was cut in a far more conservative style. He had that same easy confidence, but in a slightly slicker package. Not only were his expensive leather shoes gleaming, his teeth were too. "I hope I'm not interrupting."

Donovan popped up from the bed and hugged Austin, but it was more the bumping of shoulders and a clap on the back. "Hey, Austin. I want you to meet Lela."

Austin narrowed his sights on her. "Hold on a minute. I've seen you somewhere."

"Hello." Lela reached out for a handshake, but he raised her fingers to his admittedly soft lips. "I don't think we've ever met, but it's nice to meet you now," she said, ready to have her hand back.

Donovan closely studied Lela and Austin's interaction. "Probably the ad campaign. Austin lives in Boston. That's one of our first wave markets."

"My God," Austin said. "Lela B. Damn. Those photos

are hot."

Heat flushed Lela's face so fast she nearly passed out. She still maintained that wasn't her in those photos. It was an ideal of her, with great lighting and the right angles. "It's not me. It was all the photographer's doing."

"Come on, Lela," Donovan said in an admonishing tone. "Don't say that. It's you. It's all you. No photographer can capture what isn't there."

Lela almost asked Donovan to watch himself. If he was going to go around complimenting her and being nice like he had over the last few weeks, he might give her a reason to start thinking about stupid things like kissing him.

"I hope we get to spend some time together while you're here, Lela," Austin said.

Donovan was in her peripheral vision, bugging his eyes and shaking his head "no".

"I'm sure I'll see you around." She wasn't sure what else she should say. She didn't want to be rude.

Austin grinned. "Fantastic."

"I'll let you get settled, Lela," Donovan said. "Do you need anything?"

"I'm good. Echo and I are going to get together in an hour so I can practice on her hair."

"I'll see you at five for cocktails?" he asked, starting for the door.

"I'll be there with bells on."

Donovan and Austin left Lela to herself and she turned to take another look at the room. She found Donovan's mom's style quirky and fun. Unconventional. Whimsical. Still, she could see how if you were a kid, and she was your mom, it might come off as something else.

CHAPTER SIXTEEN

DONOVAN PRACTICALLY HAD to drag Austin from Lela's room. As soon as they were out of earshot, he delivered a warning. "Step off."

"What's that supposed to mean?" Austin trailed Donovan down the hall to his room, which was around the corner, on the back of the house overlooking the pool.

"Lela doesn't need you drooling all over her." Donovan wandered into what had once been his bedroom. Thankfully, his mother had redecorated many years ago, transforming it into something completely unrecognizable, unleashing her odd sense of style with dark navy walls, black wainscoting, and dozens of clocks that didn't work. Donovan tried not to do anything but sleep in that room. Otherwise, it felt too much like he was a prisoner of time.

"Hold on a minute." Austin grabbed Donovan's forearm and froze. "I'm just now realizing. Is Lela college Lela?"

"Yes. How many women named Lela can there be in the world?"

"How did she end up working with Echo?"

"It was total chance. A fluke."

"Are you two a thing?"

Donovan bit down on his lower lip, if only to remind himself that he and Lela were definitely not a thing. Although there'd been a noticeable softening between them in the last few weeks. He wasn't sure if that was all one-sided or if Lela felt it, too, but he had to think she did. Not that it mattered. Echo would lose it. "No. We're not."

"Hmmm...interesting." Austin narrowed his up-to-no-good eyes. "But you two slept together?"

"We did. All the more reason for you to stay away."

Austin flopped on to Donovan's bed, tucked his hands behind his head and crossed his feet at the ankles. "She's so hot, and her gray hair is sexy. I'm definitely into older women. They know what they want. There are no games."

"She's a year older than you, so not sure that qualifies. Then again, you've never been good at math."

Austin smirked. "I still reserve my right to admire her."

Donovan heaved his suitcase onto the bed next to Austin and began unpacking his things. "I reserve my right to beat on you."

"And I, you." Austin got up and wandered over to the window, leaning against the casing and looking outside. "I need to ask you something. Do you think Mom looks skinny?"

Donovan had noticed exactly that when he hugged his mom. Like his arms went around her a little too far. "I did. Do you think something is going on? Health-wise?"

"Not sure. I asked her about it and she told me that she loves being called skinny, which is ridiculous. It felt like she was deflecting."

"I wonder when she last went to the doctor." Their mom had always been skeptical of western medicine.

"I'm sure it's been years. Her room is full of crystals and astral charts, and there are countless homeopathic remedies on the kitchen counter."

"I'll try to find a way to ask."

Austin pushed off from the wall and slugged Donovan on the arm. "Finish up so we can go for a walk."

"Yeah. Yeah. Just let me hang up my tux and I'll do the rest when we get back."

A few minutes later, the two were back on the ground floor, walking out through one of the many French doors opening onto the flagstone patio and pool area. Beyond that was the rose garden tended by their mother, even though it was more than enough work to have the landscaping crew handle it. She'd always insisted on doing these things herself. Part of it was her penny-pinching ways. Part of it was her reluctance to give anyone else control.

Donovan and Austin strode down the grassy slope that led to the pond. When they were kids, they spent hours out on this lawn and in the water—swimming, throwing a football, building forts, and scheming up ways to get in trouble. There had been days during the summer when they didn't bother to come home until well after dark. Their bond had always been tight, but the dynamic was sometimes difficult to navigate, a loving tug-of-war.

The brothers came by any rivalry between them honestly. Austin and Donovan had different fathers, but they'd only known Austin's dad Noel. Cocky and irreverent, with the good looks to back it up, he was like Han Solo-era Harrison Ford. He'd been careful and kind with the boys, and

Donovan remembered always feeling safe with him. But Donovan had also been keenly aware that Noel was Austin's *real* father, and that any affection he showed Donovan was out of generosity, rather than a parental bond. Seeing it as an adult years later, Donovan thought that love freely given was better than something of obligation. But at the time, the message couldn't have been any more clear—Donovan was the one it took effort to love.

Noel and their mother had a tumultuous relationship. They were either deeply in love or despised each other, and any gray area in between was flyover country, not their true destination. Eventually, their mother cried uncle and divorced Noel when the boys were nine and seven. It was probably the right call, but in Noel's absence, her impetuous nature no longer had any guardrails. She imposed no bedtime, they could eat whatever they wanted, ride their bikes through the grand dining room, and bring home any animal they decided should be a pet. She wanted the boys to feel free. There were times when they'd craved that autonomy, but growing up with virtually no one in charge meant that they were saddled with a great deal of responsibility. One could argue that perhaps that had been his mom's plan all along. She'd been teaching them to care for themselves. There was only one problem with that theory—his mom did not plan.

As for Donovan's dad, Buck, he was little more than a sperm donor. He got Eileen pregnant, stuck around to enjoy her money and the lavish surroundings, but ultimately decided that commitment wasn't for him. The story went that he left the day before Donovan's first birthday. Eileen had baked a cake for the celebration, but she'd forgotten powdered sugar for the buttercream. She sent Buck into town, and no one heard from him again. Eileen met Noel two days later, and on the rare occasions she invited anyone to the estate, she made a grand production of telling the story—it was kismet that Donovan's dad had walked out of her life, making room for Noel.

Now that they were down by the pond, Austin asked, "How's work?"

"Great. Amazing. I love working with Echo. It's seriously one of the best things I've ever done. I feel like I'm making up for lost time. I know it's not exactly the same as being there for her when she was little, but hopefully it means more now?" Donovan drew a deep breath as he took in the view of the calm water. With cattails bending in the summer breeze and ducks paddling along, it really was peaceful. "Does it sound like I'm rationalizing?"

Austin shrugged. "I don't think so. I think you're being present and you're trying. That's all that matters."

Donovan wanted to believe that. "I hope so. I hope she feels that way."

"Maybe you should ask her."

"I don't want to do that. It'll seem like I'm asking her to absolve me of my sins. That's not her responsibility. I'm still the parent. Any blame is squarely on my shoulders."

"I'm probably not the person to consult with on this topic, anyway. Not a parent and not the best when it comes to relationships." Austin was just as handicapped in this department as Donovan was, but when it came to romance, he'd been a tad smarter, never getting married, although there had been at least two broken engagements. "Speaking of Echo, how long has it been since you've seen Genevieve?"

"Three years. Echo's grad school graduation." That had been a tense day—Genevieve was deeply annoyed with him, and he still didn't know why. She'd refused to answer when he asked. "Not exactly looking forward to it, to be honest. I always manage to make her at least a little unhappy."

"Maybe she'll be too focused on the wedding to notice you."

"Something tells me she'll find a way to get in at least one dig."

Donovan and Austin spent another half hour or so catching up, then headed back inside to get dressed for cocktails and dinner. Donovan ran into Austin in the hall a few minutes before five and they walked down to the fussy formal living room, which was where their mother liked to hold, oddly enough, *informal* gatherings. The decor could best be described as luxury taxidermy, with uncomfortable furniture upholstered in gold and white stripes while the walls were lined with mounted eight-point buck heads and the fireplace mantle home to two stuffed skunks.

Echo and Lucius were already there, as well as a handful of their closest friends, who'd just arrived. Lucius's parents were on hand, who Donovan had met once, as well as Lucius's aunt. Austin brought Donovan a gin and tonic from the bar and they retreated to the bay window seat, where it was easy to catch a buzz and stay out of the way.

Their mother made her entrance soon after, holding on to Stuart and wearing a white floor-length gown. Donovan found her choice of dress particularly odd given that Echo was the bride, but he wasn't about to say a thing, especially now that she and Stuart were preoccupied with talking to the other guests. Seconds later, in walked a pair Donovan had not expected to arrive together—Lela and Genevieve.

He popped up from his seat. "Shit."

Austin did the same. "Oh. I can see how this would be awkward."

Genevieve was wearing a royal blue cocktail dress, her long brown hair tumbling over her shoulders, still just as model-perfect as the last time he saw her. Despite Genevieve's natural ability to draw attention, Donovan could only look at Lela. Her hair was up in a high ponytail again, flaunting her cheekbones and graceful neck. Her flowing black dress had silver threads that brought out the sparkle in her gray.

"In theory, this shouldn't be too terrible," Donovan said to Austin as he studied the two women. They seemed to be having a perfectly normal conversation. "They knew each other in school. They hung out a few times back then."

"Oh, okay," Austin said, sounding entirely unconvinced. "Although, I don't know if I'd want my ex-wife and the woman I have a thing for hanging out together."

Donovan turned to his brother. "I don't have a thing for her. We're friends. And colleagues."

Austin raised both hands in surrender, telling Donovan that he doth protest too much. "Got it."

Lela and Genevieve were now approaching, tying Donovan's stomach into knots.

"Gentlemen," Genevieve started, her British accent as thick as ever. She air-kissed Donovan on both cheeks, then did the same when greeting Austin.

Lela, for her part, offered a single wave. Donovan would've gladly had it the other way around. "Hi, guys."

"Gin and tonic, ladies?" Austin shook the ice in his now-empty glass.

"Yes. Please," Lela said.

"Tell me your mother has some proper gin," Genevieve added.

"There's Hendricks and Tanqueray No. 10. Our mother takes gin very seriously," Austin said.

"Right, then. Either of those'll do."

From the other side of the room, Donovan's mother clinked the side of a champagne glass several times with a silver spoon. "Everyone. I'd like to go over the schedule for Echo and Lucius's big day tomorrow." All eyes were quickly on Eileen. "At eleven, Genevieve and I will be hosting a brunch in this room for the ladies. Stuart will be leading the men on a nature hike, followed by lunch."

Donovan stifled a groan. He didn't need to spend several hours with Stuart. By the next time he came to visit, Stuart would undoubtedly be gone and a new guy would be in his place.

"Then," she continued, "the ceremony will be at four o'clock, down by the pond, followed by dinner and dancing."

"I'm gobsmacked. Your mum is organized," Genevieve quipped. "I wasn't sure she knew how to tell time."

His mother's poor sense of schedule and ability to ignore anyone else's needs was well documented. It had driven Genevieve bonkers when Echo was a baby.

"Maybe because her granddaughter is getting married?" Donovan asked.

Genevieve shot him a searing look. "Maybe because I had to be on her about all of this for the last few months."

Just then, a chorus of barks rang out, growing louder by

the second. Everyone turned to the door. A sleek black cat tore into the room, leaping up onto the back of a wingback chair, back arched and tail fluffed, much like one of the skunks. A split second later the dogs stampeded into the room, surrounding the chair, hopping on hind legs and barking.

"And, here we go..." Genevieve said. "Gives a whole new meaning to 'dog's dinner', doesn't it?"

Donovan wasn't about to argue with his ex-wife about whether or not this was a complete disaster. The answer seemed fairly obvious. He and Austin sprang into action, tugging on collars and attempting to corral the dogs out of the room, but there were too many for two people. Stuart jumped in, then Lucius. Then Echo. Donovan's mom nearly deafened them all with one of her two-finger whistles, but this time, the dogs were not listening. The poor cat hissed and swiped, one time nearly hitting Donovan. Genevieve backed away, staying out of the fray.

"Eileen, do you have any dog biscuits?" Lela blurted, chasing a Papillon in circles. Apparently Lela was the only person with a functioning brain.

"Yes," Stuart answered. "Be right back." He sprinted out of the room and returned in a flash—who knew Stuart was so spry?

As soon as one dog received a treat, they quickly peeled off and bombarded Stuart.

Lela scooped up the poor cat and pulled it into the safety of her arms. "Well, that was exciting."

"Also known as a shambles," Genevieve said.

As Donovan found himself wanting to defend his mom a second time, a realization hit him hard—the dogs might have been his mother's pets, but an episode like that could've happened to anyone. Maybe he needed to stop thinking of his mom as an agent of turmoil. Plus, she was actually trying. It was a lot of work for her to plan and schedule. It simply wasn't in her DNA. "And it all turned out fine, didn't it?"

Genevieve rolled her eyes and walked away. Lela forced a smile, petting the cat, which was now clearly in love with her. Donovan approached the animal, ducking his head to make eye contact, then offering a sniff of his hand before he gave it a scratch behind the ears. All was okay. And he needed to relax.

"With that behind us, I think we're going to go ahead and move into the dining room," Stuart announced.

"Good idea," Donovan said. "I'm starving."

Of course, when they arrived, Donovan learned the downside of his mother's newfound organizational efforts. She'd assigned seats, and she hadn't been particularly kind to him when she'd done it. She'd put him right next to Genevieve.

Genevieve plunked her glass of wine on the table and pulled out her chair. "Well, this is a real cock-up, isn't it?"

One thing Donovan had always enjoyed about being with Genevieve was her prodigious use of British slang. Even when it was unflatteringly directed at him. "We are responsible for the bride being on the planet, so I don't think it's the worst thing in the world for us to sit next to each other."

Genevieve dropped into her chair and pinched her nose. She was so stressed it was radiating off of her in waves. "I suppose."

He sighed and reached for her hand, giving it a gentle squeeze. He felt bad. As much as things had gone completely wrong between them, he still cared for her. "It's okay. No matter what happens this weekend, our daughter will get married to a guy she loves like crazy. That's all that matters."

Genevieve did not enjoy being put on notice, and he was well aware that he'd done exactly that, but it was the only thing that made sense. Life was short. Echo's happiness was the most important thing to them both.

She turned, regarding him with an unfamiliar look, one that felt like a white flag of surrender. "I really hate saying that you're right, but you are."

"I promise to be wrong several times over the course of the weekend. Just to make up for it."

A soft smile spread over her face. "I'm bloody sure of that." She nodded across the table, where Austin and Lela were seated. "Not surprised she found her way into your life again."

"It was a total fluke. We hadn't talked in more than twenty years."

She took a sip of her wine. "Something always told me you two would end up together."

"But we're not."

"You're working together."

"And our daughter is, too."

"As I said, she's back in your life. You don't have to get defensive about it, Donovan. It's simply an observation."

He cleared his throat, watching Lela and Austin as they were chatting and laughing. Lela put her hand on his brother's shoulder, and however innocent it might have been, it made Donovan deeply uncomfortable, especially since he already knew how Austin felt about Lela. He couldn't watch them, but he also couldn't look away. It was like a sexually charged car wreck. The only cure seemed to be to change the subject with Genevieve. "Tell me what's going on at home."

Dinner was served by the cook his mother brought in for special occasions, as well as a server. They started with Waldorf salad, which Donovan had never liked because he hated celery, followed by miso-glazed salmon with veggies, Echo's favorite. As they ate, he caught up with Genevieve. She'd been dating a guy off and on, a university professor, but it was nothing serious. The literacy non-profit she'd started two years ago was doing well. Her parents, however, were not doing great, although Donovan already knew that because they'd been unable to make the trip for Echo's wedding.

When it was Donovan's turn to share, the conversation revolved entirely around Echo as he told Genevieve about the massive success of the company and how rewarding it was to work with their daughter. "It's been incredible. We're so much closer now than we were before."

Genevieve nodded, but her demeanor grew cold. "Glad you had the chance."

Dessert arrived, a salted caramel and chocolate tart, but Donovan picked at his. He'd had his time with Genevieve, they'd both survived, neither of them worse off for the conversation. He was ready to get out of there. His mom had other plans though, asking to go around the table so everyone could offer Echo and Lucius their best bit of relationship advice.

His mom started. "Love is *not* blind. It sees everything." A low rumble among the guests suggested that several people agreed.

When it came to be Lela's turn, she said, "Someone once said that you shouldn't go to bed mad, but I think it's fine. By morning, things almost always seem better." It made Donovan smile. It was such a Lela thing to say.

Austin offered, "Whatever I've done, do the opposite." That prompted a few laughs.

As did Genevieve's offering, "Never share a sink."

Then it was Donovan's turn. He wasn't good with sentimentality, and he feared his would only fall flat, but he couldn't think of anything else to say. "Just find a way to love each other." To his great surprise, a chorus of "Aww..." broke out in the room. The irony did not escape him. He was wholly unqualified to make the proclamation. Other than his love for his daughter, it had always felt far too complicated.

The crowd finished up dessert and coffee, then began to disperse. Genevieve stopped to speak to Lucius's aunt, and Donovan needed some air, so he strolled out into the hall.

"Hey, Donovan," Austin caught up with him. "I have to tell you, Lela is amazing," he muttered.

Donovan knew where this was going and he didn't like it. "She is."

"I know we talked about it earlier, but are you serious about me stepping off? Because I'm interested."

"It's a free country, Austin. You can do whatever you want. All I was trying to say is that she's a very sweet person and you don't have the best track record. I'd encourage you to tread lightly." With every word, Donovan began to feel more and more uncomfortable with this idea. "And if you do anything to hurt her, I will actually kill you."

Lela was walking toward them, an absolute vision in that damn dress, making him yet again question so many things in his life. Decisions. Choices. "Hey guys. What's up?"

"Just chatting." Donovan did his best to be casual with his answer.

"That was such a lovely dinner, but I'm beat. I think I'm going to head upstairs and crash," Lela said.

"I'll walk you," Austin blurted.

Donovan felt his hands roll up into fists.

"Sounds great," Lela said. "Good night, Donovan. See you tomorrow." She surprised him with a hug. It was warm and comforting to have her body pressed against his, but it was a fleeting moment of bliss. In a flash, she was gone.

He watched as she and his brother strolled down the hall. He didn't like anything about the idea of his brother and Lela, but he'd said his piece. Lela was not his, and his brother was under no obligation to listen to him.

He jumped when Echo put her hand on his shoulder. "Everything okay, Dad?"

"Yeah. Of course. Just tired." He turned to her and gently rubbed her arm. "How are you doing? Everything okay with your mom?"

She shrugged. "Mom is Mom. I just want to get through the ceremony tomorrow. I have a feeling she'll loosen up quite a bit after we're over that hurdle."

"We had a good conversation at dinner. She's glad you and I are working together. I told her how much I love it. How much it means to me." With every word, his voice cracked with emotion a little more, but he figured he would only have so many opportunities to tell her these things. "I feel so lucky that you gave me the chance to be a part of your life in this way. Most dads don't get this time with their adult daughters." Tears stung the corners of his eyes, but he held it all in. He didn't want to upset her. This weekend was about her, not him.

"I love it, too, Dad. I really do. We work well together. And I think Lela has been an amazing addition to our team."

"I'm so happy to hear that."

She spread her arms wide. "Coming in for a hug."

He wrapped up his baby girl and held on to her tight. She was the most important thing in his entire life. He'd found his way onto the right path with her and he wasn't going to step off it for anything. In twenty-four hours, she'd be married. And everything would change once again.

CHAPTER SEVENTEEN

"I KNOW my grandmother is calling this a Hen Party, but I think we should refer to it as the Hen *Pecking*," Echo muttered under her breath as she and Lela walked downstairs on Saturday morning for the ladies' brunch.

Lela let out an unflattering snort. "What would make you call it that?"

"Well, let's see..." She came to a stop on the staircase. "My mother is in a terrible mood. Grams is behaving strangely, which I'm guessing you've figured out is quite a statement. Plus, I've been feeling for months like I was bullied into this whole thing from the beginning."

"Bullied? Into the wedding?" Lela jutted out her lower lip. As someone who loved Echo *and* weddings, that seemed incredibly sad. "But this is your big day."

"Lucius and I didn't want any of this." She flailed her arms. "Getting married here at the estate was the compromise. We wanted something quiet at City Hall, just the two of us, but my mom had a hissy fit. She wanted a fancy wedding. First in England, then she conceded to the U.S. It was months of negotiating. Between you and me, I think she was trying to make up for what she and Dad didn't have. They had a quickie ceremony because my mom was pregnant with me."

Lela grasped Echo's arm. "Hold up a second. I thought you were born a little less than a year after they got married."

She shook her head. "Oh, no. It was a huge controversy. My mom's parents are extremely religious and they were furious that she'd gotten pregnant. She was almost four months along when they tied the knot."

Lela felt as though her head was swimming, suddenly presented with a whole new view of a defining event in her life. Not that she'd been entitled to know any of this, either at the time or now, but if she'd been aware of this one detail—that Genevieve was pregnant when she got engaged to Donovan—it might have softened the blow.

Lela had long theorized that the timing of the marriage was a reflection on her. Genevieve and Donovan were broken up when Lela had sex with him that first time, but he got back together with her days later. The sequence of events had nearly shattered Lela. Of course, it was quite likely that Donovan had been head over heels for Genevieve the whole time, and it was only after sleeping with Lela that he realized his mistake.

"You seriously didn't know that?" Echo asked as they resumed their walk downstairs. "I think my dad thought everyone on that whole campus knew what was going on. But he's super paranoid, so there's that."

"It's hard to know what's going through his head. Your dad can be pretty secretive." He'd been exactly that when he and Genevieve got engaged. He didn't tell Lela. She heard about it from a mutual friend. It was days before graduation and Lela was knee-deep in exams, so she'd shut herself off from everyone, just so she could finish the school year. The night of graduation, he had a small gathering at his apartment. Lela dragged herself to it because she felt like he deserved in-person congratulations. But there'd been no way to ask a single question about what had really happened—Genevieve was there, as well as two dozen other grads and mutual friends. Everyone was blowing off steam, drunk and having fun, and Lela felt as though her entire life had narrowed to a very dark point. The guy she loved was out of reach, but she was also losing her best friend. That was what prompted the pivot to cosmetology school. There was no way she could return to NYU.

"He does like playing things a little too close to the vest," Echo said.

"Indeed, he does," Lela agreed.

Outside the formal living room, Echo's three girlfriends, Ola, Neely, and Kendra, were waiting. Lela had met them last night, right after the dogs disrupted cocktail hour. From her vantage point, Lela spied Genevieve and Eileen inside, working away.

"Echo," Lela said. "I'm going to help your mom and grandmother."

"Sounds good," she replied, quickly returning to her conversation with her friends.

Lela found Eileen trailing behind one of the caterers who'd helped serve dinner the night before, double-checking each chafing dish as it was set out. Genevieve was hovering over a large side table, putting out supplies for what appeared to be bridal shower activities.

"Can I help with anything?" she asked Genevieve.

Genevieve straightened and granted Lela the faintest of smiles. "I think I have it all ready, but thanks."

Lela surveyed the impressive spread. There were adorable games, like a jar of foil-wrapped chocolate kisses and notecards for guests to guess, "How many kisses?" as well as a silver bowl labeled "Wishes for the couple" with small slips of paper for anyone to add their happy tidings. One activity in particular grabbed Lela's attention—a stack of clipboards with silver grosgrain bows tied at the top, each with a piece of brown craft paper featuring a simple line drawing of an undressed woman wearing a veil. In white scrolled typography, "Guess the dress" was scrawled across the page, serving as the instructions.

"I'm so impressed. You've really gone all out." Lela couldn't help but remember what Echo had said about her mom taking this too seriously. There was another side to that observation—Genevieve had put a great deal of thought into her daughter's big day.

She arranged a spray of silver and white pens in a jar. "She's my only child, and if everything goes right, this will be her only wedding. I want her to remember it fondly." She turned and looked out over the room. Eileen was busy chatting with Lucius's mom and aunt. "We didn't quite have the start I hoped for yesterday. Cocktail hour went all to pot with the dogs. Hopefully today will be better."

"I'm sure it will be."

Eileen clapped her hands as another member of the catering staff entered the room with a tray of champagne flutes topped with mimosas. "Ladies. I'd like to get started if we can. The food is hot and it's not going to be like that forever. Echo, why don't you go through the buffet line first?"

Echo cued up, followed by her friends. Lucius's mom and aunt went after them, then Eileen. At the very end were Genevieve and Lela. Lela filled her plate with all sorts of delectable brunch goodies—mini spinach quiche, roasted asparagus with a lemon butter sauce, breakfast potatoes, and a lovely fruit salad. They sat at a long table at one end of the room, with Lela seated between Lucius's aunt and Eileen.

"Hosting your granddaughter's wedding must be so much fun for you, Eileen," Lela said.

"It is. Echo is an absolute peach. I love her to pieces."

"Of course you do. She's smart and beautiful, strong and independent. Of course, her parents had a lot to do with that."

"More or less," Eileen said. "I wasn't always so sure Donovan would figure out his life. He's got an awful lot of his dad in him."

Lela struggled to swallow a bite of strawberry, so she slugged down her mimosa. "He's working hard to make up for his past mistakes."

"There's only so much making up you can do."

Lela didn't have a chance to respond, as Genevieve stood and raised her champagne glass. "I'd like to propose a toast to my daughter, Echo. Darling, you are the most brilliant and beautiful person I have ever known. May you always be happy and feel loved."

"To Echo," Lela and the other women at the table said in chorus.

"As soon as everyone's finished eating, we'll get started with games," Genevieve said.

A half hour later, they were all seated on the couches in the center of the room, with Genevieve and Eileen running the show. They ran through Genevieve's carefully planned activities, Echo seemed embarrassed for much of it, but everyone enjoyed themselves. A few times, Lela spotted Eileen, looking wistfully at Echo. There was no question that she was the true golden child of this family, even if she didn't seem to want it.

Lela offered to help Genevieve clean up after the festivities had died down and everyone else had left. She was picking up discarded pens and slips of paper when Genevieve asked a question. "You still have feelings for him, don't you?"

"Wait. What?" Lela had been unprepared for the question. It had come completely out of left field.

"Donovan. You're still in love with him. I knew it when we were in school. I see the same look on your face now."

Lela was deeply surprised to hear this from Genevieve. If she'd figured it out, why hadn't the actual object of her affection been able to see it? "I did have a crush on him in college. That's true. But it went away when you two got engaged." That last part was a lie, but she didn't want Genevieve to feel bad about what was very much *not* her problem.

"You weren't gutted?"

Lela felt like Genevieve was trying to get a rise out of her. "It wasn't a big deal. Everyone experiences unrequited love at least once in their life, right?"

"I suppose. There were plenty of guys who didn't take to me like I hoped they would."

"Plenty?"

"I got more than my fair share of inquiries." She laughed

quietly, and shook her head. "But most of them didn't stick around."

Lela could only look back on her life before Mark, when she'd wasted so much of her youth crushing on guys. Every time she got up the nerve to make her confession, she was struck down, and each of those instances pierced a hole in her heart. A few too many and she started to feel like a sieve. So she kept her feelings to herself. That was why she'd never told Donovan she was in love with him. "I'm sorry that happened."

"You still haven't owned up to Donovan, Lela."

"Sure I did. I had a crush on him."

"It was more than that. I'm pretty sure it broke up our marriage."

That was a step too far for anyone to believe, especially Lela. "Excuse me? I wasn't even in the picture. You guys were an ocean away." Lela's head was spinning. What in the hell was Genevieve implying? "If he had any feelings for me, I never knew about it. And if that's true, why didn't he reach out to me after you got divorced? I didn't hear from him. Ever."

"Because he's a bloody fool? I don't know the answer to that question."

Lela was getting more than a little annoyed. Genevieve had everything anyone could ever want—beauty, brains, and by all accounts, more than enough money to be happy. She'd also had the guy Lela had wanted. "Donovan was in love with you. He always gravitated toward you."

"Well, I saw the opposite. Do you know what it feels like to have your boyfriend do all of the fun things he likes to do with someone else? I was fine for sex, but you were the one he wanted to go see music with. You were the one he wanted to study with or talk to for hours."

Lela was hit by a realization that was difficult to wrap her head around. So much of her college existence framed in an entirely different way. That whole time she'd been spending time with Donovan, she hadn't thought about what it might feel like from Genevieve's point of view. "Oh, God, Genevieve. I'm so sorry. I never thought about it that way. I just looked at you and thought you had everything. I didn't see any way I could possibly compete, so I didn't see it that way."

She reached over and gripped Lela's shoulder. "Don't be sorry. You were friends for two years before I came along. I understand some of it. But the bottom line is that I always felt like he was carrying a torch for you."

Lela shook her head. She wasn't going to go into the details of her two encounters with Donovan, where that theory had been so soundly refuted. "Trust me. He wasn't. We've talked about it."

"Huh."

"What?" Lela asked.

"Maybe it was all in my head?"

"I really don't know." Lela needed air. She needed to escape this conversation and the room.

"It was probably for the best." Genevieve returned to tidying up. "He would've just broken your heart. Donovan doesn't stick around."

Lela didn't know many things, but she was absolutely sure of that.

CHAPTER EIGHTEEN

THE HIKE from hell was over. Miraculously enough, there had only been one painfully awkward moment during it, when Stuart stopped the expedition halfway and made a declaration to Austin and Donovan: "I love your mother more than anything in the entire world."

"Good for you," Donovan had replied, not being entirely sincere.

"I've asked her three times to marry me, and every time she's told me I'm crazy and should take a nap or fix myself a drink. One time, she turned up the volume on the TV and pretended like she couldn't hear me."

"What do you want us to do about it?" Austin asked.

"Can you talk to her? Help her see my side of things?" Stuart pled, holding on tight to his trekking poles atop the hillside, sun beating down on them. They were all sweating like crazy.

"We try to stay out of our mother's personal life," Donovan answered. "She doesn't want our opinion. We learned that long ago."

Stuart sighed heavily. "Just think about it. That's all I ask."

Donovan and Austin had a brief conversation about it when they got back to the house, quickly reaching the conclusion that Stuart was a nice guy who was oblivious to what wasn't good for him. It was best to let their mom stay the course. Plus, they'd never be able to convince her of anything.

Feeling sweaty from the hike, Donovan changed into his swim trunks and headed to the pool. Down by the pond, Stuart was arranging a handful of white folding chairs for the ceremony. Donovan had asked if he needed help, but Stuart said that he needed time with his thoughts.

When Donovan dove in, the water was cool against his skin, helping to clear his head. He swam several laps, kicking off from the side and streamlining beneath the surface for as long as his breath would hold. He tried to think about nothing. It took some work. Everyone in his life wanted to stake their claim on his thoughts, but Austin and Lela won out. What if Austin kissed her last night? What if Lela kissed him back?

What if she took charge?

It was too horrible an idea. If Lela and his brother ended up together, Donovan might lose it.

Who was he kidding? He would *definitely* lose it.

Tired of laps, he stopped in the center of the pool and floated on his back, staring up at the wide blue sky, listening to the even pace of his own breath. That was when he heard voices. He raised his head above the surface. It was Lela and Austin, out of view, probably on the other side of the rose bushes.

"You're sure you don't want to go out with me?" Austin asked.

That perked up Donovan real fast. He treaded to keep his head above water. His heart was pounding as he waited for her answer, but he was pretty sure he had one piece of the puzzle—Austin wouldn't be asking that question if he'd had any luck at all last night.

"Dating isn't a thing I do anymore," Lela said.

"Not at all?"

"Nope."

This was news to Donovan. Although he didn't have any specific intel on the state of Lela's love life, he wasn't aware she'd made such a definitive decision.

"What if the right guy came along?"

"You know, romance just isn't in the cards for me. Not anymore."

"Why not?"

"I'm over it."

Donovan snickered.

"Completely?" Austin said.

"For now, I guess. I have other things I want to focus on. My business is at the top of the list."

There were several seconds of silence, during which Donovan's imagination kicked into overdrive. The thing was, Austin did not give up on anything easily, especially if there was some aspect of beating Donovan involved.

"Okay. Well, you know where to find me if you ever change your mind."

Donovan wasn't convinced his brother had actually given up. He was simply taking care to read her cues.

"Thanks, Austin. I'm going to go for a quick walk before I help Echo get ready. I'll see you later."

"Yes, you will."

Donovan caught a glimpse of Lela coming his way and he quickly ducked his head under the water, admonishing himself for eavesdropping. When he came up for air, she was standing on the pool deck peering down at him.

"The sign says adults should not swim alone," she said.

"Yeah, well. I'm not really an adult and I'm not really swimming."

Lela laughed and grabbed a seat at the end of one of the chaises surrounding the pool. "Did you just overhear my conversation with Austin?"

Donovan swam to the side of the pool and rested his arms on the edge, looking up at her. She was stunning in a black and white checked sundress and a pair of black Chuck Taylor low-top sneakers. "A little bit. I'm sorry. I should have warned you that he was interested in you. Although I guess you were able to figure it out on your own."

"I did. It's fine. He's pretty persistent, but he also seemed to handle the rejection well."

Donovan didn't want to smile, but he couldn't help it. "Good. I'm glad to hear it."

"Why are you grinning like the Cheshire cat?"

Heat flushed his face. "Sibling rivalry. I swear, I come home and I turn into a bratty teenager. My brother wants to do something and I immediately start formulating a plan to stop him."

"Interesting. I'm an only child, so not sure I get that."

"It's the same thing with my mom. Whatever she says, I want to rebel."

Lela nodded. "Now, *that* I get. I'm like that when I go home to Wisconsin." She looked back at the house. "Although if I had such opulent digs to return to, I might find a way to be a bit more agreeable."

"How are your parents?" Donovan had met Deb and Ben once, during Lela's sophomore year when they came to visit the city for a weekend. They seemed very concerned with every little thing Lela did, which Donovan found endearing. He couldn't imagine having that much attention from a parent, let alone two.

"They're good. They're actually coming to visit soon. I have to get psyched up for that, but it's mostly just a meal or two every day and some touristy activities. Dad's allergic to cats so they always stay in a hotel."

Donovan side-stroked to the steps and climbed out of the pool, grabbing his towel from the chaise next to Lela. "You have to mentally prepare for them showering you with affection?"

"Yes. It sometimes feel like I'm being smothered. But I can't say anything. I'm their only child. It's not hard to imagine why they're like that."

Donovan sat next to her, tossing the towel on to another chair and leaning back, propping himself up with both arms. "Genevieve was really worried about Echo being an only child. She was sure she'd end up being spoiled, but I think that's just a myth. You're not self-centered and neither is Echo."

"Echo is wonderful. I can't imagine a more generous person. You must be so proud of her."

It was such an understatement, but he couldn't think of a way to express the bounds of his pride in his daughter. Not just in her success, but in the woman she'd become. She was a free spirit, strong, someone who lived in her own skin, didn't take no for an answer, and refused to let other people define her. She was everything he'd always wanted to be but never quite got there. "She's the best thing I ever did. Unfortunately, I can't take much credit."

Lela quietly scanned his face like she was looking for clues. "What happened? That you weren't able to be around when she was little?"

This wasn't an enjoyable story to retell, but he wasn't about to hide it from Lela. "Genevieve struggled after Echo was born. She had postpartum depression. Echo didn't sleep a whole lot, and she had trouble nursing. We had no clue what we were doing, and we were living in my apartment in the city. My upstairs neighbor was constantly complaining about the baby crying. We were sleep-deprived and miserable. We needed help and we needed space, so we came up here."

"To this house? To live with your mom?"

"It was our only real option. Genevieve's parents were in England and that just wasn't a leap we were ready to make. My mom seemed like the logical choice, but it was really hard. Even in this giant house. She was always offering unsolicited parenting advice, which really rubbed me the wrong way. She was not exactly the model parent." The biggest guiding force during that time in Donovan's life was that no matter what, he was not going to be like his dad. He was going to stick around, especially through the hard times. Unfortunately, every bit of criticism his mother launched at him felt like she was telling him he'd never be anything but exactly like his father. "So, yeah," he continued. "It was hard.

After Echo turned one, Genevieve said she'd had enough. We'd given my family a try and it wasn't working out, so she wanted her turn. We moved to London to be near her parents. It was great for awhile, but the happier she became, the less she wanted me."

"Oh. I didn't know that."

"She said she felt like I wasn't present in our marriage. She asked for a divorce right before Echo turned three. I agreed, left England, and came back to the states. I didn't really know what else to do. She didn't want to be married to me and I wasn't equipped to be a single parent. After that, I saw Echo maybe once or twice a year. It felt like I wasn't her dad anymore. I became more like this guy she knew. That was heartbreaking."

"I'm so sorry."

Donovan hated that their conversation had become so heavy, but it did feel good to tell someone what had happened. "Thanks. It's okay. I know it's all water under the bridge, but it still bothers me."

"Can I ask you a question? About when you and Genevieve got married?"

"Sure."

"Echo told me about the timing. I had no idea Genevieve got pregnant when you were still in school. Why didn't you tell me?"

Very little of that time was clear. In fact, the whole thing was a blur. But he knew at least some of the answer to the inquiry. "Because I thought you'd be disappointed in me."

"Why would you think that? Have I ever struck you as a judgmental person? In the slightest?"

Confronted with that question, he had to think even

more about why he hadn't told her what was going on. It tore at his heart and his conscience in ways very few things did. "Truth?"

"Please."

"I didn't tell you because getting married to Genevieve was not what I wanted to do."

"Oh."

"And I was sure that you would be able to tell that I was just talking myself into doing it." He turned and looked into her deep blue eyes, which were wide with surprise and at least a sliver of betrayal. "But I had to do it. I had to take responsibility. I wasn't going to be like my dad." He hadn't admitted that aloud to anyone, ever.

"Wow." She shook her head slowly, seeming stuck in disbelief. "It's going to take me a while to wrap my head around this. I was sure you were so madly in love with Genevieve that you didn't care about me anymore."

So many details of his relationship with Lela broke his heart, but that was especially difficult to hear. "I always cared. Always. Even when I wasn't around. Even when we didn't talk. I was just wrapped up in what I felt like I had to do. And my ego wouldn't allow me to go in a different direction. I know that now. I'm sorry you didn't know."

"While we're dredging up the past, can I ask you one more question?"

He sighed. Whatever was coming, he deserved it. "Of course."

"Three years ago. Why did you take off before I woke up?"

"I started to feel really anxious..." Donovan hadn't told a soul about this, either. He knew what Echo would say—that he needed to go to a doctor. It wasn't that he didn't want to see a physician. It was that he wasn't ready to feel like an old man, and there was something about this that made him feel like exactly that. "I started worrying about what you might expect from me, and I started to have chest pains, and I didn't want to wake you, so I left."

Her expression turned to pure horror and she reached for his arm. That one touch—there was no way she understood what it did to him. "Donovan. Why didn't you wake me up? That's super serious. I could've taken you to the doctor. Are you okay?"

He frantically scanned the immediate area. "Will you lower your voice?" He looked back over his shoulder. Luckily, there was no one there. "I don't want anyone to know about it. Okay?"

"It's okay to be human. I know you probably very rarely feel like that, but it truly is okay." She rubbed his elbow with her thumb, stirring up something inside him that he was desperate to tamp down. "What did the doctor say? I'm assuming you went straight to the hospital."

"I didn't go to a doctor. I took a cab to my hotel and eventually it went away."

Lela stood up and planted her hands on her hips. "Donovan James. What in the hell is wrong with you? You can't mess around with that. You could've died."

He shrugged. "I went eventually. Like a year later..."

She slanted her head to one side and shook it at a speed that suggested he was the dumbest person she'd ever met. "Nobody knows?"

"Nobody."

She threw up her hands, and took several steps away.

When she turned around, she flat-out scolded him. It was super hot. "Give me one reason I shouldn't tell Echo."

"It's a HIPAA violation?"

"I'm not a doctor. I don't think I'm bound by that."

"Look. I will tell her. When the time is right. I promise. The important thing is that I'm fine. And we're supposed to be having fun this weekend, remember?"

She pressed her lips together tightly. "I'm serious about this. You have to tell her."

"I will. Scout's honor."

"I'm going to hold you to that."

"Got it. What time is it?"

"Nearly two o'clock. I need to start Echo's makeup in a half hour."

"And I need to get away from the house for a few minutes." He stood and threaded his arms into his T-shirt. "Want to go for a quick spin on the Vespa?"

"The Vespa? It's still alive?"

"Yeah. It's been in my mom's garage for years. I worked on it a bit before we went on the hike. Runs like a charm."

The most stunning smile crossed Lela's lips. "I'd love to."

CHAPTER NINETEEN

LELA COULD HARDLY BELIEVE it as she stood outside the garage, watching Donovan wheel out his dinged up minty green Vespa with the chrome trim, the same one she'd ridden on countless times in college. "I just assumed this thing had died a long time ago."

He shook his head. "It'll never die. It just needs some love every now and then. Sort of like me." He bounced his eyebrows at her as he buckled the chin strap on his shiny black helmet.

Lela smacked his arm with the back of her hand, then put on her own helmet. With a kick of the starter, Donovan got it to putter to life. He revved the engine, then scooted forward on the seat to make room for her. There was no real ladylike way to do this. She was wearing a dress and she was not going to ride side-saddle like in some 1950s movie. She hiked up her skirt and lifted her leg over the seat. As she climbed aboard, she flashed back to the other times she'd done this. She wrapped her arms around Donovan's waist, pressed her chest against his back, and bracketed his hips with her thighs.

Funny, but she'd somehow forgotten how sexual it felt to do this, like she was riding Donovan, and the scooter was just this thing pleasantly vibrating under her ass.

Hello, there.

They raced down the driveway, Lela's hair flying out behind her when he picked up speed. A hearty laugh erupted from her throat when he swooped around the corner on to the asphalt, tilting them to the left nearly forty-five degrees. Donovan pushed the scooter's limits, she could hear it in the hesitation of the engine. He was totally showing off, likely for her benefit. She didn't care. It was too much fun.

She flattened one hand against his stomach, feeling his muscles twitch beneath her palm. Her other hand went to his chest, where the *thump thump thump* of his heart raced to keep time with the scooter. Pure instinct made her rock her hips into him, the hem of his soft T-shirt caressing her inner thighs while the motor buzzed between her legs. Warmth bloomed in her belly and tension began to coil. Donovan might not have managed to give her an orgasm the first time they'd slept together, but it was sort of a miracle it hadn't happened on the Vespa.

Meanwhile, she was still trying to make sense of the many revelations of that day and how they pertained to Donovan and her. Even if she'd known the truth at the time, the end result would have still been the same—Donovan and Genevieve would've been married. They likely still would've ended up divorced. But for Lela, life would've been at least somewhat different. She might have been a little less timid. She might have been a bit more bold. At least when it came to men. She'd been afraid to put herself out there for years.

Donovan took a wide curve and the warm summer air

fluttered under her dress. She closed her eyes and inhaled Donovan's scent, cedar and sandalwood, as it mixed with the faint fumes of exhaust and the sweet smell of late June while the breeze flitted through the trees. This felt like a moment to hold on to tightly and keep forever. A chance to revisit her past in a way she never would've dreamed. No matter what happened, this weekend would stay lodged in her memory. Forever.

Donovan slowed down and turned on to a gravel road, checked for cars, then doubled back the way they came. For some reason, the return trip seemed much shorter than the first leg, probably because she knew that the time on their adventure was dwindling. As they approached the house, Lela saw Echo pacing in front of the garage.

"I hope I'm not late," she shouted into Donovan's ear.

"We were only gone for a few minutes," he replied.

The closer they got, it became more apparent that she was upset. Donovan pulled the scooter into the garage and killed the engine. Lela climbed off first, removing her helmet. Donovan quickly followed.

"We aren't getting married," Echo announced to them both. She bore the sure sign of misery—smudged mascara.

"Wait. What?" Donovan asked, rushing up to her.

"I got into a huge fight with Mom, and Lucius said this isn't worth it, and we're thinking we'll just go to the airport to get on an earlier flight for our honeymoon. We can get married by a justice of the peace when we get back to the city."

"Sweetheart, take a deep breath." Donovan seemed remarkably calm given what was happening. "What was the fight about?"

"I can't tell you."

"Why not?"

"Because it will hurt your feelings for no good reason." Echo crossed her arms over her chest and kicked a rock from the driveway into the grass.

"*My* feelings? How did I become part of this?" Donovan asked.

"If I answer that, I have to tell you exactly what she said, and trust me, you do not want to know what she said."

Donovan groaned and shook his head, walking several paces away from them. "I don't want you to worry about me. We're all here. You've been planning for months. How do we get this resolved?"

"We don't. Mom is being a bitch and I'm mad."

"There's got to be something we can do." Donovan looked to Lela. He seemed completely at odds with himself. Lela had seen him like this many times, overwhelmed by the darkest forces of his mind—his feelings. "What if you talk to Lela about it?"

Lela bugged her eyes at Donovan, silently reminding him that she was not a parent and not equipped to deal with this. Plus, Genevieve only barely tolerated her.

Echo shook her head. "Lela, I don't want to bother you with our family bullshit. I like you too much."

That was all Lela had to hear. She liked Echo too much to *not* be there for her. "If you want to talk to me, I'm here to listen and offer my two cents."

"Really?" Echo asked.

"Really. Where do you want to talk?"

Echo looked at the house. "Not inside. Mom and Grams are in there."

"Down by the pond?"

"Sure. I can throw things." Echo started off.

Lela was about to follow, but Donovan's words stopped her. "Lela. Thanks for doing this."

"I haven't done anything yet."

"Something tells me you'll have no problem sorting this out."

"No promises, but I'll try." Lela turned on her heel and hurried across the grass to catch up to Echo. Echo's long dark hair was pulled into a side ponytail, and she was wearing a swishy skirt and a T-shirt, adopting a far more casual look here than she did when they were in the city. "One quick question before we launch into any of this, are you wearing Lela B mascara?"

"I am." She turned to Lela as they walked. Ahead, were the chairs arranged for the ceremony that was now suddenly in question as to whether or not it would happen. "Why?"

"It's a little smudged, that's all. I would really worry if that was the waterproof formula."

Echo shook her head. "It's the regular one. I love it. It makes my lashes thick, but still soft."

Lela smiled as they skirted the chairs and approached the water's edge. "Good. I'm glad to hear it."

Echo bent over and picked up a fat twig, casting it into the water. "Hopefully we can sell a boatload of it."

"I hope so, too." Lela didn't want to talk about work. Echo was in the middle of a crisis. "Do you want to tell me what your mom said?"

This time, Echo picked up a rock and launched it into the pond. "I was talking about how well things are going at work with dad and she got super mad. She said that I was acting like nothing ever happened. She said that he's hurt me more than any person in my life and I shouldn't let him back in so easily."

Wow. Lela wasn't really sure what to say to that. She could see it from both sides. "What did you say?"

"That I don't agree. I love having him around. He gets me, Lela. And he helps without getting in the way. Do you have any idea how hard that is to find? When JTI first acquired Echo Echo, they sent in all of these corporate idiots who were spouting all sorts of business school BS. They didn't care about what I was trying to do. They were just there to prop up the bottom line. That isn't what I wanted. At all."

"Of course. It means more to you than that."

"I'm not going to be stupid about something, but I do think there's something to be said for going with your gut."

"I completely agree."

"Well, Dad lets me do that. He lets me run with my ideas, but he also has all of this experience that comes in really handy. Like with the initial reaction to the Lela B campaign. It wasn't at all what I was expecting. Add in the stress about the wedding, and I was at a total loss. But he helped me see a path forward. One that I might not have been willing or ready to take."

"Time will tell how it will pan out, but I understand what you're saying."

Echo shook her head and confronted Lela with her big, brown, mascara-smudged eyes. "Oh, I think he was right. I think it's going to take off. It might take a month or two, but it will. We will grow your company. The products are too good."

Lela smiled. "Thank you. I appreciate that. But we aren't talking about me. We're talking about you and your mom and your wedding."

She sighed. "Yeah, back to my dad, the big thing is that I trust him. I know he wouldn't do anything I didn't want him to do. And I know he would never intentionally steer me wrong. But I made the mistake of saying something to my mom about that and she blew her top. She completely freaked out."

"What did she say?"

"That I was wrong. That I was giving him a free pass. That it wasn't fair because she'd done all of the heavy lifting."

"Heavy lifting?"

"When I was little. And a teenager. I was a pain in the ass. I fully admit to that. And I get what she's saying because Dad wasn't there much when I was young. But she's also the one who wanted the divorce, and the person who chose to stay in England. Those decisions impacted me and my dad. It definitely hurt our relationship."

Lela had always wanted to be a mom, but she could see how tangled the whole thing could become, especially if there was a divorce. Genevieve had done the hard work of raising Echo, then Donovan swept in to build a relationship with Echo when she was an adult. That could cause a lot of resentment. On the flip side was Donovan, who would've had to move to London if he'd wanted to see Echo in any regular way. "There are valid points on both sides. I can certainly see what your mom is saying about heavy lifting."

"Was I wrong to get mad at her?"

"No. There's no right or wrong in this situation. It's too complicated for that. I totally understand why you want to defend your father. He's been there for you during what I'm guessing has been the most exciting and stressful part of your life. Of course you appreciate his help. But I also see how that means your mom was there for the unexciting and sometimes grueling parts."

"I guess."

"And here's the rub. Your wedding? It's one of the exciting parts. So everything she's done to make today happen has been for you, but it's also for her. It's only natural to want to be a big part of the good times when you were also there for the harder ones. She doesn't want to feel left out. Nobody does."

Echo took a breath so deep that her shoulders rose to her ears. "Tell me what to do, Lela. Tell me how all of this is supposed to work. I feel like I can trust you. You don't have a side in this."

"All I can suggest is to listen to your mom and acknowledge her feelings. It doesn't make anyone right or wrong. My guess is that she just wants to be heard and appreciated. Like anyone would want to." Lela reached out and put a hand on Echo's shoulder. "But I also want you to know that you can ask your mom to not talk about your dad that way. It's their divorce, not yours."

Echo turned to her, eyes full of gratitude. "I wish I could just jump ahead in life to have everything figured out like you do."

Ah, the bloom of youth. "I really don't have it all figured out. Not even close. That's one of the cruel tricks of getting older. You think you should have everything figured out, but you don't."

"Really?"

"Really. You still make mistakes. All the time. I think the only difference is that you rebound faster. And you might care less about certain people's opinions."

"Was my dad a mistake?"

Lela was a little taken aback by this, especially since she didn't know exactly what Donovan had told her. "In what regard?"

Echo dropped her head to one side. "Lela. He told me."

That didn't necessarily illuminate the situation much. She wouldn't expect Donovan to tell his daughter that he made a habit of leaving in the middle of the night, but anything was possible. "So you mean romantically?"

"If that's the way you want to put it, sure."

"I don't regret anything that happened between your dad and me. It helped me learn a good life lesson."

"What was that?"

"Don't put someone on a pedestal they don't want to be on. When I was in college, I was in awe of your dad. I thought he was the coolest, smartest, most handsome guy I had ever met. Since then, I've learned that he might be a lot of those things, but he's still human. Just like me."

"So you don't have a magic wand that will make everything better? Not even for yourself?"

"I'm afraid I don't, other than good old fashioned emotional labor. As a woman, you'll do a whole bunch of it in your life. Just make sure you get the men around you to understand it's their job to do some, too."

Echo managed a smile. "I feel like an idiot for being such a drama queen."

"Don't. Every wedding needs drama. That's half of what

makes it memorable." Lela nodded toward the house. "Shall we head inside? Fix your tragic mascara?"

"I guess so."

"You are ready to get married, aren't you?"

"I'm ready to *be* married. Yes."

CHAPTER TWENTY

DONOVAN HAD PROMISED himself he wasn't going to cry. But dammit, sitting there and watching his only kid get married was overwhelming—heavy and light, sad and happy, serious and sentimental. Unable to make any sense of it, the only logical conclusion was to let the tears wash his eyes out.

"Are you crying?" Genevieve whispered, although it came out a bit like a hiss. She was seated to Donovan's right, while his mother and Stuart were to his left. Unfortunately, Lela was with Austin in the row behind them. He'd heard them giggling a few times during the ceremony, enough to make him second-guess Lela's assertion that love and romance weren't a thing she cared about anymore.

"Yes. I'm crying. Our daughter is getting married. Shhh." He sat straighter, listening to Echo and Lucius exchange vows. He couldn't help but think about the day she came into the world, when he and Genevieve were scared out of their wits and completely out of their depth. Hell, they were practically kids, too, hardly equipped to care and nurture each other, let alone a baby. That was Day One of Donovan's biggest life lesson—sometimes, you have to find your way. When a tiny, defenseless, and utterly helpless human being depends on you for everything? You figure it out.

"I now pronounce you husband and wife. You may kiss the bride," the officiant said. Eileen had hired the man, a suspiciously handsome candlemaker she'd met at a farmer's market. Apparently he was licensed to perform this ceremony? Donovan hadn't asked for his credentials. It did make him wonder, however, if said candle man might become the new Stuart. He wouldn't put it past his mom. Perhaps that was the reason she didn't want to get married. She was still playing the field.

The small gathering of guests all stood and threw confetti —biodegradable, of course—as Echo and Lucius marched victoriously down the aisle, arm in arm, gleeful grins pasted to their faces. The trip took twenty steps or less. Echo had said she'd wanted small, and that was what she got.

"It was a beautiful ceremony," Lela said, making a point to address Genevieve and Donovan's mom. "You both did a great job with organizing everything."

Genevieve did seem noticeably more relaxed now. Hopefully that would stick. "Thank you, Lela. I appreciate that."

Lucius and Echo led the parade up the grassy slope to the east side of the house, where a more formal garden and patio were situated. It was an area rarely used when Donovan was a kid, but it was a lovely space, perfect for the occasion, with room for several round cloth-topped tables and a dance floor. At one end, a DJ was setting up. String lights zigzagged overhead. Although it would be quite some time until the sun would set, the house cast a long shadow, allowing the Edison bulbs to brightly glow.

Champagne and passed hors d'oeuvres made the rounds for a while, then everyone sat for a dinner of crab cakes and rice pilaf, which was Lucius's favorite. Donovan endeavored to focus on his conversation with Lucius's father, who he was seated next to, but all too often his attention was drawn to Lela and Austin at the table next to them. They were getting chummier. This bothered Donovan, mostly because he knew it shouldn't bother him. Lela was a grown woman and could do whatever she wanted. But still feeling the effects of the Vespa ride earlier in the afternoon, he was having a hard time convincing himself that he and Lela should never be more than friends. He was stuck with phantom feelings of Lela all over his body, of her arms wrapped tightly around him, her inner thighs squeezing his hips, and the lightness in the vicinity of his heart when she laughed. Lela was haunting him in real time, from a table away.

As the meal ended, Echo got up from her seat and walked over to Donovan, crouching down to speak to him. "Are you having fun?"

"Of course. Everything's perfect." He leaned over and kissed her on the forehead. He caressed her arm, feeling nothing less than lucky to have such a wonderful daughter. It made him all the more thankful for the relationship they had now. If this wedding had taken place two or three years ago, it wouldn't have been quite the same. "The important question is, are you having fun?"

"Yes. Although I feel stupid for the drama earlier."

"Don't. I'm no expert, but I think every bride has to panic about something."

"Maybe. Thank God Lela was here. She was amazing. She really helped me sort through everything."

"Good. I'm glad. What was the takeaway?"

"That feelings can be messy. And sometimes, understanding where the other person is coming from is as good as it's going to get. Some situations aren't fixable."

He couldn't help but look at his own relationship with Lela through that lens. Everything between them had indeed been messy, but that was his track record with all women, not just her. Logic said that romance and sex were what got in the way every time, and that had been the case with Lela. But something about focusing on friendship, and only that, still didn't sit right with him. "That sounds like good advice."

"Is there something going on between her and Uncle Austin? Because he seems like he's trying really hard."

Donovan laughed, but none of this struck him as funny. "I don't think so, but it's not my place to say. You should probably ask one of them."

"Well, I'm glad you and Lela have figured out a way to be friends. She seems happy about it, too."

Donovan grinned, hiding the disappointment he felt at Echo's appraisal of the situation.

The DJ tapped the microphone, which seemed superfluous considering the size of the gathering. He could've held his hands to his mouth and yelled, and everyone would've heard him. "If I can get everyone's attention, it's time to cut the cake and then we'll put on some music and start dancing."

Echo popped up and yelled, "Woot! Cake!" She grabbed Lucius's hand and dragged him over to the table where the three-tier marvel stood. They held the knife together, posing for a few photos before drawing it through the layers and feeding pieces to each other, not being careful at all. Everyone laughed and clapped, as did Donovan, although part of his enthusiasm was for the fact that the cake was chocolate. As one of the caterers stepped in and began slicing for guests, the DJ started the music.

Only a few notes of the song—*Sparks* by Coldplay, and Donovan froze.

This was one of his favorite songs from one of his favorite bands in recent history. Echo and Lucius stepped on to the dance floor, wrapped their arms around each other and got lost in a gaze that looked exactly like true love. And Donovan was stuck between the past and the present, jettisoned back to the first time he'd heard this album. His most immediate reaction beyond falling head over heels for the music, was an intense desire to share it with one person—Lela. He was married to Tess at the time, who only liked the poppiest of mainstream music. Still, he'd tried to bond with her over it, and she'd declared it "depressing". It left him longing for his friend Lela, who understood what it was like to have a visceral connection to music. It had made their friendship special. He lost that when they parted ways.

He *had* to ask her to dance to this song. It was a compulsion gripping him with both hands. He turned, only to get stuck again. Austin was leading Lela out on to the floor. Donovan's happy heart deflated like a day-old balloon. What was he was left with? Some brilliant lyrics, a winding bass line, a sparse piano arrangement and Chris Martin's haunting falsetto. Why was he being so sappy about Lela? Was it just because of the day?

He felt a tap on his shoulder, and turned to see his mom. "Care to take your old mother out for a spin? Your brother is already out there."

"You don't want to dance with Stuart?"

She gestured across the patio with a backward toss of her head. "He's busy eating cake."

Indeed, Stuart was at their table, squarely focused on dessert.

"I'd love to." Donovan took his mother's hand, noticing how small it felt in his, and walked her on to the dance floor. Aside from the year in middle school when she'd gotten a wild hair and made him participate in cotillion classes, the culmination of which was a mother-son and father-daughter dance, he'd never cut a rug with his mom. His wedding with Genevieve had been small and not particularly celebratory, his second was on some Caribbean island his mom had refused to travel to, and the third had been hastily arranged in Vegas. Swaying back and forth with her was a nice moment to share, especially when the DJ segued to *Crazy Love* by Van Morrison, a song he adored but was far less torn up about.

"Mom, Stuart really loves you. We had a whole chat about it during the hike. He told Austin and I that he wants to marry you. Why are you giving him such a hard time about it?"

"I'm seventy-four years old. Why do I want to get married? You know what they say. Why buy the cow when you can get the milk for free?"

Donovan chuckled, even though he was inwardly cringing. He didn't want to think about his mother and Stuart and sex. "I'm pretty sure that was an excuse idiotic bachelors used in the 1950s. Nobody says that anymore."

"I say it. Then again, I'm old school." She turned her attention across the patio to Stuart, who was still eating cake. "What if it doesn't work out? Then I have to pay some lawyer to get me out of it. And it'll just make it that much harder to split the estate when I die."

"Is everything okay, Mom? Because it seems like you've lost some weight. When was the last time you went to the doctor?"

A very plain frown crossed her face. "Of course I've lost weight. Your ex-wife has been all over me about the wedding. It's been stressful."

"I'm sorry."

"It's fine. I finally learned to give in and do everything she said to do."

"Speaking from experience, that's the only way to do it."

"As for the doctor, I go every year. Believe me, they hound you like crazy until you come in. They want their copay."

"And everything is okay?" He didn't want to press the subject too hard, but he had to know.

"I have the heart of a forty-year-old. I'll probably outlive you and your brother."

"Good. I'm glad to hear it." Out of the corner of his eye, Donovan spotted Stuart as he beelined toward them. "Mom. I think Stuart wants to dance with you."

"I suppose he's entitled." She took a single step back. "This was nice, darling. It's always good to have you here."

He leaned down and kissed her on the cheek. "It's good to be here." Despite his trepidation about a weekend on the estate, he genuinely felt that way. Again, he felt like he was turning into a marshmallow on the inside. Thank goodness he only had one child to marry off. He didn't think he could take this a second time.

Stuart was standing, waiting.

"She's all yours." Donovan started to make his exit, but then he saw Lela and Austin still dancing. The song was changing to *She's Gone* by Hall & Oates. This was his chance. "May I cut in?"

Austin looked annoyed, but he gave up easy enough. "Fine. See you later, Lela." He let go of her, then sauntered away.

"Bye, Austin..." she said, but he was already gone. "Is this part of your sibling rivalry?"

"No. I want to dance with you."

Lela was a captivating vision when she smiled, but the way the light hit her face made it especially spellbinding. "Okay." She fit perfectly in his arms as they began to dance. "*She's Gone* seems like an odd song choice for a wedding reception. Isn't it about a woman leaving a man?"

"Yes. I'm sure my mom picked it. It might even be her way of dropping a hint for Stuart."

Lela looked at him quizzically. "Are things not going well?"

"He wants more than she's willing to give. Let's put it that way."

She moved a little closer to him, only an inch or two, but his body took it as a positive sign, sending pulses to every nerved ending.

"I love this song," she said. "I feel like I didn't fully appreciate Hall & Oates when I was younger. I get it more now."

"I blame *Private Eyes.* Too silly."

"Oh, no. I beg to differ. It's a perfect pop song. Just try to get it out of your head."

"I miss talking about music with you." He sensed that this little confession, however inconsequential, deserved to be made. "You know how the DJ played Coldplay for the first song? It made me think of you."

Lela reared back her head. "That record came out in 1999. That was way after college."

"Actually, it was 2000." He pulled her a little closer, and drew in the sweet smell of her hair. "The first time I heard it, the only thing I wanted to do was call you so we could talk about it."

"Oh, my God, Donovan. That's *so* weird."

Now that was disappointing. He'd thought she would say it was sweet. "I don't think it's weird at all."

"That's not what I'm saying. I had the exact same experience. A couple of times."

The goofy grin that spread across Donovan's face was too much to take. It made his face hurt. "When? With who?"

"Oh, gosh. The Foo Fighters for sure. Weezer... Macy Gray... Bon Iver... Eminem... Beyoncé. There's been so much great music since we were in college."

"Yes to all of those. I'm also thinking The Strokes. Outkast. The Killers. Arcade Fire." How he loved that she'd had the same impulse, but how he hated that neither of them had acted on it. "The big question is why neither of us reached out."

"I know. One of us should have."

"But we didn't." He sighed, resigned to the fact that he had to spill his guts again. "I didn't reach out because I thought you wouldn't speak to me. I wasn't sure I could handle that."

"I would've talked to you. I totally would have."

The regrets in his life were piling so high he was going to

need a shovel. "Tell me why you didn't call. Or send an email."

"I was worried I'd blown our entire friendship out of proportion. That maybe our friendship didn't mean the same thing to you that it meant to me."

"Of course it meant the same to me. It did."

"But you got panicky when we slept together. And right after that, like days later, you got engaged to Genevieve. So I don't know that I could come to another conclusion."

"I got panicky because our friendship meant so much. I was worried I'd ruined everything when I kissed you. That started it all."

"Another thing I didn't know."

"I'm sorry. I should have told you."

The DJ segued into *Time after Time* by Cyndi Lauper. Lela peered up into his face with a touch of melancholy in her eyes. The world around them blurred. The music wasn't helping—every lyric about looking back and putting memories in a suitcase. If he had any chance at all with her, he hated the idea of missing it. But he was also terrified to convince her of anything. If he failed, so much around him would suffer, including his relationship with Echo.

"I want to kiss you right now." The words barely made their way out of his mouth, but they were there, circling around them like birds or butterflies.

She shook her head. "You don't want to do that."

"But I do."

"But then I'll just kiss you back."

"That's sorta what I was hoping for."

"And then you'll walk away and I'll be mad and everything at work will get weird."

He sighed. "You sound like Echo."

"What do you mean?"

"You know she knows about us. Our past."

"I do know that. She asked me about it. She asked me if you were a mistake."

Donovan swallowed hard. He wasn't sure he was ready to hear what was on the other side of the question his daughter had asked. He was 99% sure the answer was yes. "What did you say?"

"That I don't regret it. And that it was just another life lesson about not putting someone on a pedestal they don't want to be on. I thought far too much of you in college."

He supposed it was better to be a life lesson rather than a mistake, but that was of little consolation. He'd messed up. He knew that. All of this was merely the logical aftermath of his choices. "Is it possible to think too much of someone?"

"In my case, yes. Don't worry. I'm very well aware that you're human now. You're not *actually* a god on a Vespa."

"Good. That's good." *I wouldn't want you thinking too highly of me.* He held on to her tightly as the song changed again—another slow one, *Don't Dream It's Over* by Crowded House. Was it over for Lela and him? It sure sounded like that. Unfortunately, that wasn't the direction his heart wanted to take. He knew he was stumbling his way through this, but he had no clue how to break his fall.

CHAPTER TWENTY-ONE

LELA TRIED to avoid excessive swearing, but sometimes it was the only thing that made sense. "Holy shit. What the fuck happened this weekend?" Standing in the foyer of the James Estate, she frantically scrolled through the notifications and texts on her phone for the first time in two days. It was... a lot.

"Dad. Lela. Are you guys seeing what I'm seeing?" Echo was in a bit of a tizzy, pacing back and forth.

"Echo. Put away your phone, love. We need to go." Lucius marched past them, ferrying bags to Austin's car. Donovan's brother was dropping off the happy couple at Logan Airport in Boston so they could get on their honeymoon flight to Turks & Caicos. The New York airports were closer, but Echo had always hated them. Plus, she wanted a little bit of time with her uncle.

"Social media is freaking blowing up with Lela B. All of the big beauty influencers are talking about it," Echo called after him, as if he actually cared. "It's everywhere. All because of Lela's gray hair."

"Don't get too carried away, honey. This doesn't neces-sarily mean anything." Donovan just had to be the voice of sobriety and caution.

Lela wasn't really in the mood for it. She'd never been so popular, ever. Also, she was exhausted after being unable to sleep at all last night after the reception. There had been entirely too much physical contact with Donovan yesterday. Between the Vespa ride and slow dancing, her body was still buzzing. And then he had to go and tell her about the many times over the years he'd wished he could talk to her, but hadn't reached out? She was tired of being turned on *and* disappointed. "I can't believe this. I have thousands of new followers. Everywhere. On every platform. What's with this hashtag? #GrayHairDontCare? How does that even happen?"

"Hey, Echo. Lucius is right. You guys need to get on the road," Donovan said, still totally blasé. It was like nothing was going on. "Have you said goodbye to your mom and grandmother?"

"I said goodbye to Grams before she went to do her medi-tation. Mom left an hour ago, remember?"

"Right. I forgot," Donovan said.

Lela was still scrolling, trying to ignore Donovan's cool and detached behavior. Why was he being such a wet blan-ket? This was exciting. She swiped at her screen and two eye-popping notifications appeared. She squealed. "Serena Williams *and* Reese Witherspoon are following me? What the what?"

"Lemme see," Echo blurted, grabbing Lela's arm and gawking at her phone. "That is so cool."

Lucius stomped back into the foyer. "Echo. We have to go or we're going to miss our flight."

Echo grimaced and dropped her head back. "Aargh! Why does everything have to take off right when I'm also about to take off?"

Donovan slung his arm around Echo's shoulders. "Come on, darling. Lucius is right." He took a step toward the door, but she didn't move.

"Dad. I can't leave. There's too much to do," she pled. "Somebody needs to talk to sales and marketing. We should probably be booking new ads. We need to get the publicity department up to speed."

"And that's what I'm for," Donovan's voice was as calm and even as Lela had ever heard it. "You have just been through several extremely trying days, on top of what has already been a non-stop three years getting Echo Echo off the ground. You and Lucius are starting your life together. It's important that you set everything aside for this. I mean everything."

Now Lela saw what Donovan was up to. He knew his daughter incredibly well, and she was not the type of person to hop on a plane and unplug for ten days when something big was going on, especially if it had to do with her business. "Your dad's right. Whatever this is, he and I can figure it out."

Echo pursed her lips and frantically nodded her head, but she was also visibly wincing. "I know. I know. It's just really hard. I've worked my ass off. So have you guys. I want to be there if things are about to blow up."

"It's ten days. I promise to keep you posted on everything that's going on. I'm sure there will be more than enough excitement to return to," Donovan said.

"Okay." Echo hugged Lela. "Goodbye. I'll miss you. You have to promise you'll text me every new celebrity follow."

Lela laughed and returned the embrace. Everything felt so surreal right now, but saying goodbye to Echo helped to bring Lela back down to Earth. "I'll miss you, too. And I promise to tell you everything."

"All right, you two," Donovan said. "Let's break it up."

Lela kissed Echo's cheek, lightly enough so she didn't leave any lipstick behind. "Congratulations. Have an amazing trip. Don't forget sunscreen."

Echo's musical laugh filled the foyer. "Spoken like a skin care expert."

Echo, Lucius, and Donovan walked to the car while Lela hung back, standing in the doorway. Mere seconds later, Austin appeared.

"I guess this is it," Austin said.

Lela felt bad about shooting him down, but there were a million reasons why it wouldn't work. First off, she felt nothing for him other than some fondness. Second, he was Donovan's brother, which seemed unfair to Donovan. Third, Austin lived in another city. As if Lela needed to juggle more in her life. More than anything, romance and dating weren't on her radar right now, especially if Lela B was about to take off like a rocket ship. "Goodbye, Austin. It was really nice to meet you and get to know you."

"It was great to meet you." He pursed his lips together and looked down at the floor for a second. "Can I tell you something?"

Lela wasn't sure she wanted to hear what came next, but she didn't want to be rude. "Sure."

"I think my brother is in love with you. But he doesn't

know how to say it. Or do anything about it. Which I totally get, because I can be a little inept when it comes to emotions, too."

"Why is that? Is it because of your mom?"

Austin shrugged. "I guess? Probably. When you don't know what you're going to get, love or indifference, it's hard to get comfortable. Your first impulse is to run away."

Lela sighed. That had certainly been the case with Donovan. "I don't know what I'm supposed to do with this information, Austin."

"Nothing. You can't figure this out for him. I just wanted you to know what I see from where I'm sitting."

"Thanks." It was a statement, but it could have just as easily come out as a question. Nothing he was saying would help her in any way.

He reached out and touched her forearm, then leaned in to kiss her cheek. "This is for my brother's benefit. I'm pretty sure he's watching right now. Maybe it'll help him wake up."

Lela peeked outside to the driveway, where Donovan, Echo, and Lucius were crowded around Austin's car. Did she even want Donovan to get in touch with his emotions? Part of her did, if only for his own sake, but part of her did not. Life was good right now. Things were going well. Love and feelings were only going to make things more complicated. "Have a safe trip back home."

"You, too."

Lela watched as Austin strolled outside and everyone said their final goodbyes in the driveway. Donovan shut the car door after Echo climbed in, then started back to the house while Austin pulled away. As soon as the car was out of sight, Donovan broke out into a jog.

"Lela. Holy shit," he blurted. "Do you realize what's happening with Lela B?"

"Excuse me, Mr. Oh I Think The Campaign Might Be Working But Maybe Not?"

"I was dying the whole time you and Echo were looking at your phones." He stepped inside the foyer and closed the door behind him. "But I didn't want Echo to bail on her honeymoon. I want her and Lucius off to the best possible start. Plus, I have a feeling things are still going to be insane by the time she gets back."

Lela was past her annoyance and was now simply feeding on his excitement. She also found it endearing that he was so focused on putting Echo first. "Do you really think all of this stuff is good? I have no clue. I've never had anything like this happen to me."

"This, Lela Bennett, is better than good. I can feel it." He slung his arm around Lela's shoulders. More physical contact, except this time in the context of happy, exciting things. Her heart couldn't take much more of it, especially after the things Austin had just said. "Case in point, a text from the president of JTI." Donovan showed her his phone.

Lela B is taking off. Moving sales resources to your team. Ramping up production. I know you're at Echo's wedding, but call me when you have a chance.

Lela had to read the message twice. Even then, it didn't feel real. Electricity zipped up and down her spine. Her brain started to kick into overdrive. Would all of the hard work actually pay off? It seemed like it might. "Wow. I'm just. Wow."

Donovan stepped in front of her and gripped both of her shoulders, with a look that was unlike any she'd ever seen on his face. Donovan James wasn't merely happy or pleased. It was like he might explode. "Take it from me, stuff like this doesn't happen very often. I don't know how long the tail will be. It could be a week. It could be months. But whatever it is, you and I need to get back to the city ASAP and figure out how to make the most of this."

"Okay. Got it. I need to go pack up the last of my stuff, but I can be downstairs in ten."

"Yes. Great. I've already brought my bag down. I just want to say goodbye to my mom."

Lela raced upstairs and crammed her remaining clothes and toiletries into her suitcase, but of course, when her phone rang and she saw Tammera's name on the Caller ID, she had to answer it.

"Tams. How are you?"

Tammera squealed on the other end of the line. "What the hell, bus lady? Your whole career blows up and I don't even get a text?"

"I didn't even know. My phone was off all weekend."

"Well, I'm telling you, there's a definite buzz."

"I still don't understand how any of this started."

"As near as I can tell, a whole bunch of women got super pissed off about the fact that people were taking issue with your gray hair. It was a bullshit response. These women clapped back. Hard."

Lela zipped up her suitcase. She was the least controversial person she could think of, but she did appreciate the idea of women standing in solidarity with other women. Any bias against gray hair was definitely bullshit. "That is so awesome."

"It's especially awesome because it happened to you."

"Donovan and I need to get on the road. Can we catch up this week?"

"I have a crazy shooting schedule, but call me. We'll figure something out."

"Great. Love you," Lela said.

"Love you, too."

Lela tucked her phone into her purse and was back in the foyer in record time. She found Donovan outside waiting for her, standing next to his car. He grabbed her bag and tossed it into the cargo area of his SUV, then rounded to the driver's side door. Lela climbed inside and they were soon on their way.

"How was it saying goodbye to your mom?" Lela asked.

"Surprisingly, a little sad. Usually I'm desperate to get out of here, but this was a really good visit. Maybe it was just because of the wedding. I think that put some much-needed perspective on everything. I realized that she got put through the ringer by Genevieve, and she was trying her best."

"It was really nice to have been invited."

Donovan settled back in his seat, leaving one hand at the very top of the steering wheel and resting his elbow on the center console. "My family loves you."

"That's sweet. I think they're lovely. Even your mom, who is not nearly as bad as you tried to make her seem."

He blew out a breath. "I know. And I feel bad about that. It's funny, but you see your family differently when there are other people around."

"I'm not saying they're perfectly normal. But I like that they're unique." Lela's phone rang with a number she didn't recognize. "I'm not even sure I should be taking these calls. I have no clue who this is."

"If I were you, I'd be answering everything right now."

"Okay." She pressed the green button to accept the call. "Hello? This is Lela Bennett."

"Oh, great, Ms. Bennett. I've been trying to hunt you down. This is Monica Figueroa. I'm a booker for Good Day USA. Are you familiar with our show?"

Lela nearly laughed. "Yes. Hi, Monica. I know Good Day USA. My mom watches every morning." It was the longest running network morning show in the country, seen by several million people every day.

Donovan cleared his throat and leaned forward to make eye contact with Lela. He silently pled for more information.

"Fantastic," Monica said. "We're hearing a lot about the ad campaign for your cosmetics line. We're wondering if you'd like to come on the show this week? Share your story with our viewers?"

"Really?"

"Yes. Really."

"Uh, sure. Yes. Of course. What day?"

"Wednesday? We'd have you on in the second hour of the show."

Lela wanted to play it cool, but deep down, she was screaming at the top of her lungs. "That sounds great."

"Perfect. We'll be in touch tomorrow about where you'll need to be and at what time. I'll talk to you then."

"Sounds great. Thank you for calling." Lela pressed the red button on her phone and shrieked. "Oh my God. My mother is going to flip out."

"Good Day USA? Seriously? What day? When? Tell me what she said."

Lela loved hearing the jubilation in Donovan's voice. She

quickly recounted her conversation with Monica. "Can I just tell you something?"

"Of course."

"This is the weirdest thing that has ever happened. Stuff like this doesn't happen to me."

"It does now."

Her mind was running at a million miles a minute, overcome with the same nervousness she'd felt about doing the photo shoot. This was going to be even more intense. More cameras, more people on set. And of course, millions of people watching. "You have to come with me on Wednesday."

"Are you sure? You don't want one of the publicists to go with you? They're probably better equipped to deal with this."

"No. Donovan. You're the only one who can keep me calm. You've known me longer than anyone." Funny, but the thought of him being at the photo shoot had been horrific, and she'd been so relieved when he hadn't shown up. But now, the thought of being on television and him not being there? Even scarier.

"If you want me there, I'm there."

She felt like she could exhale. "Perfect. Thank you."

They spent the rest of the drive talking over strategy and next steps. Much of it was Donovan talking and Lela listening and jotting down notes. He was the expert when it came to making the most of the situation they found themselves in, not her.

When they got into Manhattan, Lela's nerves kicked back into hyperdrive. There was so much uncertainty ahead of her. She liked it when she knew what was going to happen, and right now, she knew nothing. Nada. Zilch, other than the fact that she and Donovan were about to be on the front lines together, battling the unknown together. Donovan pulled on to her street, and that was when she saw a commotion. A small cluster of women were standing at the bottom of the stairs leading up to her brownstone. As they got closer, Lela noticed that a few had gray hair.

"What's going on?" she asked Donovan as he pulled up to the curb.

Her question was quickly answered when one woman turned, spotted Lela, and promptly said to the rest of the group, "She's here!"

As the crowd approached the car, Lela reflexively leaned back against the car's center console. "Are they talking about me?"

"I think so."

"How did they figure out where I live?"

"The Internet?"

"So I should fix that?"

"Probably."

"But what do I do right now?"

Donovan leaned closer to her, his chin nearly on her shoulder as he waved hello to the strangers on the street. "Smile. Wave. These are your fans," he said through grinned teeth.

"My fans?"

"Yes."

Lela was at a complete loss, so she copied Donovan and channeled Lady Diana. *Wave and smile. Wave and smile.* "This is so weird," she said.

"Welcome to your new life."

CHAPTER TWENTY-TWO

IT TOOK no time for Lela's life to turn bonkers. The morning after she and Donovan returned from Echo's wedding, there was a different crop of women outside her house. Everyone was respectful—lovely, really—but it didn't feel any less strange to Lela. When she arrived at the JTI offices that morning, there were yet more waiting for her. They wanted her autograph, selfies, and a minute of her time. Every woman within spitting distance of fifty had questions. Did she think growing out their gray would look good on them, too? How long did it take? And here was the kicker: had her love life changed because of it?

"No," was the answer to that last question, even though Echo's wedding had left her feeling a little too ambiguous about Donovan. Their attraction was still there. The tug she felt in the center of her chest every time she was around him was present, too. But beyond all of that were the doubts about what he really wanted, whether she would ever be that person, and did she even *want* to be that person? Things weren't going perfectly for her right now, but they were headed in the right direction. Did she want to mess with that?

"Do whatever will make you happiest," Lela replied to the question about whether the gray would look good on other women. "If you don't want to color your hair anymore, don't. Gray can be beautiful."

Lela had to quickly learn the art of eloquently answering questions off the cuff, as she became accustomed to navigating New York as an identifiable human being. She tried to ride the subway on Tuesday, and stupidly thought sunglasses and a hat would help her remain anonymous. It became a fail when a panhandler announced, "Hey, it's the gray-haired lady!", which caused a group of women waiting on the platform to descend upon her, asking for photos and wanting to know how she got her hair so shiny.

"Cold water rinse." She grinned for the camera phones and made a point of being kind and cordial to everyone. She knew how lucky she was to be in this peculiar situation.

On the morning of the Good Day USA appearance, Donovan arranged for a car and driver to take them. He wanted to make sure she arrived on set on time and in one piece, and Lela was thankful because she already felt like she was falling apart. He texted her when he arrived and she rushed out her front door, locking the deadbolt behind her and stuffing her keys into her bag. Luckily, there were no fans this morning. Then again, the sun was just barely up.

The driver held the door of the big black SUV for her, and she climbed in. One look at Donovan and he took her breath away, which was weird. She saw him nearly every day, so she normally didn't gawk, but he was rocking some extra mojo today. His eyes were darker and more intense, and his facial scruff a little more scruffy.

"Morning, sunshine," he said, handing her a coffee.

She took the cup after buckling in. One sip and she knew he'd ordered her favorite—an almond milk mocha. "Thank you. I barely had time to throw a cup of yesterday's coffee in the microwave."

He adorably scrunched up his nose. "You drink day-old coffee?"

"All the time. It's like the best gas station coffee you've ever had."

"I think I'll take your word for it."

When they arrived at the network studios, the driver turned into a secure parking garage, which gave them direct access to the Good Day USA set. Still, there was an odd hubbub when they got inside—Lela felt like an animal at the zoo, everyone looking at her. She decided her reaction was merely a lovely cocktail of nerves and paranoia. Also, she'd better get used to it. A whole lot of people were going to be watching her when the cameras went live.

A production assistant escorted Donovan and her to a small dressing room, with the instructions to wait until she was called to set.

Lela took the time to over-scrutinize herself in the mirror. "Do I look okay?" She'd worn a slim-fitting white sheath dress and heels, applying the Jackie O rule of restraint when accessorizing, only wearing simple silver earrings and a bracelet. She wanted to come across as successful and professional, even when inside she was just a fifty-year-old woman who sometimes felt confident and other times unsure. Stumbling into an absurd situation no one could've predicted didn't add to her confidence. It made her question the wisdom of trying so hard to claim it.

"You look amazing." Donovan seemed totally at ease, reclining on the small sofa with one arm draped over the back.

"Thanks. I hate having my picture taken, so the idea of being on camera in front of millions of people makes me want to throw up." She checked her makeup one last time, then began reapplying lipstick. "I'm trying not to think about it."

"You do seem a little on edge."

"I don't want to let anyone down. Like you. Or Echo. And I know my parents will be watching, and they'll make a big deal about it because they always make a big deal about everything."

"Are they still coming to town?"

"Yes. In a week. Which is, bonus, another reason to be anxious."

"Maybe the coffee wasn't such a great idea."

"What? No. I need it. I need to be perky and energetic."

"Okay. Because right now you're acting like a squirrel that's had too much Halloween candy."

She waved him off and grabbed her coffee. "Trust me. I come by all of this nervousness honestly. No amount of coffee will make it worse." She lifted the cup to her lips, but she was trying to be careful about her lipstick, and hit the lid with her bottom teeth. The plastic top popped off. Almond milk mocha cascaded down onto her pristine white dress. She froze, holding her arms out to the side and staring down at her front, which now looked like a Starbucks crime scene. "Oh, my God. Donovan. My dress!"

Donovan hopped up and frantically grabbed a box of

tissues from the counter beneath the makeup mirror, plucking them out one by one like a terrible magician pulling scarves out of his sleeve. He started dabbing at the stain, pressing into her breast with the side of his hand and poking at the rest of her chest. "Maybe we can get this out."

"How, exactly? It's coffee and chocolate. This will never come out. We have to find somebody to help us."

A knock came at the door. Donovan lunged across the room and flung it open. A woman wearing a headset was calmly standing there, staring at her clipboard. "Ms. Bennett, you're on in fifteen..." She looked up. Her face fell. "Oh, my God, what happened?"

"Coffee accident. It's my fault," Donovan said.

"I appreciate that you want to be chivalrous by taking the blame, but who cares? I need a dress." Lela knew she was screeching, but she didn't know what else to do.

"One minute. I'll grab a wardrobe person." The woman disappeared down the hall.

"Come on, let's get you out of this thing." Giving her zero notice, Donovan drew down the zipper.

"What are you doing?"

"Saving time."

"But I'm going to be standing here in my underwear."

"I'm seen you naked. More than once."

"So? That doesn't give you a lifetime pass, buddy."

Another woman appeared in the doorway with a rack of clothing in tow. "What size are you?"

"Depends," Lela said. "A ten sometimes, but a twelve is probably safer. Or maybe a fourteen because I don't want it to be too tight."

The woman looked at Lela like she was the candy-crazed squirrel Donovan had accused her of being earlier. "Let's go with this. It's stretchy." She handed over a royal blue dress with a similar silhouette to the white one. "Get it on as quickly as possible. And try not to mess up your hair. It's half of the reason you're on the show."

Donovan grabbed the dress and closed the door. Lela wanted to cry, and she let out a whimper, but she wasn't going to give herself the luxury. She had to soldier on.

"It's going to be okay. I promise. Let's just get you into this," Donovan said calmly. "Everything will be fine. You're going to be great."

"Funny, but you reassuring me that everything will be okay is just reminding me that everything is not, in fact, okay." She kicked off her shoes and slipped the stained dress from her shoulders.

"And you told me that I'm the only person who can keep you calm. So that's what I'm doing." Donovan was being a perfect gentleman, holding the borrowed dress open as she stepped into it while also averting his eyes. She appreciated that he wasn't taking anything for granted. She pulled on the dress and turned her back to him. As he drew the zipper up, she became more aware of his physical presence, the way his body gave off warmth and his fingers brushed her spine as he traveled north. "I promise it's going to be okay. You look incredible in blue. It makes your eyes even more stunning."

"Thank you. That's so kind." She turned and fell prey to his handsome face—the straight line of his nose and those lips she loved to kiss. She'd been at his mercy when they danced at Echo's wedding, and she'd tried to play it off, but she wasn't sure she'd done a great job. He'd said a lot of sweet things to her that day. He'd even said he wanted to kiss her. If no one else had been around, and if it hadn't felt like a big chunk of her future was hanging in the balance, she would've said yes. Just to close her eyes, draw in his smell, and have his lips on hers one more time.

"Are you okay?" he asked.

She took a deep breath and turned to study herself in the mirror. "I think so." Examining the state of her hair, it seemed to be all good—she'd used more than enough hairspray.

Donovan gripped her shoulders from behind, making eye contact with her through the mirror. The reflection of his face was right next to hers, and she tried to ignore how good they looked together. "Everything from here on out is going to go perfectly. The dress was the hiccup and now it's over. Just go out there and let America fall in love with Lela, exactly like everyone else who meets you."

"Not everyone loves me."

"Sure they do."

You don't. She knew he wasn't talking about L-O-V-E, but she still bristled at his use of the word.

There was a knock at the door, and the woman with the headset told her it was time to go. As they walked down the winding hall and stepped onto the set, Lela once again felt that her life was about to change. A tech hooked up her microphone while Lela spotted two of the Good Day USA hosts, Tilly Ann Bostwick and Renata Herrera. They were the two matriarchs of the show, true TV veterans. As soon as they cut away for commercial, the set director called the all clear, and Lela was swept up on to the set.

Tilly Ann reached out to shake Lela's hand. "I'm Tilly Ann. This is Renata. You're going to do great."

"By the way, love the hair," Renata said.

"Thanks," Lela said, getting settled in her chair. The next thing she knew the cameras were on.

Tilly Ann looked right into the lens. "Lela Bennett is the fifty-year-old founder of New York-based Lela B cosmetics, who made a splash recently with a very sexy ad campaign prominently featuring her gray hair. Ms. Bennett, welcome to the show."

Lela smiled thinly, but it felt like her face was made of plastic. "Thank you for having me."

"Can you tell us about the origins of your company? What made you want to start it?"

As Lela jumped to the answer in her head, she realized how much of this led back to Donovan. And he was standing right there in the shadows of the studio, listening to everything. "I was forty-seven and divorced. I'd been a makeup artist for years, and I didn't know what came next for me, but I really wanted a change. And I wanted to challenge myself to take some chances. I'd made several makeup formulations over the years for clients, and they always loved the products, so I decided that it was the perfect time to put myself out there."

"I think a lot of women can relate to wanting a change after a divorce," Renata said.

"I know I can," Tilly Ann quipped. Everyone knew she'd been married several times.

"How did your decision to go gray fit into that? Did something happen? Because a lot of people look at those photographs, think they're great, but then wonder why you wouldn't just color your hair."

Lela swallowed hard, but sat a little straighter. She was proud about this. She wanted to own that pivotal life moment, even when it had hurt. "It was about two months after my divorce. I ran into an old friend, a man I really liked a lot. A man I really cared about. And he rejected me..."

"I bet he feels pretty stupid right now," Tilly Ann said, apparently playing the role of comic relief.

"You know, I don't hold it against him. He had his reasons," Lela said. "And it did spur me to make a change. My hair was already going gray and I was so tired of schlepping to the salon to have it covered up. The morning after the rejection, I saw my gray sparkle in the light from my bathroom window and I had to ask myself, why was I trying to hide my sparkle?"

Both Renata and Tilly Ann lit up like a Christmas tree, smiling and eyes wide.

"What a fun way to say it," Renata said. "It sounds like something from a T-shirt."

"I wish I had the nerve to go gray," Tilly Ann said. "I'm still holding on to my ash blond for dear life."

Lela laughed, but she did want to drive this point home. "But that's the whole point. It's such a personal decision. And so much of it is decided for us. Society tells us that we have to look young, and that young is better. As women, so much of the value we're assigned has to do with youth. We're told when we're young that it's the worst thing in the world to get older, and particularly to look older. But then you get to your late forties or you turn fifty and realize it's all a lie. You don't feel that different, and so much in life is actually better."

"What do you think is better?" Renata asked.

"You're more comfortable in your own skin. You care less about what other people think. The sex can be better, too."

Both women leaned in closer. "Yes," they chimed in unison.

"You've lost a lot of your inhibitions," Lela said. "That makes sex a lot more fun." Of course, she'd only been able to really unleash that on Donovan, but she did genuinely feel that way.

"And what is it like to be this sexy beauty icon?"

"Honestly? It's very strange. I realize that I'm in those pictures, but deep down, I still see the awkward girl I was in high school or in college. I don't dwell on it now, but it's there in the back of my head. I don't think that insecurity ever goes away when you aren't someone who turns heads."

"But you are one of those women now, aren't you?" Tilly Ann asked.

"Any attention I'm getting now, I hope it helps other women feel good about embracing whatever puts them outside any narrow ideals of beauty. There is so much that can make a person beautiful. Own what you've got going on."

Renata turned to the camera. "Thanks to our guest, Lela Bennett. If you want to learn more about her line of cosmetics, visit our website for a link."

A long awkward pause played out, and then it was over. "We're clear," a voice said.

Tilly Ann and Renata both hopped up out of their chairs and were all over Lela. "We loved having you here. Thank you so much for being a voice for women over fifty," Tilly Ann said.

"Yes. It's nice to hear a different perspective on beauty," Renata added.

"Thank you for letting me say my piece," Lela said.

Another woman appeared from the shadows of the studio, and reached out to shake Lela's hand. "Lela, hi. I'm Monica Figueroa. We spoke on the phone. You did a fantastic job today."

Lela got up from her chair and stepped out from under the bright studio lights. They walked back to the spot near where Donovan was standing, hands behind his back. A production assistant chased Lela down to uncouple her from her microphone.

"We'd love to get you back on the show if we can," Monica said. "Maybe do some makeup tips with Renata and Tilly Ann? We could even talk about running a viewer contest for a makeover? Fly the winner to New York to meet you and have lunch and get a full makeup tutorial and a bunch of Lela B products?"

Lela could hardly believe any of this was happening, that people in high places wanted things like that from her. "Yes. I'd love to do all of that. Thank you."

"Great. We'll be in touch."

Donovan stepped closer. "You were unbelievable."

"She's a real star," Monica said as she walked away.

Lela's face flushed with heat. She did like the compliments, especially from Donovan. "Thank you. You really think I did okay?"

He took her hand. "You did better than okay. But I'm a little concerned about the way I played into that whole story."

"You know all of that. I told you the first day I was in your office."

"It still hurts to hear it."

Lela wanted privacy if they were going to continue this conversation, plus quiet had been called for on the set. "Come on." She led Donovan to her dressing room. There was still a puddle of coffee on the floor. Her dress, draped over the arm of the sofa, was likely ruined. "I know it hurts to hear it, but this is just part of life, Donovan. People hurt each other and hopefully we try to do better."

He pressed his lips together tightly. "I need to do better. By both of us."

"With work?"

"No, Lela. Us."

"Donovan, aside from friendship, there is no us. We've been through this."

"But I felt like there was something there between us at the wedding."

Lela picked up her dress and folded it into a small package. She thought about tossing it into the trash, but hopefully the dry cleaner could work some magic. "There's always something between us, Donovan. I am always going to be hopelessly attracted to you. It's just part of our dynamic."

"Well, good. Then we're even."

"How exactly?"

"I'm hopelessly attracted to you, too. All through the wedding, I was struggling with what to do about it. My brother was in the way, and there's work to think about..."

Lela was ready to express surprise at the first chunk of what he'd said, and agree with him on the second half, but she saw the pained expression on his face and felt like something must be wrong. "Are you okay?"

He squinted slightly and rubbed the center of his chest. "Yeah. I think I ate something that disagreed with me."

"Did you ever make an appointment to see a doctor?"

"No. We just talked about this a few days ago."

Lela grumbled under her breath. Why was this so difficult? "Come on, you. We're taking you to see a doctor."

"But I'm fine."

"Let's let a physician determine that."

"Where are you taking me?"

"To see a friend. Don't worry. You already like her."

They met their driver in the garage and Lela texted Delia from the car on their way there. As luck would have it, Delia had a patient cancel, so she was able to see Donovan right away.

"I can't believe you took me to the pediatrician." Donovan sat on the exam table, swinging one leg so his foot clanged the metal base. All around him on the walls were decals of fish and sea creatures, plus a few posters about things like not eating too much junk food and the importance of sneezing into your elbow.

"We're both busy. This was the quickest solution. Otherwise, it's the ER and you could be sitting there forever."

"I think they see you right away if you have chest pains," he said.

"All the more reason you should have done this a while ago."

Delia popped into the room, wearing her white physician's coat and with her hair pulled back. "How's my new patient?" Just to drive up the absurdity factor, she giggled a little.

"He keeps having chest pains. And he won't make time to see the doctor. I know this seems silly, but I figured this was better than nothing," Lela said.

Delia smiled. "A doctor is a doctor. I'm going to refer you to a cardiologist, but let's just make sure for today that there's nothing serious going on."

Lela sat in a chair and Delia asked Donovan a bunch of questions about his symptoms and whether there was a pattern to them. Delia listened to his heart, took his pulse, and then had a nurse bring in a small EKG machine. The nurse found it quite hilarious that the patient was a man over fifty. When all was done, Delia typed a bunch of notes into a computer then printed out Donovan's marching orders.

"Call the cardiologist today and make an appointment," she ordered. "Between symptoms like this and your age, you should at least establish care with a specialist. But from where I'm sitting, for today, everything seems normal."

"Then why is this happening?" Donovan asked.

"My guess is it's stress or anxiety. Maybe both. There's information on the print-outs about meditation, relaxation, and dietary changes."

That made perfect sense to Lela, but that also meant that Donovan's pains after he slept with her three years ago meant stress or anxiety. That wasn't fun to think about.

"Okay. Thank you." Donovan hopped off the table.

Delia grabbed a small basket and showed it to him. "Don't forget to pick out a sticker."

Lela snickered. "Too bad they don't give out lollipops anymore."

"Oh, yeah. Those were the bad old days, weren't they?" Delia asked, opening the door for them. "By the way, email wedding invites went out to you both this morning. Quicker than paper. Tammera and I really don't want to make this a big deal, so we found a tiny non-denominational church near the Flatiron Building. Ceremony in the morning then lunch at a restaurant a block or so away."

Lela gave Delia a quick hug. "Thanks for your help. Looking forward to the wedding."

CHAPTER TWENTY-THREE

NOW, when Donovan walked to work, he focused on his breath. *In... in... in... and out... out.... out.* It took a great deal of concentration to center himself while trekking along Manhattan's sidewalks. There were copious hazards to avoid—oblivious people staring at their phones, and pretzel vendors who'd parked too close to the crosswalk, and the subway grates Donovan did not trust would keep him from plummeting into the world of the New York City transit system.

He also pursued his breathing practice at his desk several times each day, reminded to do so by his smartwatch. There were far fewer distractions in the office. It was mostly just Lela and her smile and the way she seemed to float into a room. Those were the moments when he had to stop, catch his breath, and start over again.

For today, there was a bit too much excitement to make room for Zen moments. Echo was back from her honeymoon.

"Knock, knock," Donovan said at her office door. He didn't wait for an invitation, storming in to get a hug and hold on tight. He'd missed her. Desperately. "So? How was it? Awesome?"

"It was unbelievable. We have to go back. The water, the people, the food. I miss it already."

"Well, you look amazing. So relaxed. That's good."

She eased back, still holding on to him. "Thank you for being the voice of reason and making me get in the car and go to the airport. If you hadn't been there, I would've tried to talk Lucius into postponing so I could work. And I really worried on the flight that I wouldn't be able to stay away from work when we got there. But I was wrong. It was so beautiful and tranquil, I just wanted to goof off and be with Lucius. I thought I couldn't get any closer to him, but I was wrong about that, too."

Already, his daughter was better at being married than he'd ever been. The thought warmed his heart, since he'd managed to play a tiny role in her epiphany. Being able to dole out a bit of real-life guidance felt good. "You really needed it."

"I did. And now I get to see everything you guys have been up to while I was gone." She took a seat at her desk. "I just looked at the sales numbers and holy cow, it has totally exceeded my expectations."

"Things were cooking before Good Day USA, but that really blew the doors off the barn, so to speak."

"I was able to watch it on their website after it aired. Lela not only looked amazing, she *was* amazing. I loved everything she said."

Thoughts of that day had been running through his head non-stop. It wasn't easy to stand in the shadows of the television studio and hear her talk about how she'd turned his regrettable actions into a positive. It didn't matter that it had ultimately worked out well for her. It didn't matter that his gaffe brought them back together. It only underscored that he needed work.

The moment that stuck with him the most though was when she'd talked about feeling insecure. It was the first time he understood that the way he'd seen her thirty years ago and the way he saw her now, were not the way she saw herself. And that made his heart ache. It made him want to kiss her, and tell her that if she saw herself as lesser in any way, it wasn't what he saw. It had put him so close to blurting that he wanted to try again, if she could ever see beyond his mistakes. But then the stupid pain in his chest returned and reality got in the way. "I need to talk to you about Lela."

A worried crease formed between Echo's eyes. "Sounds serious. Is there a problem?"

"Not necessarily. And it's more personal than work-related." Donovan shut her office door so they could have some privacy. Lela was bringing her parents by the office at some point today. It was the tail end of their visit and they wanted to meet Echo.

Echo plopped down on the couch. "Tell me what's going on."

He didn't even know where to start, but he reminded himself that this was Echo, and he could tell her anything. "I have feelings for Lela, honey. A lot of feelings. And something at the wedding ceremony told me that I want to try to have more with her."

"Is this because Uncle Austin was flirting with her?"

That was a separate issue, but he felt confident it was one-sided, even if at the time it had truly bothered him. "No.

I've been feeling this way for a while. Really, ever since we brought Lela B on board. I tried to ignore it, but it's not going away."

"Are you asking my permission?"

"No. I mean, that would be weird."

Echo sat back in her seat and folded her arms across her chest. "Yeah. It would. Although I suppose I didn't really have any place telling you from the start not to get involved with her. You are a grown man."

"And you're a grown woman trying to run a business. That's not a small concern. Romance gets in the way at work. There's no question about it. It's half of the reason HR departments exist."

"So now what?"

He shrugged. "Lela and I need to have a conversation, which means I need to find the right time. I guess more than anything, I want you to know that I won't get myself into a situation that could hurt you, the company, or Lela."

"There are no guarantees, Dad. I don't expect you to promise me a particular outcome. Plus, what about you? Did you stop to think about whether you might get hurt?"

However unpleasant it was to think about, he didn't really care about that part. He was concerned with shielding everyone else from any collateral damage. "I did. But that's just part of the bargain when you put your heart on the line, isn't it?"

"I suppose so."

Donovan made his way for the door, but remembered that he had one more thing to tell her. "Also, you should know that I've been having some chest pains, but I saw a doctor and everything checked out. Just to be safe, I'm seeing a specialist next month."

Echo popped up out of her seat. "Dad. Oh, my God. Are you okay?" She stepped out from behind her desk.

"I'm going to be just fine. But I messed up by ignoring it and I want you to know that I won't do that again."

"I worry about you."

"Don't, honey. I'm just a work in progress. Like everyone else."

Donovan left Echo's office and disappeared into his own, diving into work for hours. Scaling Lela B was still a little rocky, but the trouble spots were smoothing out. Manufacturing had ramped up, retailers were breezing through inventory, and website sales were up 450%. Lela B was a massive success.

Around four-thirty in the afternoon, Lela appeared in his doorway. His heart lurched, but thankfully, there was no pain. "Donovan, do you have a minute? My parents would like to say hi."

"Yes. Of course." He got up from his desk.

In walked Deb and Ben, looking a fair bit older than the last time Donovan had seen them, but still very much the same adorable couple. Ben zeroed in on Donovan, delivering a hearty handshake. "It's nice to see ya," Ben said. He'd put on a few pounds and lost some of his hair, but his jovial spirit was on full display. Donovan remembered him always having a huge smile on his face.

"Hi, Donovan." Deb gave him a sweet hug. She and Lela were the spitting image of each other, except Deb wore her gray hair in a short bob, and was donning a touristy outfit of jeans, sneakers, and an I Love NY T-shirt with a big red heart.

"I'm so glad Lela brought you two by."

"What a strange set of circumstances that led us to this," Ben said, eyeing Lela then returning his attention to Donovan.

"I know, right?"

"Oh, totally," Deb said, her midwestern accent leaning on every "o".

"What are you crazy kids up to?" Donovan couldn't ignore how effortlessly hot Lela looked today, wearing a red sundress with white polka dots and a pair of flat sandals. Her hair was its usual glorious roll of pure silver.

"I gave them the tour of the office," Lela said. "They got to meet Echo and a few other people."

"Did Lela show you her pile of fan mail?" Donovan asked. "She gets letters every day. From all over the world."

"No. She didn't. Lela, honey, why didn't you show us your mail?" Deb seemed gravely concerned.

"Next time, Mom. We're on a schedule, right? You guys want to get in your final stops before you fly home tomorrow."

"That's true," Deb admitted.

"What's on the agenda?" Donovan asked.

"I want to go to that big candy store in Times Square. The one with the little cartoon characters," Deb said. "Just to pick up a few things for my book club."

"Oh, sure," Ben said. "Like you aren't going to buy a bunch of stuff for yourself."

"I do love my chocolate."

"Mom, you can get any chocolate you want in this city. You want *that* chocolate?" Lela asked.

"I do. I love it. Plus, it's fun to go there."

Donovan laughed, but he also sensed Lela's agony. Doing touristy stuff when you've lived in New York for a long time was a labor that only love could make worthwhile.

"After that, we're grabbing some pizza for their last dinner in town. I was thinking I'd take them to John's."

Donovan's stomach rumbled. He hadn't eaten anything since breakfast. He'd also been working non-stop. Air and some fun seemed in order. After all, Delia had told him to devote more energy to relaxation, and he'd seen the effects for himself with Echo. "Would you three like some company?"

Pure surprise crossed Lela's face, but it was her dad who spoke up first. "I was just about to invite you along."

Donovan knew he'd always liked Ben. "Perfect. Lela and I haven't been to John's in a while."

"Years," Lela said, arching both eyebrows at him.

"Right."

The four of them swung by Echo's office so Donovan could let her know he'd be gone for the rest of the day. The look on her face after he told her what he was doing and with whom he was going was pretty obvious. She knew something was up. He was glad they'd had a chance to talk about it earlier.

In the elevator on the way down to the JTI lobby, Donovan broached the subject of the wisdom of Lela in a large crowd of people. "Lela, are you okay walking around Times Square? Are people going to bother you?"

"I feel like I'm more anonymous in large crowds. It's

when there aren't a ton of people that I seem to get spotted. I'll just wear my sunglasses."

"You do realize they don't hide your hair."

"Of course. But hopefully people will just think gray hair is hot now, and won't know it's me."

They strolled up 8th Avenue and then cut over on 48th Street. Inside the store, it was a visual assault of colorful confections and candy characters with arms, legs, and goofy faces, all to be enjoyed while the heavy *thump thump* of dance music played in the background. Ben and Deb were quickly off on their own, heading up to the second and third floors, which left Donovan and Lela to browse on the ground floor until they were finished.

"Can I interest you in a pillow that looks like a giant piece of candy? I think it would look great with your new furniture," Donovan said to Lela.

She pretended to ponder the purple velour piece of decor. "You know, I'm worried it will just make me want to eat chocolate all the time. But thanks."

They wound around a display of snow globes and plastic Statue of Liberty figurines. "How's your week been with your parents? I feel like I've hardly seen you."

"It's been great, but I'm ready for them to go home. It's a whole lot of love and family bonding."

Donovan shrugged. "Sounds pretty good to me."

"It is. It's the best. It just makes me feel a little stifled. Like I almost wish they would criticize me for something. I can do no wrong."

"Is that why you didn't show them the fan mail?"

"Honestly, I don't know why I did that. I show it to other

people. Maybe I didn't want them to make a big deal about it?"

"It's what we talked about at the wedding. It doesn't matter how old you are. That parent-child dynamic is still there." Donovan could see how constant praise and adoration might get old, even if there had been times in his life when he'd been desperate for that from his own mother. "I'm glad you had this time with them."

"Me, too."

Two women were lurking behind Lela, whispering and pointing. "I think you have some visitors."

She turned and one of the women blurted, "You're Lela Bennett, aren't you? We love your hair. Can we take a picture with you?"

"Of course," Lela said without hesitation. "Actually, Donovan, can you take the picture? That way all three of us can be in one together?"

"Happy to play photographer." Donovan took the woman's phone and watched as Lela positioned herself between her two fans, with her arms around them and an easy smile on her face. Her big blue eyes lit up the frame, and warmth bloomed in the center of his chest, but the sensation wasn't pain. It was something else. "I got five or six good ones." He handed over the phone.

"Thank you so much," the woman said to Donovan, then promptly ignored him as they peppered Lela with questions. The woman's friend even showed Lela where she was starting to let her roots grow out. She was highly concerned with how long the phase would last.

Lela said, "It's different for everyone. Take good care of

yourself and your hair should grow faster. But sometimes it's one of those things you just need to tough out."

The two women said their goodbyes then wandered off, happy and chattering away.

"You're so good at that," Donovan said.

"At what? Being nice?"

"I've met a lot of well-known people who are not so generous with their adoring public."

"Women like that are the reason I get to have my job. Plus, I can't bring myself to be any other way. If the roles were reversed, I would want to be treated nicely."

Ben appeared from behind a rack of sweatshirts. "Well, your Mom is at the register. She's about to buy out the store, but there's plenty of room in my suitcase, so I suppose it's okay."

"Let's get out of here," Lela said. "I'm starving. And not for chocolate."

Outside in Times Square, there was the usual crush of people, and the most direct route to John's was to wade through all of it until they could cut over on 44th Street. As they navigated the crowd, Donovan had a strong urge to be protective of Lela, even when he knew she could take care of herself. And it wouldn't be right to put his arm around her in front of her parents. It would only give her something to explain later.

They arrived at John's to no line—a stroke of good luck. They were seated in one of the booths skirting the perimeter of the room, which gave them a modicum of privacy, and shielded out some of the noise, although John's was always loud. They placed their orders—pepperoni and mushroom and two diet Cokes for Deb and Ben. Donovan and Lela went for the classic meatball and a bottle of red wine.

"You must be awfully proud of Lela," Donovan said while they were waiting for their food.

She elbowed him in the ribs, reminding him how nice it was to sit close to her, even if she was annoyed with him. "We don't need to talk about that."

"Sure we do." He turned and peered into her eyes. They traded playful glances, a wordless exchange that went something like: *You're a jerk. I know I am. Stop egging on my parents. Stop being so much fun to tease.*

"Are you kidding me? Of course I'm proud," Ben said.

"It's all he talks about," Deb said. "Lela this and Lela that. But he's always been like that. A super involved dad."

"You've got a real gem of a daughter, too, Donovan. Echo is a lovely woman. And so impressive. Holy smokes, I have a feeling she's going to do a lot of big things."

"I have no doubts about that," Donovan replied, thankful once again to have such a good relationship with Echo.

Their pizzas arrived and Ben and Deb retold every minute of their trip, which Lela noted was mostly all of the same things they'd done the last time they were in the city. Ben had defended their choices by saying that life was too short to not spend time seeing the places and doing the things that you loved. Then the conversation shifted to music when *Superstition* by Stevie Wonder became faintly detectable over the restaurant's audio system and Ben declared that the seventies had been the greatest decade for music. Much debate ensued, with Donovan ultimately agreeing, with certain concessions.

Out on the sidewalk after their meal, the four walked

over to Broadway so Ben and Deb could get back to their hotel.

"You guys know where you're going, right?" Lela asked.

Ben pointed east. "Two blocks that way, two blocks up, south side of the street."

"You got it," Lela said.

"Will you see that she gets home safely?" Ben asked Donovan.

"Oh, no. Dad. It's fine," Lela said. "Donovan's apartment is in the opposite direction from mine."

"I'd like to walk you, Lela. If you're okay with it."

Their gazes connected and she smiled. "Sure. It's a beautiful night."

"It definitely is." Donovan gave Deb a hug, then went to shake hands with Lela's father—but Ben was having none of that, pulling him into a bear hug.

"Donovan, I hope we can see you again the next time we come to town." Ben playfully slugged Donovan on the arm.

"Count me in."

Lela opened her arms wide. "Bye, Mom. Bye, Dad. I love you."

"We love you, too, sweetheart," Deb said.

Donovan watched as this happy family unit exchanged a teary, and lengthy, goodbye, which was eventually put to a stop when Lela wrenched herself from the embrace. "Bye."

Deb and Ben toddled off across the street, shopping bags in tow.

"Ready?" Donovan asked.

"Yep."

They headed off to Lela's. "Your parents are great, Lela. So nice. I really like them a lot." It was funny that he and

Lela were so alike and yet their parental lot in life could not have been any more different.

"Oh, my God. My dad is in love with you. I could see it in his eyes. When you two started talking about music from the seventies? Mom and I nearly left you two at the table."

Donovan laughed, feeling so drawn to Lela it was like a drug. When they turned on to her street, he was almost disappointed she didn't have a fan or two waiting for her. It would've given him the easiest of excuses to see her inside.

"Do you want to come in for a drink?" she asked.

The sense of relief he felt was immense. He didn't need to invent a reason to be alone with her. "I'd love to."

They climbed the stairs and Lela keyed her way inside. The light in the foyer was on, making it easy to spot Rio as he padded down the stairs, voicing his displeasure at Lela's absence. She unbuckled her sandals while Donovan toed off his shoes.

"Come on, buddy," she said to Rio as she flipped on the hall light, then started off for the back of the house. "Let's get you fed."

Donovan trailed behind them to the kitchen, watching as Lela filled Rio's bowl.

"What do you want to drink?" she asked.

He couldn't think of a single beverage, alcoholic or not, that was going to satisfy what he was feeling right now, what he'd been feeling for the last several hours. What he'd been feeling for the last two months. Or three years. Or thirty.

"I don't want a drink," he answered.

"Water?"

"No, thank you."

She turned and shot him a quizzical look. "Okay... then what do you want?"

He couldn't take it. A million answers flooded his brain, all of them having to do with her. He wanted to touch her and kiss her. He wanted to take her upstairs. He longed to finally spill the sappy, lovelorn contents of his head and heart. Let them leak out all over the floor, then hope for the best.

"Lela, I don't want to be friends anymore."

CHAPTER TWENTY-FOUR

LELA HAD IMAGINED Donovan saying many things to her, but she never thought he'd say he no longer wanted to be friends. "You're breaking up our friendship?"

"Our friendship is one of the best things that has ever happened to me. So, no."

"Then what?"

He reached for her, taking her hand. He rubbed her knuckles with his thumb, back and forth, like he was marking the time he needed to think. It made tingles run up her arm, and heat bloom in her chest. "Do you remember the day we met?"

"Of course. Art history. You asked for my notes because you kept falling asleep during the lecture." It was a miracle she'd managed to write down anything at all. The view of Donovan, even when only in profile, and in a pitch-dark room, was still so enthralling that she'd had a hard time looking away.

"In my defense, no one should put a college student in a

dark classroom and show them slides of renaissance art at eight o'clock in the morning."

Lela laughed, remembering how much time Donovan spent trying to hold up his head. "Fair enough."

"We talked after class, then I walked you to your dorm and we hit it off."

She wasn't sure where he was going with this, but these happy memories of the time when everything was shiny and brand new, yet somehow familiar, made her smile. "I remember."

"I felt like something inside me was being fed for the first time. I'd never known someone who understood me from the beginning. It was like we were picking up a conversation that had been going for years. You understood where I was coming from, what I was thinking, and why."

"I felt the same way, Donovan. I always have."

"It was so great. Then everything changed."

"Well, yeah... we've talked about this."

"I sometimes wonder what would've happened if we'd never had sex."

The tingles he'd given her moments ago turned into something else—a prickly realization. How would she have felt if that had never happened? "I think we would've always sensed we had unfinished business."

"But I still feel that way."

Yes. She felt that way, too. It was this thing that loomed over her day and night. It permeated every conversation they had, even when they were looking at spreadsheets. But it wasn't just sex or getting to see Donovan naked. It was that unfinished business part. Like there was an ellipsis at the end of their relationship... Something was waiting. "I do, too."

"It's like there's an unwritten chapter between us. Maybe more."

The tingles raced back. They frantically buzzed around her body. They procreated and had tingle babies. "Careful, Donovan. That sounds romantic and sappy."

"Good." He threaded both hands into her hair, curling his fingers at her nape and lifting her lips to his. The kiss was so soft and tentative at first that it stole her breath and made it hard to stand. This was not a kiss he took lightly. This was serious business. It was time for her to take note. And she did. Every inch of her did.

And just like that, it felt like she was tumbling forward. Their mouths opened, heads slanted, tongues swirled, deep and passionate. She wrapped her arms around him and clawed at his back, arching into him. Any doubt she'd ever felt the other times they'd kissed showed no sign of life. All that was standing between Donovan and her was heat and need and too many clothes.

And one thing that needed to be said. "You'd better be sure about this." Her eyes fluttered shut when he kissed her neck, momentarily putting her off track. "Because if you leave, I will hunt you down and murder you in your sleep."

"I won't leave. I'm not going anywhere. I promise." He switched to the other side of her neck, pressing his lips against the most sensitive spot beneath her ear. It made her insides wobble.

"Well, I hope we're going somewhere. I hope we're going upstairs."

"God, yes. Please."

Lela held on to his hand tightly and led him out of the kitchen and down the hall. Adorably, he shut off each light switch they passed. *Click. Click.* Who knew that being environmentally conscientious could be so sexy? Up the stairs they went, without a word, she first and he behind. As soon as she stepped onto the landing, she turned and tugged him into her room with their fingers twined. Once inside, he made the same move he had downstairs, hands gripping her neck, possessively claiming a kiss with every bit of urgency she ever could have hoped for from him.

She wanted to counter his enthusiasm. Match him. So she kissed him harder and pushed on his shoulders until they stumbled together and with a thud, his back landed against the wall. He broke their kiss and looked at her like she'd just set him on fire. He groaned his approval and reached down for her leg, palming her thigh as she braced her knee against the wall. He pulled the straps of her dress down her shoulders, then went for the zipper.

"Buttons. In the front," she said.

"Got it." It became Donovan's turn to do the pushing, and he walked her backward across her room until her calves met the bed. He dropped to his knees and looked up at her with more adoration than she'd ever seen from any man, ever. The times she'd dreamed about him looking at her like that... they were too numerous to count. He kissed her belly through the dress, gripped her hips with his hands, then one by one, popped the buttons down the front of her dress. It only took a few until it dropped to the floor and she was standing before him, not feeling as vulnerable as the other times. Heat and blood coursed through her as he unhooked her bra and cupped her breasts with his hands. When his lips found her nipples, her eyes clamped shut as she soaked up the sensations of his warm tongue against her taut skin.

Everything about this felt right in a way it hadn't before. They'd earned this. Tiny step by tiny step. Falter and all.

Donovan stood and Lela climbed on to the bed. On her knees, she rocked back and forth to get her balance, untucking his shirt and waging her own personal war against buttons. Finally, she had the chance to spread her hands across the expanse of his glorious chest. She kissed his shoulder, then across his pecs, while her fingers traced the length of his arms, from his biceps to his wrists. Her hands went to his belt, the metal clattered, then a pop of the button on his jeans. She gazed up into his eyes, drawing down the zipper and slipping her hand inside the front of his boxers.

She loved seeing that expression on his face, the one that said she could keep her fingers wrapped around him forever and he'd never grow tired. The tension in his skin tightened with every pass of her hand until finally he groaned and pushed her back on the bed. Lela stretched out, her breasts full and heavy, and a fire between her legs. She needed him. She needed him to touch every delicate spot on her body. Every inch that only made her want him more.

He shucked his jeans and boxers, planted a knee on the bed, then tugged her panties past her hips and tossed them on the floor. She was about to remind him where the condoms were when he spread her legs apart and parked himself between them. It wasn't like she was super concerned with pregnancy. It was only a remote possibility at this point in her life, but for now, where he was headed, no birth control was necessary. He glazed his mouth along her inner thigh with wet kisses while the scratchiness of his facial hair left a lingering burn. Every step closer to her center drove her a little more wild, but he was teasing her, too, drawing out the anticipation when he switched to her other leg and started again at her knee.

When he settled his head between her legs, Lela arched her back if only to fight the buck of her hips. The tip of his tongue circled and dammit, she might have to start calling him Johnny-on-the-spot. Her thighs quivered, her knees fell farther apart and she closed her eyes, digging her fingers into his thick hair and drawing breaths in through her nose. For a split second she wondered where he'd been all her life, but she knew the answer—for most of it, he'd been out there, walking around just as aimless as she'd been. But thinking about the past wasn't going to be part of tonight. Not now.

As the pressure coiled, low in her belly and at the tops of her thighs, she realized that she didn't want this to be a one-woman show, even if it was only the opening act. So, she tapped him on the head.

He popped right up, half of his hair hanging in his eyes. "Yes?"

She wanted to laugh. And smile. And have more of him. "You are amazing. But I want all of you."

A heart-melting grin crossed his face. "Okay, then. Condom?"

"Just to be safe. Yes."

She rolled to her stomach, scooted across the mattress so she could open the bedside table and grab the box. Donovan climbed up on the bed, kissing the small of her back then following the chain of her spine. When he got to her neck, he pulled her hair aside, dotting her skin with his soft lips. She eased to her back and handed him the packet. He tore it open, handed the condom to her, then it was his turn to stretch out on his back. She figured out his plan and rolled it on him, then shifted to her knees and straddled his hips. Taking him in her hand, she guided him inside. As she sank down, she studied the look on his face. Every little happy twitch of his lips or flutter of his eyelids reflected what she was feeling—pleasure, relief, and anticipation. She lowered her upper body until her stomach rested on his and her breasts rubbed against his chest. Her elbows went on either side of his head and she kissed him deeply again as they moved together.

She'd already been so close before that this felt like it might be a quick trip, no matter how slowly they were taking things. Donovan raked his fingers up and down her back, and she ground her center against him, feeling every subtle move he made to please her. And all the while, her mind was a happy place, where nothing less than pure contentment lived.

The pressure was building, quickly approaching, and the second she hit the wall, the rhapsody started. Angels sang. There were golden harps and cherubs. Donovan knocked his head back on the pillow and his entire body froze beneath her. His breaths were short and choppy and desperate, slowly growing longer like satisfied sighs of relief.

She collapsed at his side and curled into him, burying her face in his chest and drinking in his smell. She loved having him at her house. In her bed. In her life.

"Everything okay?" he asked.

"So much better than okay."

He let out a breathy laugh and kissed her forehead. "That was great."

"I like not being friends."

She heard the dreamy quality of her own voice, felt the

way contentment was threatening to turn her into a big old truth-teller again. *Easy, Lela. Easy.* She needed to spend some time living with her feelings before she put a label on them, and definitely before she let them spill from her mouth. She'd made the mistake of making love-laced confessions to Donovan in a post-orgasm haze before. She wasn't going to make it again.

CHAPTER TWENTY-FIVE

DONOVAN HATED GOING BACK on a promise, especially to Lela. Unfortunately, there was nothing he could do about it. He didn't see a way out of his familial obligations. He also didn't really want an out. His mom needed him.

He walked over to Lela's bed and sat on the edge of the mattress, gently caressing her shoulder. Early morning strains of sun were streaming through the windows, casting beams across the hardwood floor and Lela in a soft glow.

"Good morning," she murmured.

"Good morning." He watched as she cracked open one eye then witnessed the split-second when she realized he was dressed.

She bolted out of bed, naked as the day she was born. "No. You are not doing this." She grabbed a pillow and disappointingly shielded her body from view. "You're leaving?"

"Shh. It's okay. Please. Sit down. We need to talk."

"What now?" Lela asked in a heartrending tone. Donovan couldn't blame her. She'd probably been expecting the worst of him, and from all available visual evidence, that was exactly what he was delivering.

"Just sit."

Lela crawled back under the covers, sitting with her back against the headboard and the sheet pulled up to her chin.

"You don't have to hide from me," he said.

"I'm not. I'm protecting myself. What in the hell is going on?"

"I got a call from Stuart..."

Her eyes narrowed. "In accounting?"

"No. My mom's boyfriend. Remember? From the wedding?"

"Oh. Right. What did he say?"

"I got up to pee this morning and I saw a voicemail from him on my phone from last night. My mom is sick, Lela. She has breast cancer and she's been hiding it from everyone. Including Stuart."

"Oh, my God." Lela reached for him. He took her hand as if it was the only lifeline he had. In so many ways, it felt like that was the case. "I'm so sorry. What's the prognosis?"

"I don't know exactly, but she has surgery scheduled for tomorrow."

"Tomorrow? How was she going to hide that from Stuart?"

"She tried to send him off on a fishing trip. He canceled at the last minute. He said it didn't feel right. Then he happened to answer the phone when the doctor's office called to confirm." Like so many things with his mom, he was presented with yet another mystery. Why wouldn't she have simply told Donovan and Austin what was going on? Or

Stuart, for that matter? It wasn't as if she'd ever shied away from uncomfortable subjects. Instead, she'd lied to Donovan's face at her granddaughter's wedding. She'd lied to Austin and Stuart as well. "I feel like I need to be up there. It's not really fair to Stuart to have to care for her. She'll be in the hospital for a few days, then she'll go home to recuperate. Once I know she's good, I'll come back."

"How long do you think? Tammera and Delia's wedding is a week from Saturday. Not that you have to feel like you should come. You should do whatever you need to do for your mom."

"I plan to be back for their wedding. I want to be there. I want to be there with you." He rubbed his thumb back and forth over her smooth skin. Why did the timing have to play out this way? Why couldn't he and Lela enjoy a small stretch of happiness?

She gave him a smile that sent his pulse racing. "Good. I'm happy to hear that."

He took her hand and raised it to his lips. "I know it seems like I'm leaving."

"Well, you are, in fact, leaving."

"Yes. But it won't be long, and hopefully you understand that this is important."

"Of course. You're doing the right thing." Rio jumped onto the bed and head-butted Donovan's elbow, then flopped down onto the mattress. Donovan stroked the arch of Rio's back while Lela scratched behind his ears. "Rio will miss you. I'll miss you."

Donovan's heart felt like it was breaking, but he reminded himself this wasn't a real goodbye. He and Lela would pick things back up as soon as he returned. He was ready for the next step and the one that came after that, too. "I'll miss you, too." *I love you* sat right on his lips, but he wanted the moment to be perfect, and with worries of his mom's health weighing him down, it simply didn't feel right.

He got up from the bed and Lela climbed out from under the covers. She padded to the bathroom door and grabbed her robe from the hook. He hated seeing her wrap herself up like that, but he'd keep the vision tucked away inside his head. They walked downstairs together and shared a parting kiss in the front hall. "Safe travels," Lela said as she opened the door.

"Thanks. And don't say anything to Echo. I'll call her from the car once I'm on the road. Otherwise, she's going to want to come with me. I need to do this on my own."

"I won't say a thing."

Donovan hurried down the stairs, but those words that were stuck in his mouth told him to stop. When he turned, Lela was standing there in her robe, leaning against the door-frame, watching him. He blew her a kiss, she caught it, and pressed it against her lips. It would have to do for now.

He hopped in a cab back to his place, tossed some clothes in a suitcase, and was on his way in under an hour. Once he was out of the city, he called Echo and told her what little he knew.

"Dad. I should go with you."

This was precisely what he'd feared she'd say. "No, no, honey. This is fairly routine surgery and your uncle Austin is coming down to help as well. Plus, you and Lela need to hold down the fort at work."

She sighed. "Just call and let me know what's going on, okay?"

"I will."

"Can I ask you one question?"

"Of course."

"How was it hanging out with Lela and her parents last night?"

Despite his worries, Donovan found himself grinning. "It was wonderful. We had a great time."

"Good. Glad to hear it. Drive safe. I love you."

"Love you, too, Echo."

Donovan turned off his ringer for the rest of the drive, and put on one of his favorite playlists so he could get lost in the music, and keep his mind off what was ahead. It didn't work. Every song was a reminder of something—a time in his life, or a person or event. Thoughts of his three favorite women kept circling through his head. His mom was sick, his daughter married, and Lela... well, he could only do his absolute best by her this time and hope to hell that was good enough.

When he pulled into the driveway of the estate, Austin's car was already there. The door to the house was unlocked, and Donovan stepped into the foyer, happily not greeted by a pack of ill-behaved dogs.

"Hello?" Donovan called.

"In here," Austin yelled back.

"There are more than forty rooms in this house," Donovan muttered to himself as he made his way down the hall. He was fairly certain that Austin had meant the formal living room. When he walked in, Austin and Stuart were seated on one of the sofas, drinking bourbon, or something amber and alcoholic, out of cut crystal glasses. "Cocktail hour already?"

Austin got up from the couch and embraced Donovan. "You want one?"

Stuart extended his arm to shake Donovan's hand. "I'm glad you could come."

"Where's Mom? I feel like I should talk to her first."

"She's upstairs in her room," Austin said. "Taking a nap."

"She didn't get much sleep last night," Stuart said. "She was mad that I figured out what was going on and that I called you both."

"I'll sneak up there. I won't wake her if she's still sleeping."

"You know where to find us," Austin said.

Donovan jogged up the staircase and walked in the direction opposite from the route to his own bedroom. His mom's wing of the second floor was tucked away from everything else, with a sitting room, large en suite bathroom, and a bedroom that in size, likely rivaled the queen's private quarters at Buckingham Palace. He rapped on the door quietly, and was met by a low growl, but no other answer. Somewhere on the other side of the door was at least one dog. This required caution.

He turned the knob, only to discover that one of his mom's chihuahuas was curled up next to the door in a tiny pink dog bed. It snarled at him again, and the bell on its collar tinkled, but Donovan remained undeterred. On the far side of the room was his mother's bed, heavily populated with dogs who all turned and looked at him, then put their heads back down in near unison. Despite the circus that had taken place during the wedding weekend cocktail party, the black cat was curled up next to his mom, who was nothing but a tiny lump under the expanse of a deep red bedspread.

He crept to her side and reached down to push her hair from her face. "Mom?"

Her eyes popped open, and that alone was enough to rattle the dogs. They jumped off the bed en masse and started barking at Donovan. His mom sat up in bed and two-finger whistled, then threw back the covers, stormed across the room, flung open her door and yelled, "Everybody out!" They quieted down and scampered off. She turned to Donovan. "Not you, darling."

It was nice to have the clarification. For a moment, he was unsure. "I'm sorry I woke you. Are you feeling that bad?"

"I was actually just dozing. A little tired, but some of that might be age."

"How are you otherwise?"

She rolled her eyes. "It's all anyone has asked me today."

"Mom. You have cancer. And you hid it from everyone. What were you thinking?"

She eased into one of two upholstered gold chairs near the window. She was wearing white satin pajamas that hung loosely on her. "I didn't want anyone to worry."

"Worry? You scheduled a mastectomy and then tried to send away the one person who would willingly take care of you." Donovan sat in the other chair, but perched right on the edge of the seat, hoping his proximity would underscore how seriously he took this matter.

"You don't understand what it's like to get older."

"Yes I do. I'm fifty-one years old."

She grimaced and sighed. "I count my own birthdays, but for some reason, I forget to count everyone else's."

"That still doesn't explain the situation."

She looked off, out the window, the sun lighting up her

face. If every line and wrinkle could tell a story, he had no doubt it would be quite a tale. "Saying it made it more real. I wasn't ready to accept my own mortality. So I figured that if I kept it to myself, I'd get better, no one would be the wiser, and I'd manage to squeeze another twenty years out of this body of mine."

Right then and there he had to face the truth of what he'd done when he'd dismissed his chest pains—he'd been a complete idiot. "You had to have known on some level that it was a terrible plan."

She turned and shot him a pointed glance. "You and your brother are here, so yes, I can see now that I underestimated how you both would feel about it."

"What did you expect us to do? Shrug it off and go on with our lives?"

"I certainly didn't think my two workaholic sons would drop everything at a moment's notice and come to the house."

That was fair. More than fair. "Austin and I are here for you. For the surgery, and when you come home. We don't want everything to rest on Stuart." Donovan got up from his seat and crouched down next to her chair. "Mom, no matter what, I want you to remember that we love you."

"Good. I love you, too." She reached out and brushed his hair from his face. She hadn't done that in forty years. Maybe more. "Some days, I really see your dad in you."

He'd been kept awake for countless night in his life with that worry, that there was some part of him that was inherently broken because his dad had been broken, too. Or that perhaps his mom was haunted by bad memories every time she looked at Donovan. "I hope you see *you* in me, too."

"Oh, you're mostly me. Your dad squeezed in a little, but you're a lot like me. Pragmatic. Sardonic. Dour at times."

"Sardonic *and* dour. Good use of the thesaurus."

"Learned, too."

There were footfalls coming from the door. "Am I interrupting a tender moment?" Austin asked, with just a hint of sarcasm.

"Oh, good. You're both here." She sat back in her chair. "I want to talk about my last wishes."

"Mom. Is that really necessary?" Donovan asked. That seemed like quite a leap. "I think you're going to do great. I researched your doctor online this morning. She has amazing credentials."

"I'm not talking about now. I doubt I'll die tomorrow. Or the next day. This is for later. If we talk about it now, I don't have to bring it up at an awkward time, like at Christmas or on one of your birthdays."

Donovan stood and took his seat again.

Austin poised himself next to Donovan, bracing his hand on the back of the chair. "Yeah, Mom. Go."

"This is all in the will, but I'll tell you now that I want to be cremated. I do not want a funeral. Funerals are for sadness. Plus, I know very few people I like well enough for them to be invited, and it's an awful lot of trouble to book a caterer for a small event."

Austin let out an astonished laugh. "Okay. What else?"

"I want to be cremated. I want half of my ashes spread on the grounds here. Except not in the patch of lawn where the dogs do their business." She furrowed her brow, as if she was searching her memory for what came next. "After that, I'd like you to divvy me up, and leave a bit of me wherever you think I might like the view. Austin, if you can sneak onto the field at Fenway Park, I like it there. I like the pants the players wear. And Donovan, I have two requests for New York City. In front of Tiffany & Co. on 5th Avenue, and from the Bow Bridge in Central Park."

"Mom, I can't just leave you on a sidewalk in the middle of Manhattan. You'll blow away," Donovan said.

She dismissed the notion with a wave of her hand. "So a bus comes by and I go down the subway grate. I can spend eternity riding around the city."

Austin and Donovan looked at each other, equally dumbfounded. This was one of the more remarkable conversations they'd had with their mom, which was saying a lot.

"Anything else we need to know?" Austin asked.

"The house will go to you both. Think of it as one last motherly endeavor on my part. It was always so hard to get you two to share. This will force you to figure it out."

The brothers again looked at each other. That was going to be an interesting thing to compromise on. "Okay. Thank you," Donovan said.

"I'm glad you're both here. And I'm sorry I kept the cancer a secret. Sometimes we do stupid things to protect the people we love from things we think they can't handle."

"The key word there is *think*, Mom. Austin and I can handle all of this. Just fine."

***

Their mother's surgery went off without a hitch and after three days in the hospital, she was able to come home. That was when things got a little dicey for Donovan, Stuart, and Austin. She was in a great deal of pain, but had always been leery of prescription drugs, so she refused to take what the doctor had sent her home with. Stuart was of zero help. Their mom was able to talk him into anything. That left Donovan and Austin to trade off with the battle, each of them taking a different day. They both quickly learned it wasn't easy to force medicine down your own mother's throat. Even when it made her feel better, she still didn't want to take the next dose. She could be so damn stubborn.

For a full week, Donovan and Austin were handling far more of a work load than either had anticipated. The house was in need of constant upkeep. The animals all required food and tending, and the emu in particular was a complete pain in the ass. And then there were their mother's requests. She was essentially subsisting on smoothies, but they had to be made just right, and apparently Donovan was the only one who did it correctly. More than once, he'd gotten up at three in the morning to make her one because she was hungry. Donovan didn't dare complain, but his mom did point out that she was merely getting even for the nights he hadn't slept when he was a baby.

Donovan had very few spare moments, but when he did, his thoughts drifted to Lela. They'd talked almost every day since he'd left, their conversations light and short because Donovan was too exhausted for anything else. But every time he had to say goodbye, he found himself wanting to just finally come out with it and tell her that he loved her. *Just wait*, he told himself time and again. She deserved more than a stupid phone call. She deserved the world.

He also hesitated because he wasn't sure what came next

for them. He wanted more; he just had to find the right way to finesse it, because he wasn't sure what she wanted. These things became far more complicated later in life—one person wanted marriage while another was thinking, "no more of that, thank you very much". One person might want to maintain separate households because they'd learned to love living alone, while the other person might be missing that closeness because they hadn't had it in so long. Nothing was cut and dry. Or easy. Case in point, Donovan's mom and Stuart. He was still asking her to marry him nearly every single day, and every time, even when Donovan or Austin were around to witness it, she said no.

Nine days in, Donovan was officially worried and feeling incredibly guilty, too. Their mom was still struggling with her recovery, while Donovan had promised Lela that no matter what, he would be at Tammera and Delia's wedding tomorrow. He'd asked his mom how she felt about it, but she'd simply told him to go, with every dramatic sigh of a well-practiced martyr. He needed a second opinion.

"Hey, Austin, are you up for a walk down to the pond?" Donovan asked.

Austin was consumed by a book in the library, where the shelves contained far more leather-bound volumes than anyone could ever read. When they were younger, the brothers took turns riding the ladder while the other pushed it as fast as humanly possible across the room. "Yeah. Sure."

The pair took their usual route: out the French doors at the back of the house and across the flagstone patio surrounding the pool, then down the grassy slope to the water. "Do you feel like Stuart has everything under control?" Donovan asked.

Austin shrugged. "I don't know. I mean, he's doing a great job, but I worry about what she might be able to convince him of if we aren't around. That dynamic hasn't really changed."

"She is doing better with pain, though. She not only needs less medication, she's fighting it less often."

"That's true."

Donovan cleared his throat. "Well, here's my problem. Lela's best friend is getting married tomorrow and I promised her I would be there for the wedding."

Austin smiled. "That's a problem? That sounds like a pretty great problem to me. I would love to be going to a wedding with Lela tomorrow."

That irked Donovan, but he ignored it. "The whole reason I bring it up is because I want to know that you'd be okay with me leaving."

"Yeah. Of course. Stuart and I can manage."

"Are you absolutely sure?"

"Yes. You should go."

"Okay. Good. Thank you." He wasn't good at spilling his guts, especially with his brother, but he felt like this had to be said. "Also, you should know that Lela and I are romantically involved."

Austin clutched at his chest dramatically. "Oh, my God. My brother finally got a clue?"

"What's that supposed to mean?"

"I hoped this would happen, but I was starting to wonder what your problem was. I'm just glad you actually told me and I didn't have to hear it from Echo." Austin looked Donovan square in the eye. "You keep things to yourself. You keep it all bottled up. You're exactly like Mom and it makes me nuts."

Donovan knew this about himself. He was trying to be better, but it was a bad old habit to break. "You're right. I'm sorry. Wait. Hold on a second, what do you mean you hoped this would happen?"

Austin laughed quietly and shook his head. "You don't know why I flirted with Lela, do you?"

"I assumed it was because I asked you not to. Also, she's stunning, so I get it."

"I did it to force you to spill your feelings for her. It was so obvious from the first few moments I saw you two together."

"Obvious from who?"

"Obvious from *whom*. And you, Donovan. I've always been able to read you, but I also know that you're not super in touch with your feelings. I thought that if you were jealous, you would step up."

"Huh." Donovan was still trying to wrap his head around this.

He playfully slapped Donovan's chest with the back of his hand. "Have you told her that you love her?"

"No."

"Why not?"

"I haven't had the chance. There hasn't been the right time."

"Well? Do you? Love her?"

"Yes. I do." It was liberating to finally just say it out loud, but he was mad at himself for not finding the opportunity to tell her. He now felt even more pressure to make an impression. A grand romantic gesture was in order.

"And she has no idea."

"I'd like to think she knows on some level."

Austin shook his head in dismay. "Dude. You need to get with the program. I don't know what the hell you're waiting for. God only knows how many chances at this any of us will ever get."

CHAPTER TWENTY-SIX

NINE DAYS WAS a long time to be apart, especially when thirty years of waiting off-and-on had come before it. Thus was the state of affairs between Lela and Donovan.

She wasn't going to freak out that he'd left. That was too easy. Too obvious. But she was willing to put him on the spot a little bit now that Tammera's wedding was a mere day away.

"I don't want to be the reason you leave your family behind," Lela said over the phone. "You should do what you need to do."

"No. It's okay. I talked to Austin. But I can't come back to the city until tomorrow morning. Mom made me promise I'd stick around to make her one more smoothie in the morning."

"Just let me know if your plans change. I'll ask Echo to come with me. That way I'll have someone to talk to at the lunch." Lela leaned against the kitchen island, watching Rio eat his dinner.

"That's all you want me for? Someone to talk to? I was hoping you'd want me for more than that."

"You know what I mean." She was smiling to herself like a fool. Even Rio gave her side-eye. Despite not liking the physical distance between them, she did enjoy these daily talks. It made whatever they were doing feel a little more real. Of course, given that Donovan was dealing with his mother's illness, they steered away from serious topics, which left Lela to do a whole lot of wondering. Were they dating? It seemed like they were beyond that. Would they move in together? No. Too fast. Sex and romance? *Those* seemed like logical next steps.

"Hey. Guess what?" Donovan asked.

"What?"

"I feel bad about being away, so I'm bringing a surprise to the wedding."

"A surprise? For Tammera and Delia?"

"No. For you, silly."

"What kind of surprise?"

"Lela. Are you seriously not familiar with this concept? I can't tell you that."

Like a kid eager for Christmas morning, she willed time to go faster so she could see him. "Fine. I can wait until tomorrow."

"Perfect. I will meet you at the church. Ten o'clock. Save me a seat on the aisle."

"Got it." Lela took in a deep breath. "And Donovan, I can't wait to see you."

"I can't wait to see you either."

She'd gone to bed last night with a goofy grin on her face, but now that it was Saturday morning, she was simply a ball of barely contained anticipation. She arrived at the tiny chapel near the Flatiron Building around nine o'clock, one

hour before the ceremony. As instructed, she went straight to
the bride's room where she found the brides, plural—
Tammera *and* Delia. Plus, Tammera's sister, Caprice, who
Lela had met once right after Tammera landed her show.
Caprice was Tammera's attendant, and Delia had asked her
brother, Mason.

"Hey, Caprice. And Tams. And Delia," Lela said, admittedly confused. She'd assumed the happy couple would be
spending time apart before it was time for the ceremony.

"Hi, Lela," Delia said.

"Lela's here!" Tammera hopped up from the tiny blue
plastic chair she was sitting in. This room was apparently also
a preschool classroom. The alphabet cut-outs surrounding a
chalkboard and a colorful carpet with squares for kids to sit
on were Lela's first clues. "Did you have any trouble sneaking
in?"

"People don't recognize me as much anymore."

"But you're wearing *the* dress. The pink dress from the
ads."

"Looking good, Lela," said Caprice.

"Aww. Thanks. You, too." Lela looked down at herself
and rotated her hips to make the skirt swish. "I only got to
wear this the one time but they let me keep it after the shoot.
I thought it would be fun for this occasion."

"Well, you look gorgeous," Tammera said.

"Thank you."

"Don't forget. My grandmother wants a photo with you
today," Delia said. "She went gray twenty years ago. I think
she's a little mad she didn't get famous for it."

"Tammera's the famous one. I had a few minutes of fame.
There's a big difference."

"Hey, Tammera," Caprice said. "I'm going to go check on Daddy. He was complaining about it being hot in the sanctuary."

"Thank you. That man is nothing short of high maintenance," Tammera said.

Lela set down the small makeup case she'd brought. She'd done Tammera's makeup so many times that she didn't need the full array of products she typically carried. As for Delia, she had several allergies and preferred to do her own makeup.

"Isn't it bad luck to see your partner before the ceremony?" Lela asked.

"Pfft," Tammera said. "I don't believe in that and neither does Delia. It seems silly to be separated. We've been living together for three years. Plus, have you ever hung out in a preschool classroom by yourself? It's creepy."

Lela laughed, still amazed that Tammera's normally keen sense of a disturbance in Lela's life force had not yet cropped up. Lela hadn't told a soul that she and Donovan had slept together again. "Feeling nervous?"

Tammera looked lovingly at Delia, and their gazes connected. "Nope," they said in unison.

"Do you want to get started?"

Tammera shrugged. "Sure."

Lela looked around the room. The lighting was absolutely terrible—fluorescent overheads and nothing else. "Come on. Over by the window." Lela found the teacher's chair, which was a normal size, and dragged it closer to the natural light. With a whoosh, she raised the shades, allowing daylight to flood the room. "Much better."

Tammera sat down and looked up at Lela. That was the

moment when her expression changed. She narrowed her eyes and twisted her lips. Her spidey sense still worked. "What happened? Something happened."

Lela cracked half a smile, then squirted some primer onto a sponge and began applying it. "Donovan and I are... something. I don't know exactly. But we had sex and it didn't end disastrously."

Delia hopped up and dragged her own tiny chair across the floor. "I'm listening."

"I thought you weren't going to go there again. What made you change your mind?"

Of course, it hadn't been a single moment. It had been a long string of events, much like the entire tale of their friendship. "It started at Echo's wedding. We spent a lot of time together and it was really nice. We talked about old times, including a few misunderstandings between us. Or maybe it's more accurate to say missing pieces." Lela switched to Tammera's foundation, dabbing and blending. "And then there was the Good Day USA appearance. I was freaking out and he was so sweet to me. Then, my parents came to town and he went out with us and I don't know. Things were just different. He walked me home and he told me that he didn't want to be friends anymore."

"Because he wanted to be more?" Delia asked.

"Yes."

Delia squealed. "So romantic."

"And then you got to tearing each other's clothes off?" Tammera was not quite as sentimental.

"That's typically how it happens, yes," Lela answered.

"And now what?" Tammera asked as Lela started doing some light contouring.

"We're attending the wedding of the year together, of course." Lela didn't want too much attention put on the subject of Donovan and her. As far as she was concerned, it was a lot of unnecessary pressure. *See where things go,* seemed like a passable mantra.

"When will he be here?" Delia asked.

"He's driving down from Connecticut this morning. I haven't seen him for a week and a half because he went to take care of his mom after surgery. I told him I'll save him a seat, so probably right before the ceremony?"

"That's soon," Delia said. "You must be excited."

"Delia, you're getting married. You're the one who's supposed to be excited." Of course, Lela *was* excited to see Donovan. But she didn't want the spotlight shifted.

"I am," Delia said. "We both are."

"Who did your hair? You both look amazing." Tammera's was natural and curly on top, pulled back tight on both sides with jeweled barrettes to bring out her high cheekbones. Delia's was up in an elaborate braided twist with tiny white flowers scattered throughout.

"Actually, we did each other's hair," Tammera said.

Lela couldn't help it. Her lower lip jutted out. "That's so sweet. You're going to make me cry."

"Don't do that," Tammera said. "We need you to finish up."

Lela got to work in greater earnest, and had Tammera looking completely fabulous in fifteen minutes. Since Caprice had stepped out, Lela was the sole helper when it came to dressing. She assisted Delia with the zipper on her dress while Tammera slipped into the beautifully tailored white suit she'd chosen, which really showed off her curves.

"You guys are the perfect couple. I'm so happy for you." Lela figured that if she could find a way to be half as happy as Tammera and Delia were, she'd feel so fortunate.

The three shared a group hug, but Lela kept it quick. They deserved a quiet moment alone before the main event.

"I'll see you out there," she said, then ducked into the hall.

Inside the postage stamp of a sanctuary, there were fewer than ten rows of pews. Seated on either side of the aisle was a scattering of guests. Lela recognized some from the Cook It! Studios, or from photos she'd seen of Tammera's family. Delia's parents were on hand, as well as her brother and apparently some people she worked with in her practice. Lela slipped into the very last row, and as Donovan had requested, she left a seat for him on the aisle. She silenced her phone, but kept it in her lap so she could check the time.

A tall red-haired woman appeared at the end of Lela's row. "Is this seat taken?" she asked with a nod at the empty spot on the aisle next to Lela.

"It is. I'm saving it for someone. He should be here any minute."

She grimaced. "How about on the other side?"

Lela pivoted on the seat and pressed her legs to the side. "Yes. Of course. Come on in." She smiled at the woman as she got settled. "How do you know Tammera and Delia?"

"I'm a nurse in Delia's office."

"Oh, nice. I was just there a few weeks ago with a friend of mine."

The woman looked at her strangely, which made perfect sense now that Lela thought about what she'd said. What grown woman was friends with a kid?

"I know Delia through Tammera," Lela explained. "I've been friends with Tammera for what feels like forever. I used to be her makeup artist. But then things got super crazy with my job, so I don't have as much time now. I did do her makeup for today, though." Lela clamped her mouth shut. She knew she was rambling.

"You're the gray hair woman. The one in the ads."

Lela managed a smile. "Lela."

"Nikki," the woman replied. "Are you sure your friend is coming?" Nikki whispered.

Lela looked to the back of the church, but there was no sign of Donovan. None. Tammera and Delia walked into the vestibule outside the sanctuary, each holding bouquets, ready to walk up the aisle together. Part of Lela wanted to catch Tammera's eye and give her one last thumbs up, but it was better to simply watch them fuss over each other, then gaze into each other's eyes with what was surely true love.

Lela sighed, but tears were threatening. She'd experienced what she thought was love with Donovan so many times, and had taught herself to dismiss it. She'd felt it with him the day she went on Good Day USA. She'd felt it when he came to dinner with her parents. But she'd felt it most when he finally said the words she'd been waiting thirty years to hear—that he didn't want to just be friends. That every bit of the closeness they shared meant more to him, too.

The processional music started and everyone stood. Lela watched Delia and Tammera march up the aisle together. She was so happy for her friends that it made it easier to tamp down her annoyance with Donovan for being late.

"You may be seated," the officiant said when Tammera and Delia reached the altar.

Lela sat with everyone else, but she was bursting with so much nervous energy that she started to bob her leg. Where was Donovan? Was he okay? She glanced at her phone, but only for a second. She didn't want to be *that* person at the wedding. He hadn't called. There was no text.

The officiant spoke about love and commitment, but Donovan failed to turn up. Delia read a bible passage. Tammera recited a poem. And still there was no Donovan. Lela fought her brain's most immediate inclinations, the way she wanted to assume that he was going to let her down again. She didn't believe it. She refused. They'd talked yesterday. Everything was fine. She hoped.

And then, just like that, he slipped into the seat next to her. "Hi," he whispered.

She turned and looked at him. Her normally handsome and impeccably dressed Donovan had a grease smudge on his cheek near his ear. His hair was disheveled. "What happened?" she whispered.

"Long story. I'll tell you later." He raised a finger to his lips and that was when she saw how filthy his hands were. Whatever this story was, it had better be good.

Still, she was not only happy he was there, her heart was doing a little jig. She was glad to see his messy face and smell what she thought might be motor oil mixing with his cologne. She scooted closer to him and he reached for her hand. She didn't hesitate to wrap her fingers around his. Even when they were grubby. Even when their twined hands rested on her lap while she was wearing her most precious pink dress. He was there and it felt like they were... a couple.

At the end of the ceremony, Tammera and Delia kissed, and everyone rose from the pews, clapping as music played and they strode back down the aisle. Donovan and Lela had to wait to leave since they were seated in the back, but it didn't take long. Outside the chapel, Tammera and Delia were engrossed with greetings from family, so Lela pulled Donovan aside.

"What happened to you?" She pushed his hair from his face, stopping herself from licking her thumb and wiping away the dirt on his cheek. "You're a wreck."

"I know. And I'm sorry. I just figured it was better to show up a little late as a disaster, rather than not show up at all."

"That makes sense. But you still haven't told me what happened."

"Let me show you." Donovan took her hand and walked past two parked cars. "Your chariot awaits." With a flourish of his filthy fingers, he presented the mint green Vespa. The one she'd been riding when she fell for him the first time. And the third.

"You brought it down from your mom's?"

"Something told me I should have it."

"Just too big a piece of nostalgia?"

He shook his head and wrapped his arm around her waist, pulling her close. Lela felt woozy, just like every other time Donovan had done that, which hadn't been nearly often enough, but she hoped she had time. Maybe her whole life. He pressed a kiss against her lips and it felt like she was levitating. Were those biblical sunbeams overhead or was she hallucinating? "It's more than that. I love you, Lela. I have always loved you. And I know you said you were in love with me once, but I need to know if you still love me."

She wanted to slap him silly. She also wanted to kiss him

again and never, ever stop. "I love you, too, Donovan. Of course I do. I never stopped loving you. Even when I was mad at you. There was always something pulling me toward you."

His eyes shined brighter, with a look that conveyed so much happiness. "You know, the Vespa is a thread that has run through our lives together. If we're going to move ahead, I want to start it right here and right now on this scooter, after having attended a wedding together, of course."

If anyone had told twenty-one-year-old Lela that this would be the happy ending for her and Donovan, she never would've believed it. Or maybe it was better to think of it as a happy beginning. "Don't say if." She pressed a finger to his lips. "Don't jinx us. You and I are moving ahead. Full stop."

He smiled and pressed another soft kiss to her lips. "Okay. No jinx."

"You still haven't told me how you ended up so disheveled."

"It was stupid. I forgot that if you lean too far to the right, the engine floods. I took a turn too fast and killed it. I pulled over, but the second I bent down to see what was going on, my phone fell out of my pocket and went into a storm drain. That's why I didn't call or text to say I was running late. I fixed it as fast as I could, but of course I got dirty and I couldn't do anything about it. I just raced to the church."

"So you're having a great day is what you're telling me."

"Honestly? Best day ever."

Lela grinned so hard her face was likely to stay that way. "We need to get you cleaned up if we're going to go to this lunch. It's an hour from now. I think we can make it if we're fast." She turned and caught Tammera's attention.

Tammera's face lit up, perhaps with the beautiful feelings of that day, or maybe she understood how hard-won this victory was for Lela. Lela blew her a kiss, which Tammera caught with one hand before Delia grabbed her hand and pulled her into the crowd of their guests. "And I think Tammera and Delia will understand if we're a few minutes late."

Donovan sat on the scooter and handed Lela her helmet. "I know you don't want to mess up your hair, but safety first." He kick-started the engine and it rumbled to life.

"My hair is perfect. It's not possible to mess it up." She buckled the strap under her chin and realized she was going to have to stop wearing dresses if she wanted to ride on the scooter. It was not practical. Once she was on board, she wrapped her arms around him tight. "Your place?"

"Unless you have more of my clothes hiding in the back of your closet."

"I really did think it was my R.E.M. T-shirt."

"Something tells me it's going to end up at your house again very soon." He chuckled and revved the engine, which sputtered as he pulled away from the curb.

They whizzed through the city, past the town cars and the people flirting with death on bicycles, past hot dog vendors and pedestrians going about their day, exactly like they had all those years ago. She held on to him tight, pressing the side of her face to his back when she wanted to be even closer. So much was different and yet some things remained. He was her best friend. Again. He was the love of her life. She was his. Somehow, they'd found a way to make it work after nearly thirty years. And it had been so worth the wait.

Donovan took a tight turn, nearly clipping the back

corner of a taxi. Lela's hair swung around over her shoulder. She gasped. And then she laughed, pulling him tighter. A song popped into her head, the same earwormy delight that she'd heard in Bryant Park. *You Make My Dreams Come True*. It had to be for a reason. Donovan had always been her dream, and now she had him.

Apparently even Hall & Oates agreed.

EPILOGUE

One year later

DONOVAN DUCKED into Echo's office late on a Friday afternoon. "I'm heading home to get ready."

"Got it," Echo said, wholly distracted by work.

He stepped closer to her desk. "And you're confident you can get Lela out of here and back home by seven?"

"Yes. I'm on it. I'll drag her kicking and screaming if I have to."

"You know how she gets."

"Believe me, I know. I'm forcing her to take two more people on her team. With the international expansion on Lela B, she needs all the help she can get."

Lela B never quieted down after the initial commotion. It just kept growing like a weed. Once things stabilized ten months in, Echo saw a natural opportunity and put Lela in charge of building up the beauty division of Echo Echo. Lela was working her ass off. Donovan knew what it was like to be in the weeds—there wasn't even time to ask for help. "Good job. That's exactly the kind of leadership I like to see."

Echo shot him a pointed glance. "Dad. We're not on a corporate retreat. Whatever you want to call it, I learned it all from you. Don't act too surprised."

"I'm not surprised. Just proud."

"Thanks. Now can you go be proud somewhere else?" She smiled warmly to soften the blow of her words. "Sorry. I'm just trying to catch up after getting in late this morning."

"Feeling any better?"

"I am."

"Glad to hear it. I'll see you in a bit." Donovan headed for the door, but Echo stopped him with her voice.

"By the way, I think it's super sweet that you're doing this for Lela."

He turned back. "She won't let me celebrate her any other way but by ambush."

"Then you're doing the right thing."

Donovan hustled down the hall, through reception and to the elevator. As soon as he was out on the street in front of JTI, he hailed a taxi, then called Tammera to let her know he was on his way. "I'm hopping in a cab right now. I should be there in fifteen."

"On a Friday? I don't think so. Subway might be faster."

"Too late. I've already committed." He gave the driver the address. "How's the decorating going?" he asked Tammera.

"Fine. Except the cats are going nuts with the streamers. Well, not Rio. He mostly licks his crotch and watches the other two make complete fools of themselves."

"He's the elder statesman. That's his role in our household."

Tammera laughed. "Just get your butt over here. We could use your help."

"Like I said. On my way."

Of course, Tammera ended up being right. Fifteen minutes had been stupidly optimistic. The trip ended up taking nearly thirty.

When he arrived at the house, it looked as though Tammera and Delia were done with the decorations—colorful twisted streamers dipping and swooping in a zig zag across the living room ceiling. A banner saying, "Congratulations" adorned the fireplace mantle, while clusters of balloons flanked the hearth. That might have been a mistake. They were tethered with narrow curling ribbon and the newest feline additions to the family, Bowie and Oates, were suitably obsessed. He and Lela had adopted them from the animal shelter six months ago. They were nearly full-grown, but still awfully kitten-like.

"You did an amazing job," he said to Tammera and Delia.

"It really compliments the decor," Delia countered.

Indeed, since Donovan had moved in last fall, he and Lela had acquired more furniture and some new artwork. Although the shopping and hunting had been a joint effort, everything had to pass muster with Lela, which meant nothing boring. There were pillows in aqua and pink, and dramatic light fixtures, and interesting modern art. The most recent addition to the house was a pair of near-mint vintage mid-century upholstered armchairs, which Donovan had mistakenly referred to as yellow. *They're goldenrod,* Lela had said.

Tammera pointed at Bowie and Oates. "I don't know how you and Lela get anything done with these two around."

Donovan crouched down and Bowie, the gray and white tabby, immediately ran over to him to get head scratches. He was Donovan's little buddy. "We love them to death, but they definitely keep us on our toes."

"Lela doesn't know about tonight?" Delia asked.

"I don't think she has a clue. Although I did ask her a month ago if we could celebrate after Good Day USA brought her on permanently. So maybe I tipped my hand that day? We haven't talked about it since then, though."

"I can't wait until she gets here," Tammera said. "She hates surprises."

"I know, but I had to do it. That's why I made it a small celebration," Donovan added. He glanced at his watch. "I'd better get upstairs and change. Lucius should be here any minute with the food, then Echo will text us when she and Lela are close."

"What does Lela think you two are doing this evening?" Delia asked.

"Dinner with Echo and Lucius. That's all."

"So really, Delia and I are the surprise," Tammera said proudly.

Donovan laughed. "Yes, you two and the cake. And the champagne. And the decorations."

"I still think we're the best part."

"Somehow, that does not surprise me." Donovan excused himself and ran upstairs to freshen up. As he stood in the closet, deciding which shirt to wear, he couldn't help but think about the night he met Tammera and Delia and ended up in Lela's bedroom after the takeout food disaster. If they'd been alone, he would have kissed her, and it was no big secret where that would have led—right into Lela's bed. But looking back on it now, he was glad it hadn't unfolded that way. He and Lela needed to work through a lot before their future opened up.

Dressed in a crisp white shirt with the sleeves rolled up to the elbows, Donovan went downstairs to help with last minute preparations. He realized then that he hadn't yet seen the cake, which Delia and Tammera had picked up. It was waiting for him in the kitchen, but when he opened the bakery box's lid, his heart sank. "Tammera," he called. "Did you and Delia actually look at the cake?"

She appeared in the kitchen doorway. "I glanced at it. Looked fine."

"Congratulations Lola?"

"Oh, crap. Seriously?" She rushed over and peered inside. "Shit. It does say Lola. Now what?"

"You're the chef."

"Not a pastry chef. I'm known for high-end comfort food. If you want some celebratory lobster mac and cheese, I'm the person to call."

"How do we fix it?"

"We don't."

"Really?"

Tammera sighed. "Hand me a butter knife. I'll see what I can do."

Donovan grabbed one from the drawer, but just as she was about to begin surgery, he stopped her. "Wait."

"What?"

"I don't want to make it look worse."

"It's either wrong or it's imperfect. Your choice."

That sounded more like a life lesson than a question about cake, but he had to make a decision. "You're right. Let's make it right. Even if it doesn't look great, Lela will still know it's for her."

"Excellent point." Tammera very carefully lifted a small portion of the icing that made the "o" then rotated it ninety degrees to make an "e". She did smudge the frosting underneath a bit, but at least it said Lela now. "Well?"

"Thank you. It's imperfectly perfect." If ever there was a metaphor for his life, that was it.

Lucius walked in a moment later with an armful of Vietnamese takeout, Lela's favorite. He set it down on the kitchen island, and unlike Donovan, managed to do so without incident. "Heya, Donovan. How long until Echo and Lela get here?"

Donovan's phone beeped with a text. *Almost there.*

"Any minute now. Let's get everyone a glass of champagne."

"We aren't hiding and jumping out from behind the couch?" Tammera asked.

"No. If she's mad about the surprise, it'll be easier to hand her a drink and all should be forgiven."

"Good thinking," Lucius said.

The four of them gathered in the foyer with champagne flutes in hand, and Donovan couldn't figure out why his heart was beating so fiercely. This was *not* a big occasion. It was merely what sweet, lovely, hard-working Lela deserved—a little recognition. Maybe he was feeling this way because he knew how much it meant to him. Lela was his whole life now. He wanted everything to be right.

From outside, Echo's voice filtered through the door. She was plainly talking many decibels above a normal level. The latch on the lock clicked, the knob turned, and she and Lela stepped inside.

"Surprise!" Donovan said, followed by an uneven chorus of the same sentiment from Lucius, Tammera, and Delia.

"What's all this?" A bashful smile crossed Lela's face as Donovan handed her the glass of champagne.

He leaned down to kiss her softly. "We're finally going to celebrate your big achievements over the last year."

"You really didn't have to do this."

"Oh, shush. Just take the love we all want to give you." Tammera wrapped Lela up in a big hug.

"Congrats on everything, Lela," Delia said.

Lucius and Echo got in on it last, with more embraces and well-wishes. That was when Donovan noticed that Lucius had not brought Echo a drink. "Echo, let me get you a glass of champagne."

"Dad. No." Echo looked at Donovan, then her gaze found Lucius and a smile bloomed on her face.

"What's going on?" Donovan asked.

"Oh, my God." Lela clasped her hand over her mouth.

It gradually dawned on Donovan, like he was a step slow. His eyes welled with tears. "Are you?" he asked Echo.

She nodded and pressed her lips together tightly, also trying not to cry. "This wasn't really the way I wanted it to come out. But I guess I should've been smart enough to figure out that you'd serve alcohol and I'd have to decline because of the baby."

The baby. Donovan pulled his daughter against his chest and squeezed her tight. He was a mess of emotion, an over-flowing well of happiness and hope. His baby was having a baby. "How far along are you?"

"I just passed twelve weeks. I'm due late April."

"Your grandmother and Stuart are going to be so excited to hear this news. And your Uncle Austin, too. Does your mom know?"

"I called her this morning. After I spent an hour being sick."

"That's why you were late."

She reared her head back and arched both eyebrows at him. "That's why I was late."

"Wow." Donovan slowly let go of Echo, still a bit stupefied, and watched as she and Lela shared their own tender moment. They grinned and chattered away, both wiping away tears. Delia and Tammera patiently waited for their chance to congratulate Echo, too.

Lela turned to Donovan. "Pretty amazing." She snaked her arm around his waist and leaned into him. "Somebody's going to be a grandpa," she sang.

A grandpa? Whoa. "I suppose I am."

"So what's the plan for tonight?" Lela asked.

"We got takeout, Tammera and Delia decorated the living room, and there's cake. I kept it simple. I knew you wouldn't want a big thing."

"So you threw a small thing instead."

"I might be pretty good at listening, but I'm not great at always following orders."

She planted her chin on his chest and peered up at him. "That's why I love you."

"I love you, too. Now let's eat before the food gets cold."

Donovan and Lucius went to the kitchen while the other four took a seat at the dining table, which Delia and Tammera had artfully set. The two guys ferried in lemongrass pork with rice vermicelli, fresh spring rolls with shrimp and cellophane noodles, and big bowls of pho with fragrant broth and the many fresh accompaniments. Donovan put on some music, a playlist of Lela's favorites. When *Save a Prayer* by Duran Duran came on, she pressed her hand to her chest and closed her eyes. "I love this song so much. It will never, ever get old."

All Donovan could think was that it would never get old to make her happy. To see her smile.

The conversation was brisk and lively as they skipped from topic to topic. Work came up a lot, of course. This was a workaholic crowd if ever there'd been one. Lucius had landed a publishing contract for his first novel and finally had a release date to share. He was also set to start teaching a writing class in the fall. Tammera's career was regularly blowing up in a good way, with a new line of kitchen appliances, a second show, and more cookbooks on the way.

Delia insisted her job was just the same old, same old. "But Echo and Lucius, I'd love to be considered to be your pediatrician."

"She's an excellent doctor," Donovan said. "The one time I had to see her, she took very good care of me."

Lela cast a knowing smile at Donovan. "Thank goodness we don't have to worry about that."

"Yep. Clean bill of health."

After the dinner plates were cleared away, Tammera popped the cork on another bottle of champagne and Donovan hunted down some seltzer so Echo could toast as well. He then put a single candle on the cake and walked it into the living room to present it to Lela.

"It's so pretty. Thank you," she said as he set it down before her. If she'd noticed the altered icing, she didn't let on.

"Make a wish," Donovan said.

"Are you sure? It's not my birthday."

"I still think you're entitled."

She smiled that stunning Lela smile, pursed her lips and blew out the candle. Everyone clapped and cheered. Donovan felt like his mission had mostly been accomplished when Delia started cutting and serving the cake.

"I'd like to propose a toast. Actually, several toasts. So bear with me." He raised his glass and cleared his throat. "First off, we have to acknowledge how amazing it is to have a gathering of family and loved ones like this. I love you all."

"Hear, hear," everyone said.

"And to my daughter and son-in-law and the baby on the way. It's going to take me a while to wrap my head around the idea of being a grandfather, but I can't wait for this next chapter."

"Hear, hear," they chorused.

"And lastly, to Lela, the love of my life. You are more than an amazing woman, you are a force of nature. Thank you for waiting thirty years for the stars to align." Their gazes connected, and he heard Lela's voice first. "Hear, hear."

He downed the last of his champagne, poured another glass, and gladly dug in to his cake. As they dispatched the final bottle of bubbly, the festivities naturally began to wind down. Lucius helped Donovan clean up the kitchen while Tammera, Delia, Echo, and Lela stole a few more minutes of conversation.

Tammera and Delia were the first out the door. "Good-night, all. Have a good weekend."

"Goodnight, Dad. Lela. Love you." Echo hugged them both.

Lucius, not much of a hugger, even accepted an embrace before they were on their way.

"Thank you for tonight. It was magical," Lela said as Donovan flipped the deadbolt.

"You're not mad that I forced you to celebrate your accomplishments?"

"No. Not at all. I loved having our little family together. It was awesome."

He drew in a deep breath through his nose. "I still can't believe Echo is going to have a baby. It's so amazing."

"I know. It's so exciting." She planted a finger in the center of his chest. "You are going to be a grandpa."

"How weird is that?"

"It's not weird at all, really. It's life. I do think the timing with your gray coming in couldn't be any more perfect." She ruffled his hair. "It makes you more grandpa-like. So distinguished."

"Why is my gray distinguished but you get to be sexy?"

Lela shrugged. "I don't set the standards of beauty. I'm just telling you how it is." A clever smirk crossed her lips. Surely she took great satisfaction in throwing his own words back at him, however poorly thought out they'd been when he'd first delivered them.

From the living room, the opening strains of *If You Were Here* by The Thompson Twins played.

"I love this song," he said.

"You do? It's not too poppy for you?"

He shook his head, grabbed her hand and pulled her into the other room so they could hear better. "No. It's romantic."

He tugged her into his arms, and they swayed back and forth to the music. Lela settled the side of her head against his chest, and he threaded his fingers through her silky hair, thinking about everything she meant to him and how his life had become so much fuller with her. "What if we got married?"

Lela lifted her head and slid him a look born of pure, unadulterated suspicion. "You. Want to get married."

"Fourth time's a charm?"

She laughed and smoothed her hand over his chest as their dance continued in a gentle sway. Even through the thin fabric of his shirt, her touch never failed to remind him how alive he felt when he was with her. "I love you, but do we really want to deal with a wedding?"

"You love them. Like really, really love them."

"I do." She scanned his face, eyes sweeping back and forth like she was looking for answers. Under any other circumstance, it would've made him worry about what came next, but there was a softness in her expression that he now understood to simply mean she was thinking. A lot. "I don't want you to feel like you have to do this for me. You have every reason to be reluctant to get married. And I'm in no rush."

His heart sank a little. "I'm not in a rush. I just want to get on with our lives."

"But we are. Every minute we're together is our lives. Right now. We don't need a party to tell each other that we want to be together forever."

Donovan swallowed hard. "It's more than a party to me. It's my chance to finally get it right."

Again, she surveyed his face. "You really want to do this, don't you?"

"I do."

A breathy laugh crossed her lips. "Can we go on a stupidly expensive honeymoon? A month in Italy or Ireland or somewhere tropical like Fiji?"

"You'd want to take that much time off from work, Ms. Workaholic?"

"I think I need that much time off. You do, too."

"We should probably try to squeeze it in before the baby comes."

"True. Echo's going to need our help."

She smiled and leaned into him, spiking his body temperature in the process. "Christmas, maybe?"

"As long as I get to put a ring on your finger and show the world how much I love you, I'm good."

"Ooh. What kind of ring?"

"Whatever you want. But I'm not picking it out. I learned my lesson with the furniture."

She took his hand and stepped away. "Come on. I say we talk about it upstairs."

A zip of electricity ran through him. "Right. Upstairs. Talking."

"Among other things..." Her voice was soft and warm and full of seduction.

Just then, the song changed. *One on One.* "It's so weird. I feel like I hear Hall and Oates at the most pivotal moments when I'm with you," he said.

"Really? Me too."

"Huh." They started up the stairs. "Maybe it's the

universe telling us something. Maybe it's fate that we're together, Lela."

She stopped at the top of the landing and kissed him softly. "With us, I'd say it's nothing less than exactly that."

THE END

If you enjoyed this book, please consider leaving a review online. It helps readers like you find their next great book!

ACKNOWLEDGMENTS

Like so many books, a ton of people helped me do the heavy lifting on this one. First, I'd like to thank my husband Steve, and kids, Emily & Ryan, for being the light of my life and showing me so much support.

To all my author friends, thank you for being such a bright spot. You make the ups and downs so much better. I would start listing you all, but I'd invariably leave someone out, but I hope you know who you are. To my agent, Melissa Jeglinski, thank you for always believing in whatever I throw you way. To cover illustrator Leni Kauffman, thank you for bringing my vision to life so brilliantly. To Donna Soluri for being my next-level alpha beta reader on this book. To Jennifer Gracen for jumping in at a moment's notice with your ace editorial skills. To the folks at Tantor Media for bringing this project to life as an audiobook.

To my girlfriends Sara, Ashley, Lisa, Frine, Cara, and Stephanie for solidly encouraging me to write a book about a woman who had gone gray. To Val and all members of the Backstage Antics group on Facebook, thank you for being so patient when I disappear into my writing cave. And to Margaret, Natasha, and Sandra, as well as all members of the Seasoned Romance Facebook group, thank you for bringing the enthusiasm for romance with characters who are finding their HEA later in life.

Last, but absolutely not least, thank you to everyone who has ever bought, read, or reviewed one of my books. I couldn't do what I do without you!

One final note: Traditional publishers continue to claim that romance readers don't want characters over 40. If you've read this far, that means we've proven them wrong. Yay us!

ABOUT KAREN BOOTH

Karen Booth is a midwestern girl transplanted in the South, raised on '80s music and too many readings of *Forever* by Judy Blume. An early preoccupation with rock 'n' roll led her to spend her twenties working her way from intern to executive in the music industry. Now she's a married mom of two and instead of staying up late in rock clubs, she gets up before dawn to write sexy contemporary romance and women's fiction.

Karen is co-founder of the 3500+ member Seasoned Romance Facebook group, devoted to the promotion of romance with characters 35+. She has been a finalist for RT Magazine's Series Romance of the Year, RT Magazine's Gold Seal of Excellence, the National Excellence in Romance Fiction Award (NERFA), the Booksellers' Best Award, and the Holt Medallion. Her books have been translated into seventeen languages.

ALSO BY KAREN BOOTH

Find more at karenbooth.net

CPSIA information can be obtained
at www.ICGtesting.com
Printed in the USA
LVHW052019030321
680485LV00014B/2211

9 780578 826288